The Patterdale Plot

By Rebecca Tope

The Patterdale Plot

REBECCA TOPE

Allison & Busby Limited
11 Wardour Mews
London W1F 8AN
allisonandbusby.com

First published in Great Britain by Allison & Busby in 2020.

A CIP catalogue record for this book is available from the British Library.

First Edition

ISBN 978-0-7490-2580-9

Typeset in 11/16 pt Sabon LT Pro by
Allison & Busby Ltd

The paper used for this Allison & Busby publication
has been produced from trees that have been legally sourced
from well-managed and credibly certified forests.

Printed and bound by
CPI Group (UK) Ltd, Croydon, CR0 4YY

Dedicated to the memories of
Lizzie Earl and Hilton Hughes

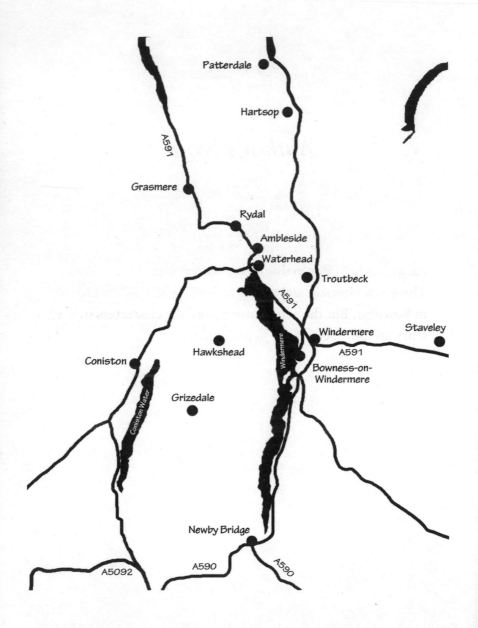

Author's Note

As with other titles in this series, the settings are real places. There is a Hartsop and a Crookabeck, and a Kendal Road in Bowness. But the actual houses and the characters in the story are products of my imagination.

Chapter One

'Still nothing for sale in Patterdale, then?' said Russell Straw to his daughter, Persimmon, generally known as Simmy. 'I told you it would never work.'

'You did,' she agreed. 'But we haven't given up hope yet.'

'The way I see it, there's a deadline.' He looked at her steadily expanding midriff. 'Another four months or so, in fact.'

'Five, nearly.'

'Except you hardly want to be moving house a week before giving birth, do you?' put in Angie, Simmy's mother. 'That's a recipe for total chaos.'

Simmy sighed. They were only thinking of her welfare, she reminded herself. And they were just as terrified as she was, below the surface. The quest for a house somewhere within reach of both Keswick and Windermere had been going on since June and was no closer to fulfilment now that they were into October. Simmy and Christopher were going to live together and have a baby and get married, probably in that order. The decisions had all been made four months ago, but putting them into practice turned out to be a whole other thing.

'We're going to have a look at Hartsop as well, probably on Wednesday,' she said. 'Somebody told Christopher it's lovely there and neither of us has ever seen it.'

'Oh – Hartsop!' Russell was suddenly enthused. 'On the banks of Brothers Water, very nearly. Easy walking distance from Hayeswater, which everyone confuses with Hawes.' He grinned happily. 'That would be like living in paradise, at least in the summer.'

'I didn't think there were more than about four houses there,' said Angie. 'Just those rather nasty holiday lodges. At least they look nasty on the Internet. I can't pretend to have seen them in person.'

'Christopher thinks they're quite tasteful, actually,' said Simmy. 'He says he's heard that they're almost invisible from most places.' But she knew there was almost no chance of buying property in what was termed a 'conservation village'. If Patterdale was difficult, Hartsop was likely to be impossible. She said as much to her concerned parents. Neither of them gave any reassurances, so she dredged some up for herself. 'At least it helps that Chris knows some of the estate agents personally. We do get early warning of anything coming onto the market. Especially Robin, of course. He's the one in Keswick who's making real efforts to find us something.'

Angie got up from the kitchen chair and started tidying the surfaces. 'Seven for breakfast tomorrow,' she muttered. 'I've got an awful feeling we're almost out of tea bags.'

'They look like coffee drinkers to me,' said her husband. 'I can always tell.'

'You mean you're right fifty per cent of the time – like predicting the sex of a baby,' Angie retorted. 'You always conveniently forget the times you get it wrong.'

He ignored her. 'You shouldn't forget Glenridding,' he told Simmy. 'Nicer views, in my opinion. Right over Ullswater to the mountains.'

Simmy nodded. 'We've been looking there as well.'

The weekend had been scheduled for some time as a chance for updating her parents on the house-hunting, as well as other things. The Windermere flower shop had enjoyed a reasonably good summer, with September especially buoyant. Bonnie Lawson, Simmy's young assistant, had survived the departure of her boyfriend to university without trailing devotedly after him as many people had expected. Ben had gently diverted her, saying he would be very poor company at least for the first term and she would be better off staying where she was. With Simmy's dramatic change of direction, Bonnie believed herself to be a stabilising factor, taking more responsibility at the shop and listening to worries. She also found the physical details of pregnancy endlessly fascinating, so long as they didn't become too graphic.

'How are your bookings at the moment?' Simmy asked her mother. The B&B had been in high demand all through the summer, but an embarrassing complaint on TripAdvisor had caused a degree of concern. Angie made a virtue of her relaxed approach to rules and cleanliness, allowing dogs in the bedrooms and crumbs on the floor. The big rumpus room on the ground floor was an untidy space for families to enjoy on rainy days, with half-done jigsaws and muddy shoes all part of the decor. When one neurotic mother found a half-eaten meat pie under a chair, she raised a great fuss and vowed to blacklist Beck View in perpetuity. Luckily for Angie, there was still a hard core of loyal clients who valued the freedom she provided, and returned faithfully, often three or four times a year.

'The writing's on the wall,' she sighed. 'I haven't had so many new people lately. And I can't afford to offend anybody else, so the cleaning's had to go up a notch.'

Angie was in her mid sixties, and Russell's seventieth birthday was looming. Having had one or two health scares over the past year, he was much less reliable than he had been as host, bedmaker, cook or cleaner. Angie found herself doing it all, with sporadic help from her daughter. The three available bedrooms meant a full house could total eight with children and nine or ten if there were babies. And a lot of people brought their dogs as well. Anyone could see that such a workload would crush even the stalwart Angie Straw before very much longer.

'You could pay someone to come in and clean,' said Simmy, for the fiftieth time.

Angie made no attempt to present the same tired arguments against this idea. The essence of her resistance was that she feared the critical judgement of another woman. A paid cleaner would want to make changes and introduce new rules. Simmy could see that the whole enterprise would be spoilt if that happened. Angie would grow defensive and irritable, and there would be no fun left at all.

Russell changed the subject with a touch of his old sensitivity. 'Time for a walk?' he suggested. 'The dog hasn't been anywhere for a while. We've got an hour or so before lunch.'

The dog was a long-suffering Lakeland terrier, who tolerated the procession of visiting canines with gritted teeth. He was quite well aware that his own life was unfairly restricted by Angie's liberal standards, with much of it spent shut in the kitchen to avoid confrontation. He was firmly Russell's responsibility, with the result that he showed little affection towards either Angie or Simmy.

'Where do you want to go?' Simmy asked, with a questioning glance at her mother.

'I can't go anywhere, can I? The meal isn't going to cook itself. You two can pop down to Bowness and back, if you like. But be sure you're here for one. That gives you time, doesn't it?'

Beck View was on the southern edge of Windermere, shortly before it morphed into Bowness. A ten-minute walk took you within sight of the lake, and in another ten minutes you could be on the Esplanade, feeding swans and watching the cruise boats coming and going. Even in October, business was brisk, despite the disappearance of school-age children. The day was breezy but fairly mild.

'We can maybe have a quick aperitif on the way back,' said Russell, with a twinkle in his eye.

'All right for some,' grumbled Angie, but Simmy could see she was relieved to have the house to herself for a while.

Her father's legs were as functional as ever, after half a lifetime spent tramping the fells of the Lake District, and he set a brisk pace down to the lakeside. 'Hang on,' complained Simmy. 'You're going too fast.'

'The dog doesn't feel he's had a walk if he can't go at a trot. He really needs to be up your way, where he can run free.' Simmy lived in Troutbeck, where there were fells just outside her door. From Windermere there were few suitable walks where a dog could be safely liberated.

'You're welcome any time,' she said.

'Until you move, that is,' he reminded her.

'Will you mind? You hardly ever do come up to me these days, do you? We had that big walk, ages ago, when there was that dog business, but we never did it again. And now . . .' She trailed off, thinking that pregnancy, motherhood, commuting and marriage would all curtail her time with her parents, and that this would be a deprivation more for Russell than for Angie.

'I like Patterdale,' he reassured her. 'And Ullswater has always been my favourite of all the meres.'

They reached a point from which the lake could be seen between buildings. 'The cruise boat's looking nice,' said Russell. 'I always think of postcards when I see it. Must have picked up the Bowness contingent not many minutes ago.'

Simmy had never taken one of the tourist trips around the lake, considering herself too much of a permanent resident for such a thing. She had, however, allowed herself to be ferried across once or twice, with her car. 'Oh, look!' She was pointing to a group of people causing an obstruction on the pedestrianised area beside Lake Windermere. 'What's happening here?'

'Protest of some sort,' he observed cheerfully. 'It's a wonder your mother isn't part of it.' But they both knew that Angie's demonstrating days were long past. She hadn't been on a march since 2003.

'Not another zipwire?' She was trying to read the placards, but they were still too far away. The Friends of the Lake District, or some similar organisation, had gone overboard in repelling an attempt to erect a very long zipwire through Grizedale Forest. A year or two previously, the plan had come close enough to success to worry all concerned locals that it would come back in a modified form and be waved through on the second attempt.

'Looks like another tourist village,' said Russell, squinting at the slogans. 'That one says "Enough is Enough". Very informative. And there's "Nothing's More Precious than Our Landscape". Bit wordy, don't you think?'

'Your eyesight's better than mine,' she noted ruefully.

'Oh, I like that one. "Keep Tourism in Proportion". That's almost clever. I mean – there's a logic in there somewhere. If you let too many millions come, they'll just ruin it for themselves and everybody else. Like wind farms,' he finished obscurely.

'Mm,' mumbled Simmy, heading across the road. 'I can see someone I know.'

'So can I. Three, in fact, at the last count.' He followed her to the lakeside and accosted a man in a bright-green zipped-up anorak. 'Tristan! What brings you out onto the campaign trail?'

'Russell. Good to see you. I'm not campaigning, exactly. It's this business at Patterdale that's got us agitated. Another whacking great chalet park, would you believe? Here, have a leaflet.' He thrust a sheet of A5 into Russell's hand.

'Impossible. Where would they put it? Don't they know the place floods almost every year, so they can't be thinking of that level area between the road and the fells?' Russell's knowledge of the entire Lake District was legendary. 'And anywhere else is far too steep and rocky to be practical.'

'That's not true at all, I'm afraid. Read the leaflet.'

Russell stood obediently scanning the page, while the other man chatted to him. Simmy turned away, watching the people and wondering how much any of them really cared if a new chalet park appeared in remote little Patterdale. 'Can't see much wrong with it, personally,' said Russell.

'You should,' his friend informed him. 'There's dirty work afoot, you see if there isn't.'

'And he should know,' Russell muttered to Simmy, a minute later. 'Finger in every pie, has old Tristan.'

'Who is he?'

'Leading light in the Lib Dems for a while. Now he's something environmental. Or do I mean ecological? He grows things in a glasshouse. He's started talking about removing all the sheep from the fells, so the trees can grow back. I think he calls himself a consultant, which we all know means nothing in the real world.'

'Sounds as if he's one of the good guys, all the same.' Simmy rather fancied the idea of forest-covered hilltops.

'That's what he'd like you to think,' said her father darkly.

They each had a leaflet, printed on both sides, with a map, and a quote from Caroline Lucas. The point was made that there were empty slopes on the western side of Patterdale that were apparently vulnerable to

16

development unless strenuously protected. The threatened proposal was for a 'modest' two-acre site, with ten small chalets specifically designed for 'low-tech' tourist use. The protesters made their sarcasm unambiguous by repeating the words 'modest' and 'low-tech' in a second paragraph, with acid commentary. Simmy read it with a sinking heart. While she did not agree that the 'lodges' made of timber and discreetly positioned were particularly intrusive, it did seem a pity to keep on adding more of them to the landscape. Her own home village of Troutbeck, above Ambleside, was host to a very large number of the things, which had become grudgingly accepted by local people, over a period of time. The visitors brought cash with them, after all. But nobody pretended that the park in any way enhanced the landscape.

Another of the people Russell had recognised came up to them. 'Coming to join us?' she asked him with an air of challenge. Simmy watched her, noting the wispy hair and unhealthy skin. The woman was somewhere in her mid fifties, thin and tired-looking. Probably very hard-working, Simmy thought charitably.

'Candy,' Russell greeted her, with far less bonhomie than he had shown Tristan. 'This is my daughter, Persimmon. You might have seen her in her shop. Simmy, this is Candy Proctor. She's got a B&B two doors along from us.'

'Answer the question,' the woman insisted, having barely glanced at Simmy. 'Can we count on your support?'

'Let me think about it,' he said evasively. 'We've got to get back now. Angie's doing a Sunday roast.'

'Still eating meat, then?'

The voice came from behind Simmy's right shoulder, soft and unthreatening. She turned and smiled. 'Ninian! I saw you just now. Yes, I still eat meat. My mother would disown me otherwise. How are you? It's ages since I saw you.'

He bowed vaguely, his gaze on her rounded shape. 'Is that what I think it is?'

She laughed. 'Hadn't you heard?' Ninian and she had been in a relationship not so long ago, which had petered out with no recriminations. Ninian Tripp the potter lacked the energy for recriminations.

'Not in so many words. I assumed it was on the cards, that's all. Please accept my congratulations. And I forgive you for eating our fellow creatures, under the circumstances.'

'Thank you. You're not part of this protest, are you? Just about everybody we know seems to be here.'

He shuddered melodramatically. 'Perish the thought! Although I admire their spirit. They've been at this since before eleven this morning. I saw them when I came down into town earlier on. They've got right completely on their side, but they'll lose, of course. What's another handful of tasteful little chalets, more or less, in the great scheme of things? That's what the planners will say, mark my words.'

Russell and his near-neighbour were arguing in a desultory fashion, without any real conviction on his part, and an air of weariness on hers. The dog stood patiently at Russell's heel, well accustomed to such slow perambulations, where its master repeatedly paused to converse. Eventually, her father reached out a hand to Simmy. 'Come on. We're going to be late,' he urged, as if the delay had been all her doing.

Candy Proctor raised her chin and addressed Ninian. 'I heard what you said just now,' she accused. 'And I'll have you know we will not be beaten. The whole population of Patterdale is with us.'

'All twenty-seven of them,' muttered Russell, as they walked away.

'It's more than that,' Simmy corrected him. 'But what I don't understand is why are they protesting in Bowness? Patterdale's nearly fifteen miles from here.'

'And that's a very good question,' said her father.

Chapter Two

They had got as far as the Baddeley clock tower when yet more familiar faces came into view. 'Uh-oh,' said Russell softly. 'Here's the people from the back room.'

'What?'

But it was too late for elaboration. 'Well, hello!' crowed the family patriarch, putting a restraining hand on his wife's shoulder. Their seven-year-old son kept walking until called back. 'Look who it isn't – mine host, Mr Straw. Taking a constitutional, is it?'

'Mr . . .' said Russell weakly. 'This is my daughter.'

It gave Simmy a pang to realise he had forgotten the man's name. Less than two years ago, that would never have happened. She sighed and tried to form a polite smile for the little family. Meeting guests in the street was a horror for both her parents. Once the house had emptied for the day, they both liked to pretend that their lives were their own until the people began to trail back in the late afternoon. Such encounters as this risked more interaction, questions, observations and even complaints than they felt were reasonable.

But it seemed they were to be spared. 'Sorry, can't stop,' said the man. 'Lunch down in the fleshpots of Bowness, and then up on the fells. We'll be back around five, I should think.'

'Lovely,' said Russell, and pushed on up the hill to Beck View.

'Shouldn't that boy be at school?' Simmy wondered. 'How long are they staying?'

'Most of the week, I think. They're not bothered about the lad missing school as far as I can tell.'

When Angie asked after their walk, they regaled her with a list of people encountered. 'A mad social whirl, in fact,' Russell summarised. 'And there was that ginger-haired chap from Ambleside as well, holding a placard. I didn't get a chance to speak to him.'

'What ginger-haired chap?' Angie waited impatiently for enlightenment.

'You know. Great mane of orange down his back and wears bright pink shirts. Looks like something from a 1970s sci-fi film.'

'You mean Stuart Carstairs,' said Angie. 'You can't have forgotten his name.'

'I hardly know the man. He's more your friend than mine. Anyway, he's objecting to holiday chalets near Patterdale, along with the rest of them, for some reason.'

'He forgot the name of your people in the back room, as well,' said Simmy treacherously. 'We saw them just now.'

Angie merely nodded, and Simmy realised how tired her mother was, just as poor Candy Proctor had been. It was a weariness that came to all B&B proprietors after a hectic summer, and which was compounded, in Angie's case, by a sense that the valiant struggle to keep going was inexorably heading for failure.

'Are you going to be full all week?' Simmy asked.

'The man in the little room is staying until Friday. The Watsons in the front, with the little boy, are here till Wednesday. They're nice. They've been before. The ones with the seven-year-old are called Tomkin. They've got three more nights as well.'

'I think you should close down right through November and give yourselves a proper rest. I know I keep saying it, but you'll never get through the winter if you don't recharge your batteries while you get the chance.'

'Easier said than done,' argued Angie.

'Much easier,' confirmed Russell. 'Although if we took a break we could go to Patterdale every day and sabotage the new buildings. We could do all sorts of things if we didn't have all these beds to make.'

'At least you're not insisting we go on a cruise.'

'I know better than that.' He twinkled at Simmy, with a flash of his old mischief, but far from reassuring her, this reminder of former times only depressed her further. There had been a time, not so long ago, when he would make quips, puns, wry observations and criticisms of contemporary lack of grammar, several times an hour. Now the quips were feeble and infrequent, and even his impatience with poor English was blunted.

Lunch was a roast chicken, which was consumed with

a slightly forced relish. It seemed to them all that every viable topic of conversation had been covered during the morning. So rather than endure an awkward silence, Simmy enquired further about the current guests. 'Who's the man in the small room? Is he a walker?'

'Probably.' Angie was clearly not very interested. 'I've hardly seen him, to be honest. He went out early this morning, without breakfast. I think he might have come back while you two were out, but it could have been somebody leaving that flyer about pizza delivery. I actually don't know whether he's in or not. Without the dog to alert me, I don't always hear the door. It would be odd for him to be here in the middle of the day, but I can't forbid it. He's got a laptop with him, so maybe he's a writer or something. The good news is that he asked me not to clean his room today.'

'Maybe he was being thoughtful, given that it's a Sunday,' Simmy suggested.

'Possibly. More likely he just wants the room to himself.'

'Unusual not to want breakfast, as well. Isn't that the whole point of a B&B?'

'Not these days. Do you know – we had *four* different vegans last month?' Angie took veganism as a personal insult, since she made a feature of her local sausages and eggs, and insisted on using butter and full-cream milk unless actively prevented.

'Yes, you said,' Simmy nodded. 'Sign of the times.'

'Anyway, we do only about half as many full Englishes now. Quite a few go without completely. I always expect them to ask for a discount, but hardly anybody ever does.'

'I should hope not.'

'I think I would. I mean – most hotels charge extra for breakfast. It's usually quite a lot, as well.'

'Ten quid,' said Russell, clearly proud of his knowledge. 'Each.'

There followed another silence, while the food was finished, and plates cleared away. Then Russell spoke again. 'So we don't know for sure whether or not he's up there now. That's unsettling. I do like to know exactly who's in the house.'

Angie had to think hard. 'I think the stairs squeaked. It was about half an hour after you two went out. Didn't you meet him in the street? Wherever he went was on foot, because his car hasn't moved.'

Russell frowned. 'I doubt if I'd recognise him. I barely saw him when he arrived.' He wriggled his shoulders. 'I really don't like not knowing if he's in or out.'

Wife and daughter both gave him looks that said *Now he's really losing it*. 'Well, if we haven't found out for sure by the time it gets dark, I'll go and tap at the door,' said Angie. 'There's no law that says he has to go out, after all.'

'It does seem rather odd, though,' said Simmy, experiencing a very faint flicker of alarm. 'He's not ill, is he?'

'Looked perfectly fit yesterday. Forget about him. It really doesn't matter where he is. Who else did you see in Bowness?'

'A few vaguely familiar faces, from the shop,' said Simmy. 'It was a lot busier than I thought it would be. The weather's mild, of course. That must be it.'

'Isn't it nice to think,' Angie burst out, 'that just as the winter's ending, we'll have the baby. Spring babies are special, somehow.'

It was brave of her, Simmy had to admit. The many minefields had been trodden a few times already – the date, the first scan, the countless uncertainties – but they never got safer. 'Edith was a spring baby,' she said firmly. 'Pity I didn't keep the maternity clothes. They'd be just the right thickness for this time as well.'

'This one won't come on the same date,' said Russell with unwarranted confidence. 'You'd have to be ten days late.'

'Yes, I know, Dad,' said Simmy. Discussing the strange behaviour of the man in the little upstairs room would have been a lot easier than this. Almost anything would have been – which impelled her to return to the subject. 'He can't still be in his room, can he? He'll be hungry.'

'I told you he had a laptop with him. Maybe he's writing a book,' said Angie again. Neither parent seemed the least bit worried about their guest, so Simmy did her best to suppress the flickering concern she was feeling.

'What did you say Christopher was doing?' Russell asked. 'It would have been nice to have him join us.'

'He's covering for Josephine. She's got shingles, and the results of yesterday's sale haven't been logged on the website. He's in the office for most of the day.' The language and procedures of the auction house had gradually become familiar to Simmy. 'There's a backlog of queries to deal with, as well. Everything's got to be cleared by Wednesday, when stuff starts coming in for the next sale. It's relentless, and they can't let it fall behind.'

'I see,' nodded Russell, slowly absorbing the information. 'But he's happy in his work, is he?'

'Oh yes. He's found his vocation well and truly. He gets really excited – and he's learning such a lot.'

'Lucrative, too,' said Angie. 'Or so I understand.'

'It's amazing what people will pay,' Simmy agreed. 'With all the talk of decluttering and peak stuff, there's still an insatiable appetite for it all. A box of old postcards can go for eighty pounds, easily. And anything Chinese. They bid online from China and pay fortunes. The commission's amazing sometimes.'

'That's another thing,' said Russell, with a flash of anger. 'Charging the vendor *and* the buyer is scandalous.'

'I think it's a stroke of genius,' said Angie.

Russell was adamant. 'It's daylight robbery. I couldn't believe it when I first realised.'

'They've got to live,' said Simmy calmly. 'And nobody seems to object.' She had come to terms with the occasional greyness of auction ethics, and its consequences for Christopher. There were times when he had to compromise with standards of absolute probity, in order to protect the business and keep the right people happy. He had assured her that deviations were minor and infrequent, and little more than normal imperfect business life.

'Well, at least it means you can afford a decent house on the banks of Ullswater,' smiled Russell, suddenly relenting. 'That's my girl.'

'That's all very well—' Simmy began, when a strange unearthly voice coming from the floor above interrupted her.

'Help!' it screeched. 'Somebody help me!' And then there was a series of thumps followed by an even more unearthly silence.

Chapter Three

Angie was first on the scene by a wide margin. Russell had to disentangle himself from his dog, and then pause to ask himself just what was afoot. Simmy was doing nothing in a hurry, permanently aware of the precious little life inside her, which must not be jeopardised by falls or shocks or careless moments.

'Good God!' they heard from the top of the stairs.

They joined Angie to find her kneeling beside the prostrate body of a man, who had froth coming out of his mouth and nose, and was curled up in evident agony. 'Poison!' he gasped. 'They've poisoned me.' His body spasmed, the knees pulling up to the chest, hands opening and closing. Through a clenched jaw, he uttered one final word: '*Why?*'

'Great Scott, woman, what have we been feeding him?' said Russell. 'He looks as if he's just taken strychnine.'

'Call an ambulance,' Angie ordered. 'He'll die otherwise.' She bent over the man, her whole body taut with strain.

Simmy watched her as she reached out a hand and took hold of the man's shoulder in an effort to calm him. His eyes flickered and his teeth clattered.

Russell skittered obediently down the stairs, while Simmy held tightly to the bannisters and tried to subdue a rising hysteria. Long seconds passed. The man had rolled over, despite Angie's efforts to restrain him, and his face was in shadow, but his fists were visible, tightly clenched and pressed into his middle. As she watched, the hands relaxed and flopped away, the acute tension throughout the body softened, and the head lolled sideways, to face her. 'Mum,' she faltered. 'I think . . .'

'Too late for the ambulance,' Angie confirmed, her own body loosening as well. Simmy's thoughts ran wildly from one black joke to the next. *At least we won't have to perform mouth-to-mouth* was one. And *What are we going to tell the ambulance people?* And *Won't Ben and Bonnie love this one!*

'Poor man,' she said aloud. 'He must have been lying in bed all day feeling awful, and left it until now to call for help.'

'I don't think so.' Angie looked up. 'I'm sure he went out earlier this morning, and I was obviously right that I heard him come in again. And this doesn't look like something that's built up gradually to me. Didn't you hear what he said?'

To Simmy's certain knowledge her mother had never witnessed a death before. She had seen a few bodies lying tidily in their coffins, but she hadn't seen the stark brutality of the transition from animation to wholesale inertia, in a single irreversible second. Simmy herself had seen a man

28

shot in the street, and had been confronted by an untidy body or two in recent years. But nothing like this. 'He looks ghastly,' she murmured. 'What's that froth?'

'Lung damage, I would guess. Your detective friend is going to be up to his eyes, if I'm right in what I'm thinking.'

'What?' Simmy stared at this calm woman who seemed to have leapt many miles ahead already. 'What *are* you thinking?'

'Your father said strychnine. He might not be very far wrong. It has to be poisoning – that's for sure. Even if he hadn't said what he did, it would be pretty obvious.' She looked around, as if wary of being overheard. 'Here on my landing, damn it. This is going to finish us – you see if it doesn't.'

'For heaven's sake! You're rushing ahead much too fast. If it is poison, he must have taken it by himself, as a deliberate act. That makes it suicide. I can't see any need for Moxon to be involved. We needn't repeat what he said, especially as he can't have really meant it.'

'Don't be so stupid. Didn't you *hear* what he said?' demanded Angie. 'His very last word was "Why?". Nobody who'd decided to kill himself would ask that, would he? It's probably the absolutely most unlikely thing a suicide would say. And he clearly accused somebody of poisoning him. There's no chance that he did it himself. Any fool can see that.'

Simmy stuck doggedly to her point. 'He could just have been confused. Delirious.'

'Russell!' Angie called down the stairs, ignoring her foolish daughter. 'Is that ambulance on its way yet?'

There was no reply, and Simmy realised her father

was still on the phone. 'Shush,' she told her mother. 'He's talking to them.'

There was a sound from the man on the floor, as if he was heaving a long sigh. 'Hey, Mum – he's still alive!' Simmy was aghast. They had been far too quick to write him off, failing to administer first aid of some sort. 'What should we do?'

Angie leant over the body. 'I don't think he is,' she said. 'He's not breathing, look.'

'Can you feel a pulse? In his neck – that's what they do, isn't it? This is terrible. We're being totally pathetic, just letting him die without even trying to help him.'

Angie laid a tentative finger against the side of the man's neck. Simmy instinctively felt the same area of her own body, trying to establish the correct spot. 'I can't feel my *own* pulse,' she said, after a few seconds. 'What about his wrist?'

'There's nothing. That sigh was just an escape of air. I remember we had a dog die on us, when I was young. That did the same thing.'

Then Russell was beside them, looking from face to face in wonderment. 'Did he die?'

'Before you started calling 999, probably,' said his wife. 'He just went limp and stopped breathing.'

'Poor man,' he said, just as Simmy had done. 'What a thing!'

'How long will the ambulance be?' asked Angie.

'I don't know. They're not terribly busy. Ten minutes or so, I think. It's all very strange. Nobody poisons anybody these days. It's the stuff of the 1930s. Not like this, anyway. Could have done it to himself, of course, but you'd expect something nice and gentle like codeine – this looked alarmingly painful.'

'Stop it, Dad,' begged Simmy. 'You're making me feel ill.'

Russell grimaced. 'Distraction strategy,' he muttered.

'More like the exact opposite,' Angie accused him. 'Why don't you two go downstairs and leave it to me? You'll have to let the ambulance people in, and tell them we need the police.'

Simmy was more than happy to follow this suggestion, but her legs evidently had other ideas. She had been kneeling a foot or two away from the body, and standing up proved beyond her. 'Help me up,' she ordered her father.

Awkwardly, he pulled her to her feet. They were on a good-sized landing, with doors on two sides, and the open stairway at the end. The dead man's room was the closest, its door standing open. Glancing in, it seemed that there was considerable mess in there. 'He's been throwing things about,' she observed. 'That must have been the thumps we heard.'

'Isn't that what happens when people eat poisonous mushrooms?' Angie spoke distractedly, her eyes focused on empty space.

Simmy stood still, breathing heavily. The sheer horror of the situation swept over her. 'Mum . . .' she faltered. 'Will you be all right?'

'Me? Of course I will. What do you mean?'

'This is just so horrible. Look at him! What was his name? Where did he live? *Why* . . . ?' The unfinished question seemed to cover just about everything that had just taken place.

'Hush, girl. Time enough for all that when the police show

up. This isn't your problem. Let me and your father handle it.'

Somehow she got downstairs and into the kitchen. Russell was soon summoned to the front door, and there were voices, heavy footsteps, and short, ominous silences. Simmy sat at the cluttered table, reliving the last half-hour, struggling to make sense of it. The man himself had claimed to have been poisoned – but wasn't that just something anybody might say, if suddenly taken ill? There were surely some medical conditions that could explain what had happened. What about an aortic aneurysm? Or a burst ulcer? Internal bleeding, peritonitis, sepsis – the terms flittered around her head, with little underlying knowledge to confirm their relevance. Her ignorance made it easier to cling to the notion that it had been a natural death, with no sinister implications.

The doorbell rang again, and she waited to hear whether Russell would come down to answer it. He didn't, so she got up and went to do it herself.

The familiar face on the doorstep gave rise to a slew of emotions. Disappointment, reassurance, admiration for his promptness, and a sense of warm friendship. 'Hello,' she said.

'Where is he? This is Detective Sergeant Emily Gibson, by the way. Mrs Brown, daughter of the homeowners,' he completed the introductions.

'Upstairs. On the landing,' she told Detective Inspector Nolan Moxon.

The next thing she knew, it was half past three. She had phoned Christopher with the news that a man had died in

Beck View and there was a crowd of police people in the house. The plan to spend the early evening in Patterdale, visiting the bar of the hotel to check, for the fifth time, whether anyone knew of property coming onto the market, was postponed. 'I don't know when I'll get away,' she said. 'I can't leave Mum and Dad until things have settled down. The other guests will be back before long, wanting to know what's been going on.'

'Sounds like a nightmare,' her fiancé sympathised. 'Should I come and help?'

'That's very sweet of you, but I don't think Mum would welcome yet another person here. They haven't even removed the body yet.'

'Where is it exactly?'

'On the landing, outside the back bedroom. They've got police people stripping the room and none of us is allowed up there. The real worry is what happens when the other guests come in. Nobody seems to know what we're meant to do with them.'

Christopher's mind was evidently working well. 'Will they be suspects, then, if it's murder? *Is* it murder?'

'Who knows? They're taking it all very seriously, because my dad told them the man said he'd been poisoned, just before he died. So I assume they think it could be, or at least have to give it serious consideration. I don't know why they don't rush him to a pathology lab somewhere and do a post-mortem to see what killed him.'

'What about his family?'

'Mum's got an address for him, so the police will send somebody there and see if there's a wife or something – I suppose.' Then there were new voices in the hall, and she finished the call, promising to let Christopher know as soon as she felt able to leave.

At four o'clock all the Straws were in the kitchen, as well as their dog, drinking tea and listening to the many heavy footsteps above their heads. 'I think I'm in shock,' said Angie. 'I'm going to put two sugars in this tea.'

'You've been very calm so far,' said Simmy. 'We all have, really. I wonder what they're thinking about us.'

'Your Moxon man is a godsend. It's so lucky he knows you. I've never met such a nice policeman. I remember in the seventies . . .'

'Yes, Mum, all right. Don't get started on police brutality now. He might hear you.'

Angie drank her sweet tea with uncharacteristic meekness. Russell was restless, shifting in his chair and irritating the dog. 'We must be suspects,' he said. 'At best, they'll think we fed him rancid sausages.'

'He hasn't eaten anything from this kitchen since he got here,' Angie retorted. 'So that's not something we need to worry about.'

'It could still easily be suicide,' said Simmy. 'In fact, that's much more likely, it seems to me.'

'We've been through all that,' sighed Angie. 'They obviously think the worst, or why are they bothering with all this forensic business?'

'Because of what Dad told them he said.' Simmy couldn't quite refrain from throwing an accusing look at her father. It would all be so much easier if that detail had never been reported.

'You'd rather a murderer got away with his crime, would you?' Russell enquired, as if he really wanted to know her

34

response. 'I can see that might be tempting in the short run. But it won't do, will it? You know it won't.'

Simmy sighed, knowing he was right.

Two hours passed, during which the body of Mr Grant Childers of Halesowen near Birmingham was taken in a special vehicle to the mortuary at Barrow Hospital. DI Moxon spent twenty minutes explaining procedure to the Straws, showing them the G5 form that had to be filled in for a sudden death. He commiserated briefly and apologised for the disruption. The other guests would be permitted to continue with their existing plans, after being questioned. 'Just their names and addresses, basically,' he reassured Angie. 'Until we know the precise cause of death, we won't have much idea of what to ask them. As far as you're aware, they didn't know Mr Childers, I presume?'

'I'm sure they didn't,' said Angie. 'They were all here before he arrived.'

'It still might have been suicide, don't you think?' Simmy asked.

Moxon scratched his head. 'The whole picture indicates otherwise, I'm afraid. Whatever he took caused considerable pain, which very few suicides would opt for. Then his cries for help – and even the timing doesn't fit the usual pattern. He'd have known you were all downstairs enjoying a family Sunday. Only the most extraordinarily self-obsessed person would wilfully blight that by killing himself at that particular point in time.'

'Aren't all suicides self-obsessed?' said Angie sourly.

Nobody argued with her, but nor did they agree. Moxon met Simmy's gaze, with the slightest eye roll to indicate he knew better than to engage with one of Angie's many dogmatisms.

Angie had been questioned more exhaustively than the others, concerning any food she might have carelessly provided the man. 'Nothing at all,' she insisted. 'He arrived quite late on Friday and went straight to bed, as far as I could tell. No breakfast yesterday or today.'

'But he could make a drink in his room?'

'There's a kettle and tea and coffee. But I give them proper milk in a jug, if they want it – and he didn't ask for anything. The kettle was exactly as I left it, so I'm pretty sure he never even made a drink. He was out the whole of yesterday.'

'It could have been an accident,' Simmy went on, still clinging to the hope that this was not another murder. 'Something he brought with him – berries or mushrooms, perhaps. It is the season for that sort of thing. Or he could easily have picked something up this morning, when he went out.'

'That's possible,' Moxon agreed, with hardly a hint of scepticism. 'But if so, he ate every morsel, because there's no sign of any food or drink in his room.'

'So the same goes for if somebody gave him poison,' Simmy pointed out. 'He ate the whole thing, whatever it was, without leaving any evidence. Isn't that terribly odd?'

'It's all terribly odd,' said Moxon darkly. 'If ever you wanted a mystery, this is it.' He smiled ruefully. 'And your young Ben Harkness is going to miss the whole thing.'

Next morning, in the shop, Simmy had to break the news to Bonnie. 'A man died at Beck View yesterday and it looks like murder,' she began, without preamble. 'And Ben's not going to have any chance to play detective.'

The girl stared at her. 'At Beck View?' she repeated. 'How can that be? Who died? How? When?'

Simmy gave as detailed a description as she could, knowing that anything she left out now would be held against her later. 'I still think it could easily have been suicide or an accident,' she concluded.

'No.' Bonnie shook her head decisively. 'Not a chance. He'll have been trying to hide from somebody who was out to get him, but they were too clever for him. Gave him a bottle of something laced with poison, or a doctored bar of chocolate, or . . .'

'There's no trace of anything like that in the room.'

'Didn't he go out at all?'

'Well, yes. He was out all Saturday, as well as yesterday morning. Mum heard him come back while I was out with my dad walking the dog.'

'There you are, then!' Bonnie waved a triumphant hand. 'That's when it happened. He came home with stomach ache, lay down for a bit, then when it got bad he shouted for help. Simple.'

Simmy had to admit that the hypothesis fitted the known facts with almost embarrassing tidiness. She was going on to enumerate her reasons for nonetheless continuing to doubt these conclusions, but Bonnie interrupted her.

'It'll be brilliant for your mum's business,' she enthused. 'Everyone's going to want to see the place where a murder happened.'

Simmy gulped at this. 'My dad thinks the exact opposite. He thinks it'll finish them completely.'

'He's wrong,' Bonnie assured her. 'People are going to love it.' Then she changed tack again. 'So I'm guessing you didn't get to Patterdale yesterday?'

Simmy shook her head. 'I didn't leave Beck View till seven. I didn't see Chris at all over the weekend. Saturday was an auction day and he was logging all the results yesterday. Josephine's off sick.'

'That's not good.' Bonnie's mouth turned down. 'But I know the feeling. I won't see Ben for a *month*.'

'We're both abandoned by our menfolk. It was ever thus, as my dad would say.'

'Yeah . . . well,' said the girl vaguely. 'First customer incoming, look.' She nodded towards the street door, where a man was hovering on the pavement outside. 'We haven't got the pots out yet.'

'Too much chatter. Is he anyone we know?' Simmy was standing at an angle that made the man's face hard to see.

'Don't think so.' But then the door opened, and there was a clear view. Simmy recognised the man her father had addressed the previous day as Tristan.

Chapter Four

It could not be a coincidence. Hazy memories of protests over holiday chalets near Patterdale and local politics filled her head, along with her father's acquaintance with this man. Wilkins was his surname, she remembered. And his first name carried implications of good breeding and horses, for some reason.

'Hello?' she said. 'Didn't I see you yesterday?'

'You're Russell Straw's daughter, if I'm not mistaken. I hope you'll forgive me, but I saw some of the commotion outside Beck View yesterday and thought I should check that all's well. I know poor old Russ has had a few problems lately, so I didn't like to intrude if there was anything . . . you know. And I'm not so well acquainted with your mother.'

'Everything's absolutely fine, thanks,' she breezed, with unwarranted confidence.

'Oh good. That's good. So – what happened, if you don't mind my asking?'

Simmy calculated that the story would be public

knowledge before the end of the day, making it futile to try to keep it quiet. 'Well, I suppose it's all right to tell you that a man died in the house. One of the guests. It was very sudden.'

'Good Lord! That must have been dreadfully shocking. Were you there at the time?'

'I was, yes. But everything's settled down now. These things happen, I suppose.'

Bonnie made a small, sceptical throat-clearing noise behind her, but Simmy ignored it. The man seemed at a loss for more to say and began to look around the shop as if thinking of buying some flowers. Then another thought appeared to strike him and he started rummaging in a sort of satchel on his shoulder. 'Here – I thought you might have a place I could put these, for your customers to pick up. I'm thinking they'll mostly be residents, rather than visitors, and might be on our side.' He produced a bundle of the leaflets he'd been distributing the previous day. 'Would that be all right?'

Simmy hesitated. She had been asked for similar favours before, as well as requests to stick posters in her window, and almost always declined on the grounds of limited space. But Patterdale was beginning to feel like home territory, a place that must not be despoiled or excessively invaded. 'Well . . .' she said, 'I suppose we could stack them next to the till.' She eyed the small table where all the shop business was conducted. Whatever happened to old-fashioned shop counters, she asked herself, with acres of space for putting things. Even before she had taken it over, when it had been an off-licence, there hadn't been a full-sized counter.

'What are they about?' Bonnie enquired, peering at the top leaflet.

'A plan to build a bunch of tourist chalets on the fell above Patterdale,' said Simmy quickly, not wanting Tristan to embark on a long tirade. 'My dad and I met him giving out leaflets in Bowness yesterday.'

Bonnie gave this a moment's thought. 'Why in Bowness?' she wondered. 'I mean – we're *miles* away from Patterdale.'

'My dad and I wondered the same thing,' said Simmy.

'We explained,' said Tristan irritably. 'Bowness is the best spot for maximum publicity. And most visitors don't stay in one spot. They explore the whole area, with Kirkstone and Ullswater high on their list. They want that whole northern section to be unspoilt. You locals might see it differently, but believe me, we know what we're doing.'

'Is that why you did it on a Sunday?' asked Bonnie.

'Right,' he said shortly. 'Lots of people about.'

'Still seems pretty weird to me,' said the girl, with little consideration for politeness. 'They'll never let anybody build something like this in Patterdale in a million years.'

'You'd be surprised,' he told her, with a severe look. 'They've done it in Hartsop, which is barely two miles away.' Bonnie was eighteen, but looked a good three years younger. Her frizzy fair hair and elfin features gave her a cheeky expression, even when she was trying to be serious. The man continued to lecture her. 'They've been clever about it. Everything's eco-friendly, low-impact, and so forth. Tucked away out of sight, like in Hartsop.'

'So why's it such a terrible idea, then?'

'Come along to our meeting on Thursday evening, and we'll tell you.'

'Why not tell me now?'

He opened his mouth to reply, but Simmy got there

first. 'Bonnie, we haven't got time to stand about arguing. Listen, Mr Wilkins, we'll take a few of your leaflets, but I'm not going to push them at people. Bonnie's right, in a way. We need to find out more about the plan before we reject it outright. I know my father isn't sure it would be such a bad thing. I'm hoping to find somewhere to live in Patterdale myself, as it happens, so however this turns out, it might well affect me directly.' She paused, then added, 'I don't suppose you know of anywhere that might be for sale up there, do you?'

He gave a slow smile that made his broad face considerably more benign than when he was in hectoring mode. 'You know – I just might. It's not certain by a long way, but I do know somebody who might be able to help. I'd have to make a few enquiries first.'

'Oh yes! Please do.' Simmy's excitement rose out of all proportion to the dubious offer. 'That would be great.' She gave him a card. 'Let me know if anything comes of it – you can phone me, all my numbers are on there.'

'Who is he?' Bonnie demanded, the moment the man had gone.

'According to my dad, he was a Lib Dem – on the council, I presume. And now he does some kind of environmental work. If I got it right. It didn't sound as if Dad liked him much, although they did have a bit of a chat yesterday.'

'Hmm,' said Bonnie. 'Well, he's certainly obsessing about this Patterdale thing.' She picked up one of the leaflets. 'I still think they're overreacting. These things never get permission. And if it's so eco-pure, then it might not matter anyway.'

'He seemed quite interested in the man who died,' Simmy mused.

'Anybody would be. What was his name, by the way? The dead man, I mean.'

'Childers. Grant Childers. From somewhere in the Midlands.'

'What else do you know about him?'

'Practically nothing. He looked about thirty-five, although I can't say I got much sight of him. Stayed two nights, on his own, and was due to leave on Friday. He had a laptop with him and was out all day Saturday. And now I've told you all I know. Some of it twice, probably.'

Bonnie was clearly frustrated, but the timely arrival of a genuine customer diverted her from any further speculations. Simmy left her assistant to deal with a complicated enquiry, and disappeared into the small room at the back of the shop, where she had tasks waiting. Fresh flowers were due that morning, to replace the drooping blooms from the previous week. An online order meant she had to create a bouquet and deliver it that afternoon. The next day would see a funeral at the Windermere church, for which she had three wreaths to make, and at the end of the week there was a wedding in a hotel, requiring substantial floral decoration.

Her thoughts revolved around poison and all the toxic plants she had learnt about on her floristry course. Many were not lethal, but would cause illness to some degree. If you excluded fungi, and those plants that required complex processes to extract the poison, it mostly came down to rare and exotic species, with hardly any berries and seeds that might be found in ordinary gardens. She recalled one of her fellow students drawing attention to the phrase 'and might even cause death', which came at the end of numerous descriptions of toxic plants. 'What does that really mean?' the girl had asked. The tutor had been forced to check actual statistics, eventually coming back with the clarification that actual known deaths caused by the great majority of the listed plants amounted to a very small handful, most of them young children. 'So we don't really need to worry that we're selling anybody something they might use to kill their husbands,' laughed the student.

Why was she thinking of this now, Simmy asked herself. Was she afraid that her role as a florist might find itself implicated in Mr Childers' death? Moxon had given no hint of that, and neither had Bonnie when she heard the story. Besides, poison came in many guises, most of them chemical. That was to say, in substances used in industries far removed from her innocent flowers. Acids, medicines, rat poison, fluids associated with cleaning and bleaching . . . her imagination quickly ran dry, and she forced her attention back onto her work.

When she emerged, Bonnie was alone in the shop, looking much more sombre than usual. 'What's the matter?' Simmy asked.

'I can't tell Ben about this murder, can I? He's still trying to settle down and understand his course syllabus and everything. Helen made me promise not to distract him until at least November. That's more than two weeks away.'

'Well, if you promised, you'll have to stick to it.'

'I know. And I would anyway. But how was I to know something would happen so soon? And it's such a *good* one.'

'Don't say that, Bonnie. A person being murdered is never good, is it?'

44

'You know what I mean.'

'It might yet turn out to be an accident,' said Simmy, with forced optimism.

Angie phoned at lunchtime, with the news that DI Moxon had been back to tell her and Russell that Grant Childers had died from ingesting a plant-based toxin more likely to have been in the form of a drink than anything solid. 'They've got to do a whole lot more tests before they know exactly what it was,' said Angie. 'But it seems he didn't eat anything much all day.'

'Do they know how long it was between him taking it and dying?' Simmy asked.

'He didn't say. He wasn't supposed to tell us as much as he did, but he wanted to reassure us that we weren't under suspicion.'

'Oh? Why do they think that? You might have made him some herbal tea or something.'

'Except we told them we didn't and they believed us. It would be insane to accuse us. We've got no reason to want the man dead.'

'It could have been an accident – in their minds, I mean. In fact, that's surely still more likely than deliberate murder. Some horrible mistake in a cafe somewhere has got to be what happened.'

'Not if there's been absolutely no sign of anyone else in Bowness or Windermere or anywhere within twenty miles having the same thing.'

'Oh. Well, perhaps there will be. It's still a bit soon to say for sure. If there's a contaminated batch of orange juice or something, it might be days or even weeks before it's drunk.'

'Clutching at straws,' said Angie tiredly. 'With all the checks and health and safety rules, it's almost impossible for that to happen. And if it did, it would probably be deliberate, so that's still murder. Believe me, your father and I have talked this through ad infinitum since you left yesterday.'

'But Moxon didn't say what sort of plant poison it was, exactly?'

'No, they can't tell that yet. He did say there's quite a lot of Childers family, all wanting to come up here and find out for themselves what happened. Mother, father and two sisters, I think he said. No wife, luckily.'

Simmy was trying to keep up with the poison theme. 'So it could have been someone in town, who gave him something lethal to drink?'

Angie sighed. 'Presumably. But I can't imagine they'd have done it by mistake. I keep trying to come up with a sensible story that doesn't involve murder, but nothing seems very convincing.'

'Well, Bonnie says that a murder would be great for the business. She thinks you'll get flocks of guests wanting to see the room where a man was poisoned.'

'She's mad,' said Angie, with real anger. 'Any normal person would want to keep as far away as possible.'

Privately, Simmy thought that many of her mother's guests were quite a distance from 'normal' – but she didn't say so. 'Well, keep me posted,' she said. 'I've got to go now. There's a customer.'

'Yes, but—' Angie said urgently. 'I haven't told you what the other guests are saying.'

'Sorry. I really do have to go. I'll phone you again this

evening. I'll have to do some shopping and catch up with Christopher. And we're going to be busy here for most of the week.' Suddenly she felt the pressure of it all. 'And I've got an antenatal appointment on Wednesday,' she remembered.

She ended the call before her mother could say anything more. Her parents were quite capable of getting through the next few days without her holding their hands, she reminded herself. The most they could reasonably expect was a listening ear and reassurances that everything would settle down again eventually. If this crisis precipitated a decision to give up the B&B, then that could be dealt with too. It had been in the air for most of the year anyway. Christopher had gone so far as to hint that the sale of Beck View would release a great deal of equity, which Simmy might reasonably expect to benefit from, as the Straws' only child.

'Except they might need it all for their nursing homes when they lose their wits,' Simmy had objected. That prospect did not seem so distant, or so improbable, as it had a year or two earlier.

The customer was deftly satisfied, as was the one who came rapidly on her heels. People were anxious to fend off the oncoming winter with bright colours and summer scents. They wanted freesias and roses and lilies and dahlias. Simmy kept a generous stock of these and others, ordering more every second or third day. Bonnie kept the window display vibrant and fresh with primary colours and only the most subtle hints of autumn. Time enough for that after Halloween was over. Simmy was forced to sell pumpkins, but she resisted any other offerings. 'The whole thing's gone mad,' she grumbled. 'They can get their broomsticks somewhere else.'

Bonnie, somewhat to Simmy's surprise, did not argue the point. 'I don't like Halloween either,' she confessed. 'There's something dark and nasty about it.'

'Same as Bonfire Night, really,' Simmy remarked. 'That's even nastier when you think about it. And it's daft that they're less than a week apart.'

'That's what Ben thinks. He says they're basically the same pagan ritual, which got split up after Guy Fawkes and all that. The problem is the way the Americans have gone so overboard about Halloween, and sent it back here with bells and whistles on. Corinne says when she was young they just did apple bobbing and nothing else at all.'

Corinne was Bonnie's foster mother. Their relationship went back eight or nine years, after Bonnie was rescued from a non-functioning mother whose succession of unpleasant boyfriends had been very bad news for the little girl. Her school career had been blighted by anorexia and other problems. And yet here she was, bright and cheerful and the devoted girlfriend of the brilliant Ben Harkness, who had just gone off to university to study forensic archaeology.

The afternoon proceeded with no hiccups, once Bonnie had been updated on the death of Grant Childers. She snatched some moments to learn about plant poisons on her phone and treated Simmy to a shortlist of likely culprits, along with their effects on the human body. 'It's unusual these days,' she said, more than once. 'Poisoning, I mean. Most things are very difficult to get hold of, for one thing. And hardly anybody understands plants any more.'

'That's true,' Simmy agreed, thinking of the profound ignorance displayed by most of her customers.

'Moxon might call in, do you think?' Bonnie's tone was hopeful. 'You know how he likes to see you.'

'He saw me yesterday. It's really nothing to do with me. He'll have enough with my parents, without adding me into the mix.'

'You always say it's nothing to do with you, and then you jump right in with both feet. And this one's much closer to home than anything that's happened before. You were *right there* when he died. Was he actually in your arms?'

'Definitely not. Stop it – I don't want to think about it. The poor man. He must have been so scared.'

'Did he look scared?'

'I don't know.' She thought about it. 'I didn't see his face very clearly. He was all tensed up and then suddenly he went limp. Just like that.'

'Awful,' Bonnie murmured, obviously trying to imagine the whole scene.

The last hour of the working day went slowly. Nobody came into the shop, and no new orders arrived, either by phone or computer. Simmy found herself unconsciously braced for the arrival of another person connected to the death of Mr Childers. One aspect of running a shop was that everybody knew where to find you. She couldn't count the number of times she had been cornered by suspects, witnesses, bereaved relatives and police officers in the days following a violent death. Most times, Bonnie was there as well, eagerly vacuuming up all the information that got spilt in Persimmon Petals, and passing it on to Ben, the boy detective, who had, two years earlier, been on the street in Bowness when a man had been shot, while Simmy watched it all from her car. From that moment on, he had been addicted to the whole business of murder and was now putting his obsession into practice with the beginning of his degree course.

'Home time,' Simmy announced at last. 'I'll have to go to the supermarket first. There's no food in the house.'

But before either of them could make a move, the shop phone rang and somehow they both knew it was not going to be an order for flowers.

Chapter Five

'Simmy? It's Ninian. Were you just leaving for the day?'

'I was, actually. Why don't you use my mobile?'

'I can't remember the number. Does it matter?'

'I suppose not. What can I do for you?'

'I've been thinking of you since we bumped into each other yesterday, and then I just heard on the radio that a man died at a Windermere B&B. I called someone I know, who told me it was at your mother's. At least, she thinks that's right, so I phoned to check.' His voice was as languid as ever, wrapping everything he said in an easy, relaxed blanket, where no crisis could be serious enough to agitate him.

'That's right. I was there.'

'Who was he?'

'A B&B guest, from the Midlands somewhere. It's a police matter.'

Bonnie was hovering, trying to work out who was calling. Simmy flapped a hand at her, indicating that she should go home, and there was nothing to concern her. With a small shrug, the girl obeyed.

'Sounds nasty.'

'Yes, it was. But I'm trying not to let it bother me. You'd approve of that, I'm sure.'

'Stay serene,' he agreed. 'Especially in your condition. I wanted to say something about that, actually, if I'm not crossing a line. I do remember that this isn't the first time, you see. And maybe it's all somewhat stressful and scary. And I know a bit about past traumas coming back to bite you. So – all I wanted to say, really, is that if you want to chat about it any time, I'm available. No strings, nothing ulterior. But we were good pals, Sim, for a bit, weren't we? And good pals don't grow on trees.'

She laughed, feeling decidedly soothed by his individualistic way of putting things. 'We were,' she said. 'And that's very sweet of you. I'm not doing too badly so far, fingers crossed. It's going to be at the end that everything gets tricky. I don't know how I'm going to be, but I'll have to tell them to stand by with the sedatives.'

'Are you going to find out what sex it is?'

'No.' The word came out with real emphasis. 'Absolutely not.'

'Good for you. Very wise.'

'I'm not sure Chris thinks so, but somehow it helps not to know. If I persuade myself it's a boy, that already makes it different from before.' She stopped, hoping he would follow her tangled logic.

It seemed that he did. 'Makes sense,' he said. 'So, I'd better let you get off now. I'll pop in and see you sometime, then.'

'You do that,' she said warmly. 'Thanks for phoning.'

She spent the next hour in a small glow of satisfaction that she had managed to retain the friendship of such a gracious man. She still sold his pots in the shop, whenever he could stir himself to supply them, and thought fondly of their time together. It was hardly his fault if he hadn't quite met her prerequisites for a long-term committed relationship. Ninian would never want children, and that for Simmy had been enough to disqualify him.

She did not call her mother until she was safely back in her Troutbeck cottage, with a ready meal warming in the oven and a large mug of tea in her hand. It was a short conversation, because Angie was overwhelmed with the number of people in her house. 'The Childers family are coming any minute, and the guests have all come back for the day. I didn't think they'd stay on, but they all seem determined to carry on as usual, at least for another day or so.'

'Is Moxon going to be there as well?'

'What? Oh no, I don't suppose so. There'll be one of those liaison people, won't there? They haven't wasted much time, I must say. Three of them have dropped everything to come and see where their loved one died. Can't quite see the point, personally.'

'No,' said Simmy, wondering how she would react under similar circumstances. 'Remind me who they are.'

'I think they said father, sister and sister's husband. Too much for the old mum, presumably. There's another sister somewhere, but she doesn't seem to be coming.'

'Well, good luck with it. Call me later, if you want to talk about it.'

'Thanks, but I doubt if I'll want to. What about you, anyway? You were there as well – are you getting flashbacks?'

'Not yet,' said Simmy. By an obvious association, her mind filled with the memory of holding her dead baby daughter on her lap After that, she did not believe any dead body would have the power to traumatise her. 'I don't think I was unduly affected by it, actually.'

'No. I don't expect you were,' said her mother.

The October evening ended well before eight, as far as the sky outside was concerned. Simmy closed her curtains and eyed her woodburning stove with affection. Another week or two and she'd be using it for the cheerful glow and the pleasing warmth it threw across the room. The existence of the stove had been a strong selling point when she first bought this Troutbeck cottage. Now she would have to adopt a brave face and use it to woo prospective buyers. The whole business of selling and buying property was beyond difficult, she had quickly realised. Combining it with running the shop, keeping things going with Christopher, being pregnant and watching over her parents was proving almost impossible. Given that there were virtually no properties for sale in the chosen area, and that the restrictions resulting from living in a National Park could be draconian, she often came to the conclusion that it was never going to happen. She would live with her baby in Troutbeck, and Christopher would have to move in, squeezing himself, his possessions and his car into far too small a space. It would work financially, of course. And the commute to his Keswick auction house was probably less than the average distance that working people drove each day. There were no real plans as to the future of the shop in Windermere, but Simmy had assured Bonnie and others that she would not be giving it up, whatever happened.

This assurance was both rash and pessimistic. The baby was due during one of the busiest times for floristry, for one thing. But there was a frightening sense of tempting fate in assuming there would really be a live baby at all. Underneath the brave face and words, Simmy had a dreadful certainty that this one would die as well. And if that happened, she would need the shop in a whole lot of ways.

Christopher understood at least some of this, but was at a loss as to what to do about it. By nature he was an optimist, with more than a dash of the same laissez-faire approach to life as Ninian Tripp possessed. He had spent several years travelling, picking up casual work, enjoying brief relationships and then moving on again. The eldest of five siblings, he had been born on the same day as Simmy, their mothers bonding in the maternity ward. Summer holidays had been spent together for years. When they found each other again after a gap of twenty years, it was at his mother's funeral. Sometimes Simmy found herself believing that this had been an omen, which she should have had the sense to observe.

Now he was an auctioneer, selling objects that were beautiful, peculiar or simply old to avid collectors and slightly shady dealers every other Saturday. His work was controlled by this rigid fortnightly routine, with the necessity of producing a comprehensive catalogue two days before each sale a powerful taskmaster. Crises arose frequently, with lost purchases, challenged provenance, bewildered vendors and sudden breakages all demanding patient diligence on Christopher's part. His full-time team of workers comprised of Josephine, who controlled the computer, three other women and four men. In addition, there were van drivers, house clearers, porters and cleaners who came when needed. The operation was growing, with Internet sales expanding dramatically and not a hint that the appetite for antiques, collectables and general junk was ever going to abate.

Everything was perfectly doable, according to Chris. The important thing was that they remain united, them against the world, determined not to let anything divide them. The new house would happen in its own good time, whether in Patterdale, Ambleside, Rosthwaite or somewhere they had never even thought of. Their first idea had been to find a home in Grasmere, and that was still under consideration, too. But Simmy had perversely set her heart on Patterdale, for no logical reason other than that she found it magically beautiful. To bring up a child there seemed to her the most perfect piece of parenting she could imagine. And now Mr Tristan Wilkins had hinted that he might be able to help, which was a detail she should waste no time in conveying to her fiancé.

So she phoned Christopher and told him she'd had a good day, and nothing had occurred to disturb her unduly. They made arrangements to go together to the antenatal check, and the twenty-week scan, which had slipped to almost twenty-two weeks, and agreed to close their eyes when it came to examination of the foetal genitalia. 'And don't you dare cheat!' she ordered him.

'I wouldn't dare,' he said. 'And I've come round to your way of thinking, anyway. I'm going to enjoy the suspense of not knowing.'

The feeling of relief surprised her. Until that moment she had not realised how defensive and anxious she'd been feeling about this apparent conflict. She had anticipated reproach and argument from the baby's father. 'You lovely man!' she told him. 'I really don't deserve you.'

'Aw, shucks,' he said in a silly voice. Simmy laughed, suddenly cheerful.

They confirmed a plan in which he would spend the following night in Troutbeck, then they would go together to Barrow, where they had reluctantly agreed to use the maternity services, rather than Whitehaven or Carlisle. Not one of the three was quick or easy to reach, either from Troutbeck or Patterdale, and the uncertainty of where they would be living made the decision almost impossible. Barrow had a very unfortunate history when it came to new babies, which made it hard to trust them. But as Angie said, this would have concentrated their minds considerably, making them sure to be the safest option. 'Like after a bomb,' she said. 'That spot becomes the safest place to be.' It might be rational, but Simmy had privately felt it left out a major aspect of human nature.

But she knew the way there and had no personal complaints against them. She and her father had both been patients in Barrow General, with no unfortunate outcomes. 'If necessary, we can stay at Beck View for the last few days, which is only half an hour away,' she said.

The consultant she had seen six weeks earlier had urged her to agree to an elective Caesarean section at thirty-eight weeks, to ensure the best possible outcome for the baby. But Simmy had resisted, hearing her mother's howls of outrage at the very idea. 'That would be fine if there was any cause for concern,' said Angie afterwards. 'But if everything's going normally, it would be a terrible idea.' Ever since she had heard a man refer to his child's birth as 'coming out through the sunroof' Angie had been loud in her condemnation of this mechanical approach. Simmy mildly agreed with her, on the grounds that on the whole nature knew best. The prospect of coping with a large fresh scar at the same time as a startled new baby did not appeal.

'See you on tomorrow, then,' she told Christopher.

'It's going to be great,' he said. 'I can hardly wait.'

She knew he was being deliberately upbeat, and was grateful for it, even if he was missing the point that it was not this scan that she was anxious about. All the hazards would come later, when the terror of history repeating itself would come flooding in.

Chapter Six

'Oh Lord, that must be them,' sighed Angie, as the doorbell rang. 'Now, mind what you say, all right? Don't start one of your rambling stories, and don't go making any wild guesses about poison.'

'I'll stay quietly out of the way, then,' said Russell mildly. 'I don't want to upset any apple carts.'

'You'll probably have to talk to the guests, anyway. Once that kid's asleep, they'll want to be downstairs for a bit.' It had long ago struck her that families and B&Bs did not go well together. Often, there was no downstairs space available at all, except for the dining room, which was generally closed during the day and evening. The choice was to stay out until the children were asleep on their feet, or huddle together in the bedroom, reading or watching television, until everybody crashed out together. Beck View had an all-purpose downstairs room with games and books, but no TV, which was at least some improvement on the usual pattern.

'I still can't remember their name,' said Russell tetchily. 'Simmy and I met them yesterday and I couldn't address him properly. The other lot are Tomkins. I do remember that.'

'So your job is to keep them away from the Childers people.'

'Thank you,' said her husband meekly. 'I'll do that.'

Angie was already halfway along the corridor, talking over her shoulder. The imposition of having to speak to the grieving relatives of a man she had hardly exchanged fifty words with – and all those the usual spiel about keys and breakfast times – was making her cross. Nobody seemed to consider how it had been for her, having the wretched guest expire on her landing. And Persimmon, in her condition, should never have been witness to such a thing. She pulled the door open with the faintest of smiles. Two men and two women confronted her, one of the women in uniform.

The only place she could take them was the private sitting room used by her and Russell. That in itself felt like an unfair intrusion. When they got there, the police liaison officer made introductions, beginning with a man about Russell's age. 'This is Mr Childers, father of the deceased,' she said awkwardly. 'And Mr and Mrs Gorringe, one of his sisters and her husband.'

Angie shook hands, wanting to say *Yes, I know. It's obvious from what you already told me*. Instead, she maintained the stiff smile and said, 'It's an awful thing to happen. You must be terribly shocked.' Angie Straw would rather die than say 'I'm sorry for your loss' or anything from a pre-existing script.

'Yes,' said the son-in-law. 'We really can't believe it.'

He was short and wide, with pale-coloured hair and bulging blue eyes. His wife was an inch or two taller, in her late forties and an unsettling replica of her father, who stood with his hand on her arm. Both had long beaky noses, narrow dark eyes and lank brown hair. As far as Angie could recall, Grant had not looked like them at all.

'He was three years younger than me. We never really did much together, even when we were children. We saw very little of each other in recent years. I've got the business, and he never seemed to have much to say for himself. But it's dreadful to think he's *dead*.' The bereaved sister wiped away a small tear. 'Can we see his room?' asked the sister. 'I know it seems a bit silly, but we'd like to be able to visualise it. We didn't know he was coming here, you see. We had no idea where he was.'

'Come on, Suze. You make it sound like some sort of mystery,' chastised her husband. 'When did he ever tell us where he was going, anyway?' He cast a nervous glance at the police officer. 'We've already explained that, haven't we?'

Nobody spoke, and Angie led the way up the stairs. The police had taken Grant's laptop and all his luggage, leaving nothing that his family would find meaningful. Even the sheets from the bed had gone off in evidence bags in case forensics could find anything interesting on them. Another guest had been booked in from the end of the week, but was eager to cancel when Angie contacted her with the story. 'No, no – I don't think so,' had been the response.

'Where exactly did he . . . I mean, what happened in those last moments?' It was the sister who asked, while managing to imply that all three of them wanted to know. 'They've told us very little, you know.'

'It's still under an initial investigation,' defended the policewoman. 'We have to be absolutely sure of the facts before we can issue any information.'

'Yes, dear, that's all right,' said Childers Senior, with a strong Birmingham accent. 'I'm sure it will all be made clear eventually.' As he turned back to Angie, she caught a whiff of whisky on his breath, which went some way towards explaining his lack of tension or emotion. 'The thing is, we simply can't understand why the police are so interested. It seems to us absolutely obvious that poor Grant ate something by mistake. He always did have a delicate stomach, and perhaps he was silly enough to buy some dodgy mushrooms out there in one of these funny little villages. Or even picked something out of a hedge that looked tasty. He was quite keen on natural history, you know. Berries and nuts and that sort of thing. His mother thinks that was why he came up here on his own again. He wanted to have a few days in the wilderness, by himself. He's been a bit low, I think. All this politics, and the doomy talk about climate change. He worries about animals, as well. Pollution – all that plastic. Poor chap, it's just one thing after another.'

'He wasn't that bad, Dad,' his daughter corrected. 'You'll have them thinking he did this to himself on purpose, if you're not careful. All that misery stuff was years ago now. He's been loads better lately.'

'Maybe so,' nodded the elderly man dubiously. 'So

you're saying the police have it right, and some swine did this to him deliberately?'

'I'm not saying anything, Dad.' The tone was weary. 'Just let's leave it to the experts, shall we? We can take a few pictures of this room for Mum, and let this lady get on in peace.'

'Your poor mother,' moaned Mr Childers. 'This is going to be the death of her, you know. However she's going to face the funeral, God alone knows.'

'People are tougher than you think,' said Angie, unwarily. 'I expect she'll surprise you.'

All three family members gave her the same long, unfriendly stare. 'You don't know her,' said the son-in-law. 'You don't know anything about her.'

'That's true, of course. I was speaking generally.'

Suzy Gorringe took several pictures with her phone, while the men hovered in the doorway. 'Nice room,' she said finally, as if offering an olive branch. 'How did he come to find you, I wonder? Did he say?'

Angie tried to think, but could not differentiate Grant Childers from a host of other people who had booked rooms with her over the past months. 'It must have been online,' she said vaguely.

'We knew that he came up here quite a few times, but we'd never asked for details. We rather assumed he always stayed here with you.'

'No. This was his first time,' said Angie.

'Oh. Well, perhaps he fancied a change. That would be a bit surprising, given what a creature of habit he was, but as I say, we never really asked him about it.' The sister had the grace to look sheepish at her lack of interest in Grant's movements.

'Just getting away from the rat race,' said her father. 'Recharging his batteries. Nothing sinister about it.'

Angie privately thought the whole thing sounded decidedly sinister. Suzy Gorringe read her expression and said, 'We still think it's ludicrous to suggest that someone *murdered* him. I mean, if you'd known him, you'd think the same. He never did anyone any harm. To be honest, we all thought he was pretty much of a wimp.'

'Suze!' her silent husband protested. 'The poor chap's dead. You can't talk about him like that.'

'It's true enough, all the same,' said Childers Senior. 'Everybody thought so.'

They trooped untidily back to the downstairs hallway, and stood in an uncertain cluster like sheep, with the police officer a somewhat hesitant collie dog. No way was Angie tempted to offer them tea, or even take them into her sitting room, unless forced to. There were voices coming from the guests' room, including that of a young child. The Watsons and Tomkins, by coincidence, had both brought a small son with them, but the Watson one was only three. *Long past his bedtime*, thought Angie, with a sigh. The kid would get overtired and probably make another fuss about the strange bed, as he had since the family had arrived.

'Well . . .' she said. 'If that's everything?'

The Gorringes exchanged a look. 'I suppose it is,' said Suzy. 'Thank you very much, Mrs . . .'

'Straw,' said Angie. 'I hope it's helped, somehow.' They could surely hear the implication that it really couldn't have been the least bit helpful.

'It's always good to get a complete picture,' said Mr Gorringe. 'As complete as you can, anyway. There's nothing worse than not knowing how a person died. It's like never hearing the end of the story. You don't know what to tell people.'

Angie gave him a surprised look. He was both more sensible and less upset than she'd first thought. His brother-in-law had clearly not been one of his best-beloved relatives. 'Yes, that's true,' she agreed. 'You need to be able to tell the whole story, even if only to yourself.'

'The police understand that, too,' said the liaison officer, still on the defensive. Angie supposed it went with the role – foisted onto bewildered grieving families whether they wanted it or not, in a clumsy attempt at making them feel valued and cared for.

'Good,' she said.

Then they somehow got out of the house, and Angie closed the door firmly behind them. Squaring her shoulders, she went to find husband, dog and guests.

Not until they were in bed did Russell and Angie manage a coherent conversation. The Watson child had refused to let his parents out of his sight, so the whole family had decamped to their room. The Tomkins had embarked on a somewhat uneasy game of Monopoly, which had to be aborted long before its rightful conclusion, the seven-year-old nodding sleepily over his properties. The Straws, in the kitchen, watched their small television with sporadic attention, and hardly spoke. 'Catching up with us,' said Russell at one point. 'Delayed reaction.'

Angie wanted to argue, but hadn't the heart for it. He was, after all, probably right. Though there had been some small consolation in the discovery that Grant Childers had not been the great love of anybody's life, or the sole provider for a vulnerable family. His mother was apparently the only person who would be severely affected by his death. It seemed he had occupied a very small place in the world, leaving a negligible hole in the fabric of which he had been part. Nobody had mentioned his line of work, she noted. Most likely a minor civil servant was her best guess.

'So why in the world would anybody want to murder him?' she said aloud to her husband, as she got into bed beside him.

The question haunted her dreams and was still at the front of her mind next morning. Up before seven, the whirlwind demands of the second B in B&B occupied at least two hours. Whatever diets or fads were favoured by the guests in their home lives, the majority of them succumbed to the Full English when it was offered as a non-negotiable part of the holiday package. Coffee had to be made and kept fresh, toast had to be warm, juice cold, milk untainted. Every egg had to be cooked to precise specifications and sausages must not be burnt. The necessary juggling act was second nature after almost twenty years, but nothing could be left to chance. Russell's role had always been as waiter, convivial host and source of local information. He would loiter beside one table after another, issuing facts about weather, history, traffic conditions and topography. In his glory days he had relished this part of the business, sending people in all directions on his latest whim. Brantwood and Brant Fell, Kendal and Keswick, Grasmere and Grizedale – he would rattle off the names with a mischievous intention of causing confusion. There would be an anecdote to go with every hamlet, and most large houses. Wordsworth and

Beatrix Potter seldom got a mention. Russell very much favoured John Ruskin and Fletcher Christian when it came to local heroes.

But over the past year, Russell's abilities had diminished, his memory less reliable and his sense of mischief sadly absent. Anxiety had him in its grip, resulting in a complete change of personality. Doors had to be locked, news headlines scanned, guests repeatedly warned of dangers lurking on the fells. When a mini-stroke assailed him, his wife and daughter had feared it would only exacerbate his distress. Instead, it seemed to shift something, and since then he had been more relaxed, but nowhere near his previous levels of competence.

Now he pottered in and out of the dining room with cafetières and racks of toast, on Angie's instruction. None of the guests looked happy, and it came as no surprise when the Watsons announced that they would, after all, be cutting their holiday short by two days. Only mildly apologetic, they explained that there was too much disruption for comfort. And surely the Straws would be glad to be rid of them, under the circumstances. It was nobody's fault, of course, but really, they couldn't face another evening like Sunday.

The Tomkins heard this with evident indecision. Should they do the same, or stick it out as planned? They were due to stay until Friday, and Jason had set his heart on taking the ferry across Windermere. They wanted to go to Coniston and Ullswater. There was just so much to see!

These musings were overheard, in part, by Russell, who hovered close by, ready to advise. 'We'd really like you to stay,' he urged. 'And what will the school think if you take this young man back two days before they expect him? They'll mark it down as a moral victory.' Mr and Mrs Tomkin had already regaled Russell with the story of their royal battle to obtain permission to remove Jason from school in term time. 'We'll have to pay a fine,' sighed the father. 'Sixty quid. The lad's only seven – what do they think he's going to miss?'

The mother looked less than convinced by the wisdom of this. Clearly she had been overruled in the original decision. 'We could keep him at home,' she said. 'That might be quite nice – just doing nothing for a day or two.'

'You'll have this place to yourselves if you stay,' Russell encouraged. 'And I think we can safely say there won't be any more interruptions from anyone connected to poor Mr Childers.'

Both parents glanced at the boy, who remained oblivious to the fact of a sudden unexplained death a few feet from the room he shared with his parents. A year or two older, and he might well have shown a ghoulish interest. 'We'll stay one more night, and go back tomorrow,' said Mr Tomkin decisively. 'Coniston today, and then cut and run. Sorry if that's a blow to you, Mr Straw, but it doesn't look as if things are going to get any better here, are they? Police and so forth, I mean.'

As he loaded the dishwasher, Russell reported this exchange to his wife. 'I told them there probably wouldn't be any more visits from the police,' he admitted. 'But it didn't make any difference – they've lost their nerve. Do you think we should worry about our reputation yet?'

'I do a bit,' she admitted. 'The Friday people have cancelled. At this rate, we'll be all by ourselves over the weekend.'

'It's your own fault. You shouldn't have said anything.' Angie had phoned everyone booked into the B&B over the coming days, offering them the option of changing their plans. 'They probably think you *want* them to cancel.'

'I do, mostly. It feels almost disrespectful to carry on as usual. And I don't actually feel altogether well.'

This was tantamount to an admission that she was severely ill, and Russell looked at her in alarm. 'You don't look poorly,' he observed. 'What's the matter with you?'

'Oh, nothing to worry about. Just sick and tired, literally. Worried. A bit scared, to be absolutely honest. I wish Persimmon hadn't been here on Sunday. It has to have had a bad effect on her and the baby. That blasted man – why did he have to die here?'

'Very thoughtless of him,' Russell agreed. 'Sim's going to be all right, though. She was on tremendous form before lunch on Sunday.' He was awkwardly trying to change the subject, searching for some diversion. 'Did we tell you we saw that Candy Proctor woman protesting about the Patterdale plan? Very strident, she was, shouting at poor old Ninian.'

Angie showed a flicker of interest. 'Sounds as if half the population of Cumbria was there.'

'Not quite. But it was quite busy. Tristan Wilkins, and quite a few I knew by sight. The whole thing strikes me as a bit silly, actually. I'm not sure it would be so terrible for a few new chalets to go up in a discreet valley over there.'

'Was Ninian protesting?'

'No, no. He was just hanging about. I told you – the Proctor person was arguing with him. He seems to think it's all a foregone conclusion and protesting's just a waste of time.'

'And you're sure you didn't see Mr Childers?'

Russell sighed at the failure of his ruse. 'I told you before – even if he'd walked right past us, I wouldn't have known him. I'm not too good at faces at the best of times, and that would have been a miracle, after seeing him for about five seconds on Friday.'

'I have to admit he was very ordinary-looking. The picture they showed of him on the news last night could have been anybody.'

'Within certain parameters, of course,' Russell corrected. 'And I dare say anyone who knew him would recognise him.'

'Poor man,' she sighed. 'Nobody should die as young as that.'

'Oh well. It'll be all the same in the long run,' he said weakly.

'In the long run we're all dead,' said Angie.

'That's what I meant,' said her husband.

Chapter Seven

Simmy awoke on Tuesday morning to the shreds of a jumble of bad dreams. Her father's dog had consumed something poisonous and lay twitching on the kitchen floor, Bonnie and Ben had unaccountably run headlong into the waters of Windermere and a beautiful house in Patterdale had collapsed into rubble as she watched. As she went downstairs, she felt the strongest fluttering so far from the baby. A strange, unreal sensation that brought a rush of euphoria at the very definite miracle of new life. A cliché, admittedly, but no less true for that. All the time-worn phrases went through her mind. A new little person, dependent and demanding, vulnerable and life-changing, nestling there inside her. The real truth was that nothing else mattered very much, at that moment. Christopher had asked her, not so long ago, whether she would want to be married to him if there was no baby. It was, of course, impossible to give an answer – and now there was no need, anyway. She had the man *and* the baby – if she could manage to keep the child alive.

* * *

Bonnie was ten minutes late to work. 'Sorry,' she mumbled. 'I overslept.'

'No problem. The mornings are getting darker now, aren't they? Makes it harder to get out of bed.'

'Mm,' said Bonnie.

Simmy wanted to share her sentimental baby thoughts, but decided against it. Bonnie was too young, too fragile to fully grasp the complex immensity of parenthood. She and Ben, as far as Simmy knew, still had not consummated their relationship. Wary of inflicting new and unpredictable damage on her, the young man had nobly refrained – apparently with Bonnie's full agreement. There were still aspects of life that she found deeply stressful, still moments of paralysis and panic.

'Well, work to do,' Simmy said fatuously. 'I've got to take the funeral wreaths first, and then I'm supposed to go down to Newby Bridge at lunchtime, aren't I?'

'Gerberas and carnations,' Bonnie nodded. 'With plenty of purple.'

'How's Ben?'

'Busy. He says the timetable's in chaos and they left him off one of the most important lists, so he's missed three lectures already. I think he's feeling disillusioned.'

'He'll probably do them a spreadsheet, so they can get it right in future.'

'An algorithm, actually. But he likes most of the lecturers so far. And there's a woman tutor, he says has to be at least eighty, who reminds him of your mother.'

'Gosh.'

'It's a different world,' Bonnie said sadly. 'I can't even imagine it, most of the time.'

'But you'll go and see him next month, won't you? Then you'll get a much better picture.'

'Yeah,' she sighed.

'You didn't mention the dead man at Beck View, I presume?'

'No.' This, Simmy guessed, was the source of much of the melancholy. 'But I wanted to.'

'I'm sure you did. Let's just hope the police get it all sorted quickly. The family went to see the room last night, apparently.'

'We don't know *anything* about him, do we?' Bonnie burst out. 'He's just a tourist from the Midlands who ate something that killed him. There's no *story*. It might not even be a murder at all. I'm going to try not to think about it, because then I can tell myself that Ben's not missing anything. Does that make sense?'

'Fine by me,' said Simmy heartily, as she pressed a gentle hand against her belly. 'I've got plenty of other things to think about.' Then she added, 'You haven't forgotten you'll be on your own tomorrow, have you?'

'All day?'

'Oh no. The appointment's at ten, so we should be away easily by eleven. We did think we might dash up to Patterdale for lunch, and then back here, maybe around half past two. You can phone me if there's any problem, and I can come straight here instead of Patterdale.'

'Yeah, yeah. That'll be okay. I hadn't forgotten, anyway. I thought I'd do something about the cards. They're looking a bit tired.'

Persimmon Petals sold ribbons, cards and 'favours' for people who wanted to construct their own floral tributes, rather than leave it to the florist. Not very many chose to do so, which meant the same cards languished on the rack for months on end.

'Good idea,' said Simmy.

The day drifted on in much the same vein. The trip to the undertaker was quickly accomplished, and two new orders duly processed. The drive down to Newby Bridge was made memorable solely because a black cat ran across her path as she passed Storrs, which she chose to regard as a good omen.

Customers were sparse, and the atmosphere was dreamy and distracted, each woman preoccupied by her own thoughts. And then at three-thirty the door opened, and for a moment Simmy was transported back in time. 'Hiya!' chirped the new arrival. 'How's things?'

It was Tanya Harkness, Ben's young sister – one of three younger sisters. Four years junior to him, she had the same lanky shape, and carried a rucksack on one shoulder just as Ben always did. She had the same intelligent expression, and the same light-brown hair.

'Gosh – I thought you were Ben for a second,' laughed Simmy. 'He comes in here just like that.'

'Tsch,' said the girl dismissively.

Bonnie came forward in a rush. 'Hey – good to see you! You okay?'

Tanya set down her bag and looked from face to face. 'There's been a murder,' she said accusingly. 'Hasn't there? And don't pretend you don't know about it, either.'

'How on earth do *you* know?' Simmy demanded.

'Police all over one of the cruise boats on the lake. Some tweets about people dying in B&Bs. And my mum was accosted by a woman because she knows Simmy's folks and saw police activity there on Sunday, and there's something about somebody sabotaging conservation efforts up by Ullswater, which I didn't really understand.' She rattled off her evidence with total confidence, again reminding Simmy of Ben. 'There's sure to be something on the news by now, as well. I haven't had time to look yet.'

'None of that gets us very far,' Bonnie observed. 'Apart from the tweets, maybe. Some relative of the dead man must have posted them.'

'Why do people do that?' Simmy asked, more of herself than the girls. During a fairly recent episode in Staveley, Twitter had been awash with vitriolic assertions that she had found deeply shocking.

'How do you know all this, anyway?' Bonnie went on. 'Haven't you been at school all day?'

'Yes, but Natalie's at home with conjunctivitis, and she's been texting me all day with a whole lot of stuff she's gleaned. She went out for a bit at lunchtime and saw the police on the boat. And Mum was in such a rage about the woman who ranted at her that she splurged it all on poor Nat just now.'

'It might be about something else entirely,' said Simmy, who was floundering badly. 'You're connecting up a whole lot of separate issues.'

'I don't think I am,' said Tanya, yet again uncannily channelling her brother. The same air of patient forbearance in the face of adult dim-wittedness was impossible to ignore. 'Because it happened at Beck View, didn't it? And you were there, and the man was into conservation, and there's something going on up in Patterdale.'

'Stop it!' Simmy ordered sharply. 'It's just not possible that you've put together any remotely coherent picture from scraps of texts from your sister. Especially when you must have had lessons all day, and school's only been out for about twenty minutes.'

'You'll have to listen to her, Sim,' said Bonnie. 'From what I can gather, she's got quite a lot of important things to tell us. And if we don't let her talk, she'll go to Moxon and we'll miss all the excitement.'

Tanya laughed. 'No, I won't do that. He'll know most of it already, so there wouldn't be any point. But I might go to Ben instead,' she finished darkly.

'Don't you dare!' Bonnie and Simmy spoke in unison, equally appalled at the suggestion.

'All right, then. So just listen for a minute, will you?'

Simmy had already known she had no choice, from the moment Tanya mentioned Patterdale. The place already had deep personal implications for her, the name imbued with heightened significance. 'Go on, then,' she sighed.

'Firstly – it looks as if your man went on the cruise boat on Sunday. Assuming it's his murder they're investigating, that seems an obvious deduction. What I don't know is exactly how he died. Did somebody follow him after the boat ride, and get at him somehow? You know – I was there on Sunday morning myself, watching all the tourists.'

'He was poisoned,' Bonnie volunteered, with an eagerness that Simmy found insensitive. 'So maybe somebody gave him something on the boat, and he didn't eat – or drink – it until later. Pity you didn't know him. You could have been a brilliant witness if you'd seen him.'

'Perhaps I did, without realising. Wouldn't that be great!'

Simmy was getting cross. 'Stop it, both of you,' she ordered. 'It looks as if practically everybody was in Bowness on Sunday. My dad and I walked the dog down there, as well. We didn't see you,' she said to Tanya. 'And there's absolutely no reason to think Mr Childers was there.'

'Childers? Is that his name?' Tanya muttered the name again, to fix it in her memory. 'I was there from eleven to twelve, more or less. Natalie was meant to be with me, but she couldn't face being seen with her eyes all red and crusty. She does look disgusting, I must admit.'

'I think it's very likely the man was there as well,' Bonnie insisted. 'You said he went out on Sunday, and most likely came in while you were having lunch. Right? Where else would he go? He was on foot, I assume?'

'I don't know. He might have gone for a drive. I don't remember anybody saying one way or the other. Probably nobody actually knows. And we're not sure when he came back in. My mum thought she heard him earlier, but she wasn't very definite about it.'

Bonnie wouldn't stop. 'That's quite important, surely? Won't they have searched his room for traces of food or drink containing poison?'

'I expect they have. I don't know everything that's been going on.'

Tanya joined in again. 'We've been daft not to think of it before. It means he might have brought the poisoned whatever-it-was from home, and it's his girlfriend who's responsible.'

'Has he got a girlfriend?' Bonnie wondered. 'Didn't you say he only had a mother and two sisters?'

'The point is that if he did eat something that killed

him, there are about a hundred places he could have got it, even if he didn't bring it from home. But it's quite likely that he *did* have it with him before he arrived here,' said Simmy, feeling a surge of relief at this thought. It not only exonerated her parents, but everyone she knew in the whole of the Lake District.

'You're worried that your mum's going to get the blame,' said Tanya soothingly. 'I can see that must be scary.'

'That was my dad's instant reaction. He said something like, "Good God, what have we fed him?", which was understandable, I suppose. But he didn't have breakfast, so they didn't feed him anything.'

'That's lucky.'

Bonnie was scowling, which was unusual. 'Hey, what's the matter?' Simmy asked.

'Nothing, really. Just missing Ben. It feels all wrong without him. All we're doing is making silly guesses, without any evidence. Even with Simmy having actually *seen* the man die, we still don't know any of the important facts. Who exactly was he? Did anyone around here know him? Where do we even *start*?'

'The police have plenty of facts already,' Tanya reminded her. 'And they'll want Mr and Mrs Straw to remember every word the man said – including when he booked the room. There's sure to be a few clues, like whether he did know people here. Has he stayed at Beck View before?'

'I can answer that, at least,' said Simmy. 'No, they'd never seen him until he arrived on Friday evening. He had a laptop with him. Presumably the police will be examining it for that sort of information. They don't need us getting in their way, do they? We can just leave everything to them and get on with our lives.'

There was a short silence, during which the two girls exchanged meaningful glances. 'It's because you're pregnant,' said Tanya kindly. 'I get that. But think of your poor mother. Surely you want to do anything you can to get everything settled and back to normal, for her sake?'

'Within reason,' said Simmy, feeling humiliatingly patronised by a child of fourteen. 'But I really don't see how we can add anything to the police investigation. They've got all the right tools for it, plus it's what they're there for. It's different this time, in all sorts of ways. We don't have any special knowledge of the person who's died. We don't know his friends or relations. He's just a stranger who ate something that killed him. The fact that he was in my parents' house isn't very relevant, when you think about it.'

'Hm,' said Tanya, momentarily lost for words.

'But somebody local probably did kill him,' said Bonnie thoughtfully, much to Simmy's disappointment. 'Because if he arrived on Friday with food or drink in his car, surely he'd have finished it before Sunday? And that means we can at the very least ask around, to see if there's a connection with the lake cruise. If Tanya's right, then that's what the police are thinking. They might have found a ticket in the man's pocket.' She lifted her chin triumphantly at this thought. 'I bet you that's what happened. It fits beautifully.'

'And if it did, the police will be questioning everyone they can about what happened on the boat. Do they have a passenger list?' asked Simmy.

'Of course not. You buy a ticket at the kiosk and just

walk on. They don't ask you your name, or even film everybody.' It was Tanya speaking. 'I know, because Wilf worked on that boat when he was sixteen.' Wilf was her older brother.

'That was years ago. It might be different now,' said Bonnie. 'I bet most people get their tickets online, for a start. And then there would be a record of them.' She produced her phone and began the familiar swiping and thumbing until the information was laid bare. 'Yes, you can book online. We're right at the end of the summer season. Chances are he chose the Yellow Cruise. Ninety minutes, up and down the lake. Good way to see the scenery and pass the time.'

'All of which the police will already know,' said Simmy tiredly. Where were her customers when she needed them? The conversation was irritating her more all the time, the two girls making her feel old and slow and very much detached. 'Go home, Tanya. I'm sure you've got homework to do.'

'Yes, but—'

'But nothing. You're coming in on Saturday, aren't you? If there hasn't been any progress by then, you can talk about it all morning. I'm going to need a day off, with all that wedding stuff to do on Friday.'

As if by some malign telepathy, the shop phone began to ring. Simmy answered it, to be informed by the local undertaker that there was a big funeral due to take place in Troutbeck on Friday afternoon. The unusually short notice was sending everybody into a tizzy, especially as flowers were being actively invited from all the mourners. 'You'll be deluged,' said Janice, who was the woman in the office, who knew everything and had control of the diary. 'All hands to the pump.'

Simmy conveyed this news to both girls. 'That's Thursday sorted, then,' she said. 'As well as tomorrow afternoon, most likely.'

'Good to be busy,' said Bonnie bravely. 'Can I make one or two wreaths, do you think?'

'I expect you'll have to,' sighed Simmy.

Tanya finally decided to leave. 'Bye, then,' she chirped. 'See you on Saturday, Bon. If not before. Call me if there's anything . . . you know.'

'Right. And you the same. You're closer to it than me. Keep an eye out, okay?'

Tanya turned to go, but had to pause to allow a woman to come into the shop. With a polite smile, she waited for the doorway to be clear, but her courtesy went ignored. The newcomer headed straight for Simmy, words already tumbling from her lips.

'Somebody was *killed*, at Beck View – and I've only just heard about it this afternoon. In your parents' B&B, which is only two doors up from mine. What's this going to do to our reputation? The whole town's going to be tainted by it. And it *would* be Angie Straw, wouldn't it? As if she hasn't caused enough trouble already with her sloppy ways. And you were there – I saw you with your father, just before. It *must* have been soon after that, from what I've heard. I want you to tell them from me—'

Simmy put up a hand to stop the flow. 'Mrs Proctor – is that right? I remember you were handing out those leaflets about Patterdale. You had a little chat with my father. I thought you were his friend, actually, so I'd appreciate it if

81

you'd stop shouting at me. If you've got something to say, perhaps you can do it more quietly.'

The woman almost visibly subsided. 'It's Miss, not Mrs.'

'Okay,' said Simmy. 'So what is it you want to say?'

She swallowed and her eyes grew moist. 'The man who died. They're saying it was Grant Childers. *Grant Childers*, of all people.'

'Why? Do you know him?' It was Bonnie, bursting in, wide-eyed.

'I should think I do know him. He's stayed with me four or five times over the past three years. He only went to Beck View this time because I was full. And then he goes and gets himself killed.' She turned her distraught gaze onto Bonnie for a moment, before returning to her attack on Simmy. 'And I want to know why.'

Chapter Eight

'Well, it certainly wasn't anything my mother did to him,' Simmy defended. 'Which is what you seem to be implying.'

'Have you told the police you knew him?' Bonnie asked.

'Obviously I have. They came to me today, as it happens. They found my email on his computer, from September when I had to turn him away. They told me the whole story – about him collapsing on Sunday afternoon and test results showing it was not a natural death. I was so *shocked*. They said they were treating it as homicide, and anything I could tell them about him would be relevant to their enquiries. Honestly – I've *never* been involved in anything like this before. I really didn't know what to say for myself.'

She was almost calm now, talking herself into a much quieter frame of mind. Russell had greeted her warily on Sunday morning, Simmy recalled. She had been an active participant in the protest, arguing with Ninian and clearly passionate in her opposition to the proposed chalets.

'You're not really involved, though, are you?' Simmy ventured to say. 'The police will only be hoping for a bit of background on him. If he's been here several times before, there are probably locals who know him as well. Has he got friends here? Or work contacts? Why does he keep coming back?'

'Fell climbing? Birdwatching?' Bonnie suggested, without giving Candy time to reply. 'Lots of people come regularly for that sort of thing.'

'Had you seen him this time?' Simmy wondered. 'Did he call in to say hello?'

Candy Proctor looked from one to the other. 'He comes here because he's interested in wildlife and conservation. He counts red squirrels and the big birds. He's told me a lot over the years. And I don't know whether he tried to come and see me. If he did, I must have been out. Honestly, it's been so hectic. I had three families arrive on Saturday, and the girl who helps me has got flu or something, so I was left doing it all myself. The breakfasts weren't finished till after ten on Sunday. I nearly didn't go out with the leaflets, but I'd promised, and I didn't want to let Tristan and the others down. It was clever of him to think of tackling the tourists in Bowness. Right on the doorstep, and all the right sort of people. Nearly all of them agreed with us at the protest.'

'But why, when it's so far from Patterdale?'

'It's all down to human psychology,' said Candy, who appeared to be quoting the sainted Tristan. 'The point is, tourists never think of themselves as part of a problem. They're always the virtuous ones, respecting the countryside and preserving the landscape. They want to keep others –

who are exactly the same as them, in reality – away, so they can have it for themselves. So it makes sense to hand out the leaflets and gather support in places where there are lots of them, like Bowness. We go to Ambleside as well – or Waterhead, where there are always swarms of them.'

'"Swarms",' Bonnie repeated softly. 'That's not a very nice word to use, is it?'

'It's perfectly accurate. Do you know how many millions of people visit the Lake District every year?'

'A lot,' said Simmy briskly. 'But it seems to me there's space enough for everyone.'

'The entire population of the world could stand on the Isle of Wight,' said Bonnie, with minimal relevance. 'Or they could, a decade or two ago. It might have to be the Isle of Man now.'

'Well, I can't stay,' said Candy, picking up on the briskness. 'Must be closing time by now. My people will be coming back any minute.'

'I'll have to go and see my parents,' said Simmy. 'I haven't heard from them today.'

'They'll have had to cancel all the bookings,' said Candy with certainty. 'You can't have guests when there's just been a murder in the house.'

'You can, actually. There's just the one room they can't use.' Simmy found herself still keen to reject the notion that there had been an actual murder at all. Were there not still several other reasonable explanations? Looking from Candy to Bonnie and back again, she realised she was alone in clinging to such a hope.

'But – they must have to *tell* people,' Candy said. 'Give them the option.'

'Maybe. I haven't asked about that.'

The woman left on a much less aggressive note than the one on which she'd arrived. It was five past five.

Bonnie watched her go, her expression thoughtful. 'Was she *really* as shocked as she said? Or was it all a big performance for our benefit?'

'Pardon? You can't be saying you think she could have poisoned him, can you?'

'Why not? You don't know her, do you? She might be a brilliant actor. She seems to be in the thick of all this protest business, as well as knowing the dead man.'

'Nobody can act that well,' Simmy asserted, with a feeling that she had said much the same about other people on previous occasions. 'Or am I being too trusting again?'

'She did seem genuine, I suppose.' Bonnie sighed. 'And not very clever. What Corinne would call "dull" – meaning "dim".'

'I think she's just tired,' said Simmy, with her own mother's exhaustion in mind.

'Could be,' said Bonnie dubiously.

'Tomorrow,' Simmy remembered to say. 'Can you open up and see to everything until after lunch? Be sure to take exact details from people ordering flowers for that funeral.'

'Yes,' said Bonnie firmly. 'Do we know who died?'

'Somebody in Troutbeck,' said Simmy vaguely. 'Janice gave me the name.' She picked up the notepad. 'Dorothea Entwhistle. Miss,' she read. 'Do you know her?'

'Good God, Simmy, of course I do. Everybody knows the famous Miss Entwhistle.'

'Well, I don't want to hear any more about her now. Leave it till I get back tomorrow.'

Bonnie shrugged. 'Fair enough. So – good luck with everything at the hospital. I'll phone if there's a problem.'

Beck View was quiet as Simmy walked in at half past five. The door to the breakfast room was open, and she noted that two tables were laid ready for the morning. In the kitchen, she found her mother on her own, sitting beside the ever-warm Rayburn, just staring into space.

'Where's Dad?'

'Out with the dog. He's been gone half an hour already. I suppose he'll be hungry when he gets back.'

'Do you want me to do it? You look as if you're half-asleep.'

'You could find something in the freezer for me. There's a thing of bolognese sauce I made a while ago. Should be enough for three, if you're staying.'

Simmy went and rummaged in the big chest freezer and located a plastic box duly labelled 'bol sauce'. A further search revealed a new packet of spaghetti. 'No problem,' she said. 'Ready in half an hour. He'll be back by then, surely?'

'Let's hope so. If not, we can start without him.'

'What's made you so tired? Aren't you sleeping?'

'I drop off well enough, but then I keep having the most dreadful dreams, and they wake me up. There was one where the Childers man vomited all down the stairs, like a river of sick. Did you know that you can *smell* in dreams? I could, anyway. It smelt like cow muck. It got on my shoes and I screamed. Must have made a noise because I woke myself up.'

'That sounds like PTSD to me.'

'I don't care what it's called. I just want it to stop.'

'They can probably give you pills for it.'

'It might yet come to that,' said Angie gloomily. To Simmy this was a startling admission. Her mother had, to her knowledge, not swallowed a pill for the past twenty years or more. Adamantly opposed to excessive medication, she had gone to the furthest extreme in resisting it wholesale. When Russell had his mini-stroke, he had been put on a low-level dose of blood thinner, which he was supposed to take indefinitely. To Angie, this was a personal affront, which she could only deal with by ignoring it. 'As long as it's only for a short time,' she added.

'That Proctor woman came to see me this afternoon,' said Simmy. 'The one with a B&B along here somewhere.'

'She's in Greenwell Haven. It's next door but one. She disapproves of me.'

'So I gather. Even more so, now you've let somebody die under your roof. She thinks it'll taint the whole B&B industry in Windermere. We saw her on Sunday, actually. Did Dad tell you?'

'He might have done – I don't remember. I always felt a bit sorry for her, actually. She's so thin and worn-out looking. But she's very popular. I've had to take her overflow a few times.'

'Mr Childers was one of them. Didn't he tell you?'

Angie looked hunted. 'How am I supposed to remember what everybody says to me? She should be glad it was me that got him, in that case. Or does she think she'd have been able to keep him alive, and I let him down somehow?'

'She didn't say anything like that. But the main point is – he's a regular visitor. He comes to the Lakes a lot. He knows people, and counts red squirrels for a hobby.'

'Knew. He *knew* people. He is no more, remember.'

'Right. Yes. Funny how hard that is sometimes. Even when I never even met the man. Or only for two minutes before he died,' she amended ruefully. She was warming the sauce in a large pan on the Rayburn, stirring it every minute or two. 'Is Dad usually this long when he goes for a walk?'

'It varies. If he meets someone he knows, he might stay out for hours. He's been known to walk down by the lake nearly as far as Storrs. Makes the dog happy, when he does that. But with things as they are this week, he probably won't be very long.'

'Well, he's got another twenty minutes. Can we phone him?'

Angie pursed her lips. 'Best not. It'll put him in a flap. He's probably got it switched off, anyway.'

'It'll be dark soon.'

'You're not *worried* about him, are you? He might be a bit soft in the head these days, but he's not going to come to any harm. What do you think might happen to him? I can't stand it if you start getting all paranoid as well.'

'I'm not. I'm cross with him, if anything. He knows it's supper time.'

And then, barely two minutes later, Russell was heard stamping his feet on the doormat, chirping at his dog, and generally making his presence felt. He came into the kitchen smiling broadly. 'Wind blowing up out there,' he announced. 'Very bracing it is.'

'You look like a shepherd, back from a night's lambing on the fells,' said Angie. 'What happened to your hair?'

He put a hand on top of his head and stirred his thin grey locks uncertainly. 'It's still there,' he announced.

'It needs cutting,' said Simmy. 'It's sticking out over your ears. I'm making spaghetti bolognese for you. Ready at seven.'

'Lovely,' said her father with an even wider grin. Then he added, 'You'll never guess who I've been talking to.'

Both women looked at him, and Angie sighed. 'Just tell us,' she instructed him.

'Your red-haired chum, Stuart. Can't get away from the fellow these days. He was very ancient-marinerish, I can tell you. Wouldn't let me go until he'd told me all about this brother-in-law of his, lives near Patterdale, and wants to sell half his garden in Hartsop as a building plot. That's more or less in Patterdale. He knows Sim and Chris want to live there – I imagine you must have told him – and now he's practically got the foundations in without a by-your-leave. Thinks it would be absolutely ideal.'

Simmy was dumbfounded. 'Really?' was all she could say.

'They'd never get planning permission,' said Angie.

'They might. The brother-in-law's got some sort of influence, apparently, and people don't so much object to a one-off new-build, do they?'

'What about those chalets?' wondered Simmy, slowly assembling her thoughts. 'They'll have made everybody up there super-sensitive to any suggestion of a new property.'

'That did occur to me,' Russell agreed, with a satisfied little nod. 'But it could go in your favour. If they reject the chalets, they'll feel they're in a sort of moral credit, which might make them more inclined to pass a modest new house for a local couple with a baby. If you follow me.'

She did, with only minor difficulty, and was instantly reminded of Candy Proctor and her psychological analysis of public attitudes to new buildings. 'Ninian says they'll pass the chalets,' she remembered.

Angie made a scornful sound. 'What does Ninian Tripp know about anything?'

'Did Stuart give you any details? We're going up there tomorrow. Maybe we could have a look, at least.'

Russell produced a scrap of paper with the name and phone number of the brother-in-law. Simmy made no secret of her admiration for his efficiency. 'That's brilliant,' she gushed. 'And did I tell you that Tristan Wilkins said he might know of a place, as well? The grapevine seems to be working at last. We'll be spoilt for choice if it goes on like this.'

'You've your father to thank for that, as well,' said Angie. 'He asks everybody he meets if they can find you somewhere. He's made it his mission. You know what he's like.'

'I like a man with a mission. Thanks, Dad.' She gave him a quick hug. 'For that you get extra bolognese.'

She stayed until eight, chatting comfortably with her parents, as all three of them gradually relaxed. They veered away from the subject of the dead man, once Simmy had heard the story of the family's visit, and indulged in local gossip, and vague plans for the future. Christmas was looming, with Simmy already invited to join the large Henderson family for the day. Christopher had two brothers and two sisters, who had all agreed to get together for the festivities, in honour of their deceased parents. Simmy had grown up knowing the whole family well. As an only child herself, she had learnt lessons, sometimes painfully, about the rough and tumble of a large litter of children.

'So we're to be left in the lurch,' said Russell, half-seriously.

'You could probably come as well. They'd be happy to have you. You're like uncle and auntie to them, after all.'

'Where is this vast gathering to take place?' asked Angie.

'Not yet decided. Probably a hotel – but they're likely to be all booked up by now. Hannah's supposed to be in charge.'

'Ten weeks 'til Christmas Day,' said Russell. 'We're closing for a fortnight, you know. Giving ourselves a nice break.'

'Yes, you said. I think you should go somewhere nice. Barbados or Dubai or Sri Lanka.'

'I vote for Sri Lanka,' said Russell, with a laugh that said he knew it was all fantasy.

Then, with some reluctance, Simmy felt herself dragged back to the topic of the murder. 'Just one question,' she said. 'Have the police examined Mr Childers' car? Are we sure he didn't bring something poisonous with him from home?'

'Nice thought,' Angie nodded. 'But they took it away on Sunday night, and from what they've said since then, there's absolutely nothing suspicious in it at all.'

'Pity,' said Simmy, with a sigh.

Christopher arrived at Simmy's cottage just before nine-thirty. They were to leave at eight-thirty next morning and drive down to the hospital at Barrow. They speculated about timings, and whether they'd have a chance to get to Patterdale and have a look at the putative building plot as well as check out any new information at the pub. 'Bonnie won't mind if I'm a bit late back,' said Simmy confidently. 'She's been very capable lately, I must say.'

'Compensating for the absence of young Ben.'

'Probably.' Somewhere deep down she noted a flicker of apprehension about leaving Bonnie to manage the shop all day on her own. Nobody could deny that there was an awful lot that could go wrong.

At ten, they watched the television news, waiting for the local items at the end. Too often Simmy had neglected to keep track of what the media was saying about crimes she had personal involvement with. It was with a sinking sensation that she watched her parents' house appear on the screen. In front of it was a man she had never seen, who was introduced as 'Martin Tomkin, guest at the B&B where a man died on Sunday of an undisclosed poison.' He was then interviewed about what he had seen or heard, which turned out to be almost nothing. 'The chap was very ordinary. I only saw him for a minute, on Saturday. He didn't come down to breakfast on Sunday. At least, not when the wife and I were there. It was a dreadful shock when we heard what had happened. We were due to stay until Friday, but with all this disruption and unpleasantness, we decided to cut it short. We might find somewhere else to go to.' He looked straight at the camera as if inviting viewers to help him relocate to another bed and breakfast establishment.

His contribution was worthless, Simmy concluded. The interviewer had extracted no information whatever that could possibly enhance the existing picture. Much as usual, in fact. Grab a person who had glimpsed the victim and make them say something, anything, on camera. Where, she wondered, was Mrs Tomkin? Had she resisted the blandishments of the news reporter? Had her husband elbowed her aside, so as to have all the limelight? Well, good luck to him. To Simmy's eye, he didn't look very nice.

Chapter Nine

The scan on Wednesday morning was oddly underwhelming, in the event. Having a very full bladder took some of the enjoyment away, but worse than that was the echo of earlier times, when her baby Edith waved at her, at twenty-one weeks' gestation, and boasted a healthy heart and full set of organs all in the right places. In a fierce determination to overcome this, she had to damp down all emotions, and just lie there until it was over.

'Don't tell us the sex,' said Christopher, at the outset.

'Don't worry,' said the woman operating the machine. 'We always ask first if you want to know.'

Fortunately, the blurry picture made little sense to either parent, with only the outline of the plump little profile looking like something human.

Christopher saw no reason to hold back on his excitement. 'It's a baby! A real baby!' he trilled. 'Isn't that incredible! It's like a miracle.'

The women both treated him to tolerant smiles,

the radiographer evidently aware of Simmy's history. 'Everything's absolutely fine,' she said. 'A perfectly normal pregnancy. Now you'll be wanting to scoot along to the loo.'

'Thank you,' said Simmy. 'Thank you very much.'

They were away ten minutes before eleven, the atmosphere in the car slightly uneasy. 'You're very quiet,' said Christopher, after a few minutes.

'Sorry. She was nice, wasn't she? Very understanding.'

'Hmm? What did she have to be understanding about?'

'Chris – please don't be thick about this. I've had scans before, remember? I've seen a baby at the same stage as this one, and I can't just forget all about her. I know it's different for you, and there's no way you can get how it feels, but give me a bit of leeway. Cut me some slack, as they say. I'm happy and sad, scared and excited, all at the same time. I thought that seeing this one would help me move on, but I'm sorry to say it's done the opposite. It's sent me right back to where I was in my first pregnancy. And I can't force myself to change that. It'll come right eventually. I know enough about grief and denial and processing and all that jargonny stuff to trust that once this one's born alive and well, I'll be fine. But it's risky. If I try to pack Edith away and pretend she never existed, that'll rebound on us. People kept telling me that doing that leads to post-natal depression when you have another one. I even know somebody it happened to. A girl at school called Jackie, had a cot death and never really faced up to it. When her next baby was born, she was a complete mess, and spent weeks in a mental hospital.'

'I do get it,' he said softly. 'I've known people crash into horrendous depression years after losing someone, because they didn't grieve properly at the time. But *you* need to cut *me* some slack, as well. I'm allowed to be euphoric and proud and madly excited, aren't I?'

'Absolutely you are. The baby deserves that. It's lucky to have you.' And she wept for the next few miles, which seemed the only way the emotions could get themselves acknowledged.

It took nearly an hour to get to Patterdale, passing through Bowness, then Troutbeck, before climbing up to much higher ground through the famous Kirkstone Pass. Even after some years in the area, Simmy still felt a strong sense of adventure every time she used this road. The landscape was bare and desolate and timeless. It was almost always windy, and when the wind dropped, mist replaced it, making any walkers seem crazily intrepid. If it was misty, sheep and oncoming vehicles would loom in front of the car like ghosts. Whatever the season, Kirkstone was alarming. In winter, it was liable to be impassable for several days, and even weeks. If they lived in Patterdale, Simmy would have to drive this way every day, on her commute down to Windermere.

When they came to Brothers Water on their left, barely four miles distant from Simmy's cottage in Troutbeck, it felt as if they'd entered a different land.

She was aware of a shameful loss of nerve, perhaps induced by the poisoned man in Beck View, perhaps by the prospect of the oncoming winter. 'Do we really want to live right out here?'

'Don't we? Should we consider the downside, while we still can? We'll be snowed in a few times each year, even if I get a four-wheel drive. You'll be stuck indoors with Junior when it's raining, with nothing at all to do. It's not too late to change our minds.'

'I really hate changing my mind.' She gazed out of the window at the fairy-tale scenery all around them. 'And I do still think it's fabulous here. Would we ever get tired of it, do you think? Would we crave bright lights and loud music? Ought we to think of my parents, getting older? Would they ever manage to drive up here to visit us?'

'We've said all this before,' he reminded her. 'I'm fine with it, if you are. I feel the same as you do about it. Besides, it's all in the lap of the gods anyway – we just have to hope that fate's on our side. Otherwise I'll be squeezed into your cottage, and we'll be driving each other mad. I guess I could keep the flat on, just as somewhere to store all my stuff, but that's pretty bonkers financially.'

'At least we've got that as a backup. And my dad's straining every nerve to find us something. He's asking everyone he knows. That's how I heard about the building plot in Hartsop. I've got the man's phone number, if you think we should go and look at it now.' She pointed away to the right, where the village of Hartsop nestled. 'It's over there somewhere.'

'We haven't got time to build a whole house from scratch. Besides, if we did it properly, with local stone, in keeping with the current kind of houses, it would cost a fortune. You don't easily get a mortgage for a building plot, you know. And where would we live while it was being built? Who would build it? And above all else – we'd never even get planning permission.'

'Okay. I get the picture. It's a nice idea, though, don't you think?'

'If the timing was different, maybe.'

'It would be feasible if we carried on where we are while it was being built. And it's got to be cheaper than buying a house.'

Christopher sighed. 'The *hassle*, Sim. Haven't you watched those building programmes on telly? The people end up exhausted, depressed, thin. Some of them have nervous breakdowns. And those are the ones who actually *finish* the thing. I know of at least three self-builds that still aren't half-done after about five years.'

She was grateful that he didn't add, *And all that with a baby as well.* 'You're probably right,' she conceded. 'So let's get to the pub. I'm starving.'

They covered the short distance between Hartsop and Patterdale, rounding the final bend to see the village in its entirety. Dark slatey buildings to the left, open water meadows to the right, with a landmark white house nestling into the foot of the fell. A big white-painted hotel with a generous car park gave the village an air of solid respectability. Fells rose with their customary drama on both sides, creating a valley along which a little river ran into Ullswater. Water was everywhere, with a pretty bridge on their right crossing the small river.

'Have you ever been over there?' Simmy asked.

He snatched a quick look. 'No. Shall we go and see what's there?'

'Now?'

'Why not?'

He veered off the road and over the bridge. There were

several houses scattered ahead – many more than Simmy had expected. 'They'll all be holiday lets or second homes, I suppose,' she said.

'Probably.' Closer inspection revealed 'Tourist Board' stickers in one or two windows, and on a gatepost. 'But there's a working farm or two, as well.'

They followed the little road around another bend, where it soon dwindled to a track. 'Crookabeck, look,' said Christopher, pointing to a sign. 'It's got its own name.'

'Never heard of it. It's fabulous, isn't it?' From one moment to the next, Simmy had made a decision. This was where she wanted to live. She could see her toddling child fearlessly playing in the fields, climbing on the mossy tree trunks, mingling with the shaggy Herdwick sheep. There had to be a cottage for sale, by some miracle. There were other little tracks leading to further buildings. Perhaps there would be a barn they could convert.

'Crookabeck,' said Christopher again. 'Do you think we've gone through a portal and this is all an alternative reality?'

'Could be. That bridge is a bit magicky.'

They laughed and turned the car around in a gateway. 'Wouldn't it be amazing, though . . . ?' She sighed. 'If we could only . . .'

'Where there's a will, as they say. Nothing's impossible. Look, this track leads to Hartsop. Two miles of easy walking, fantastic views. Are you *sure* you won't let me have a dog?' It was a topic they'd discussed a few times already.

'Pretty sure,' she said. 'Sorry. It would only chase the sheep and get itself shot.' *And it might eat the baby*, she added silently and foolishly.

'Time for the pub,' he said.

The landlady welcomed them like old friends, which Simmy assumed was the default response to everyone who came through the door. The thousands of visitors who must eat and drink there every year could not possibly all remain in the woman's memory. But then she confounded these thoughts by cocking her head at Simmy's bump, and saying, 'I hear there's been some trouble at your folks' B&B.'

Simmy was dumbstruck. 'How? I mean – it was only three days ago. I didn't think you knew who I was – that they were my parents, anyway. What have you heard?'

'"Mysterious death of B&B guest. Man dies of suspected poisoning." Headline news, duck. Looks as if somebody done the poor chap in, as they say.'

'But it didn't name Beck View, did it? How did you know it was us?'

'Word of mouth. Police camped outside for half a day was the biggest giveaway. Not much about the victim, mind you. Keeping that a bit darker than usual, for some reason.'

'They had to find his family,' said Christopher, evidently not relishing this line of conversation. 'And we haven't come to talk about that. You might remember we've been a few times before, looking for somewhere to buy up here. Are we chasing a rainbow, do you think?'

The woman shrugged. 'Hen's teeth, lovey. Though there's talk of a building plot going on the market, just this side of Hartsop.'

'Yes, we know about that,' said Simmy. 'We don't think that's going to work. It'd take too long.' She looked down at herself. 'And we're a bit short of time.'

'So I see.'

Simmy leant on the bar. 'Do you think there's anything in this plan to build a tourist chalet park somewhere right here in Patterdale? Do you know exactly where they want to put them?'

The response was a blank stare. 'Pardon?'

'There was a protest about it on Sunday, down in Bowness. Leaflets and everything. And a public meeting on Thursday. A modest two-acre park, apparently, somewhere in Patterdale. Must be like the one with the chalets in Hartsop, I assume.'

'You've got something wrong somewhere. I've not heard anything about any such plan.'

A man spoke up from a table by the window. 'Best hope it's all in someone's imagination. If something like that went through, there'd be ructions.'

'There are already,' said Simmy.

'Did you say Bowness? Why would they care what goes on up here?'

'That's what some of us have been wondering,' said Simmy. 'They say it's because people down there are very keen to keep everything just as it is up here. Or something.'

The man at the table nodded sagely. 'It'll be a set-up. There's wheels within wheels, backhanders, dirty tricks.' He looked at Christopher. 'You'll know a bit about all that, in your business.'

Christopher groaned softly and then forced a tight smile. In his role as auctioneer, his face was well known to anyone who had ever been to the saleroom. It was clear to Simmy that he had no idea who this man might be. 'Nowhere near as much as you think,' he said. 'And nothing approaching the scale of a whole new estate of tourist chalets.'

'Granted,' said the man, turning back to his lasagne and chips.

'Are you eating?' asked the landlady, proffering the menu.

Simmy was trying to decide how greedy to be, when a person came up to her from the other end of the bar. 'Hey, remember me? You are the florist, aren't you? You'll have forgotten, but you delivered some flowers to me, near Coniston, ages ago now.'

Simmy frowned. It seemed that she and Christopher were both uncomfortably famous in their own ways. 'Sorry. Remind me.'

'I grabbed them off you and threw them across the yard. Farmyard, to be exact.'

'Oh gosh, yes. How could I forget?'

'It was terrible of me. I felt so bad afterwards. What a thing to do! But you were the final straw. I've been wanting to apologise ever since, actually.'

'Don't worry about it. It was funny, really. It made a good story. I've learnt that you can never be sure what reaction a bunch of flowers might evoke. It's often quite different from what you might expect.'

'So what brings you all the way to Patterdale? Isn't your shop in Windermere?'

'We're house-hunting.' Simmy allowed a quick flash of hope – had this woman been sent by fate to solve their problem? 'This is my fiancé, Christopher.'

'Hi. You want to live up here, do you?'

'Ideally, yes. It's sort of midway between my shop and his auction house in Keswick. We don't want to give either of them up, you see.'

The woman blew out her cheeks. 'Complicated! What about the winter? It gets a lot of snow here, you know. And you can still see the effects of the storm, back in 2015 and the flood the year after. Neither of you would be able to get to work, maybe for weeks at a time.'

'Come on, Tina! It's never as bad as that!' The landlady was hovering, waiting for them to choose their food. 'With a four-wheel drive you can mostly get out after a day or two.'

'You never know,' said Tina mulishly. Then she leant closer to Simmy. 'I've moved up here myself, as it happens. Left bloody Martin and his farm. Living with this lady's brother, now, just down the road.' She nodded at the landlady with a complicated expression. Simmy detected a world of tangled relationships and wounded feelings. She thought she remembered a small child on the fringes of the farmyard drama.

Christopher had had enough. 'Pie and chips for me,' he said loudly.

'I'll have the ploughman's.' Simmy quickly followed up. 'We're in a bit of a rush.' Which wasn't entirely true, but she sensed her fiancé's impatience.

A moment later the door burst open to admit a group of windswept walkers, who stamped their feet and tore off their woolly hats and generally made a great commotion. 'Quick,' said Christopher, 'before they start ordering food.'

Tina drifted away and the food order was processed with reasonable alacrity. They had been eating for a few minutes when Simmy's phone warbled for attention.

'It's Bonnie,' she discovered. 'I hope she's all right.'

Bonnie was excited but not in any trouble. 'Mr Moxon's here,' she said. 'He wants to talk to you.'

'He's not *Mr*, he's Detective Inspector,' she corrected.

'I can't say all that, can I? Anyway, talk to him. He wants to ask you something.'

Simmy's first words were, 'Sorry about Bonnie. She's never very good at job titles.'

'Don't worry. I'm not offended. I'm sorry to bother you on your morning off, but it's just a quick question.'

'Fire away.' Forgetting that she was within earshot of half a dozen pub customers, she became entirely focused on what the detective was telling her.

'Are you familiar with a plant called "datura"? Or thorn apple, I gather is its other name.'

'Vaguely. Nice flowers, but I don't think I've ever used them. I've heard it called the devil's trumpet. Isn't it poisonous? Oh!' The implications dawned on her. 'Are you saying . . . ?'

'It's still only one of several possibilities. We've been scouring all sorts of websites and checking anything that looks likely. Another batch of lab results came back this morning, but it's all a bit general, still. But there was toxic plant material in his system, definitely taken as a fluid. That's as much as we've got to go on so far.'

'I thought maybe it was mushrooms. The sort that make a person frenzied, with hallucinations and violence? There was some noise in those last few minutes and the room was in a mess.'

'Doesn't look like it was mushrooms. He'd knocked a few things over, but I've heard reports of people clawing at the wallpaper and turning furniture upside down. And they'd have been ingested as a solid, not a liquid.'

She understood that he was sharing more with her – again – than was usual. Nolan Moxon regarded Simmy as a friend, rather than a witness who regularly popped up when there was a murder investigation. He was concerned for her welfare and aware of her painful past. 'I know he said he'd been poisoned, but it could have been accidental, surely? Don't people often say things like that without meaning it? Maybe someone sprinkled the wrong seeds on a salad – something like that?' She looked down at the little pile of chopped cucumber, lettuce and tomatoes on her plate. No seeds – but it wouldn't have been unusual for there to be some. Then, as Moxon went on speaking, she realised that the whole pub had gone quiet and that Christopher was trying to catch her eye.

Moxon was saying, 'Possible, admittedly. But there haven't been any reports of similar cases, and it's very unlikely that he'd have been the only victim, if it was a matter of mixed-up seeds. You can't buy anything really toxic in a health food shop.'

'Oh.' She looked round in embarrassment.

'So you've never stocked them here in the shop? The thorn apple plant, I mean.'

'No. Absolutely not. I was asked for one, a year or so ago, and I looked it up. When I realised how toxic it is, I refused to supply it.'

'Very sensible.'

She detected a hint of relief in his tone, and read his thoughts with little difficulty. Turning away and speaking more softly, she said, 'So you can rest assured that my mother didn't get any kind of lethal plant from me and use the seeds

106

to kill her guest. If that was what you were thinking.'

'Not me personally. But there is a certain logic to it that I couldn't help but follow up.'

'Understood.'

'There are some places in the world where poisoning is still a popular method of disposing of somebody.'

'Right,' she said, aware of pitfalls. 'And I expect there's plenty about it online.'

'Indeed. Well, I'll let you get back to whatever you were doing.'

'Thanks. Eating lunch in the Patterdale pub, as it happens.'

'Very nice.' He gave an avuncular little laugh and must have handed the phone back to Bonnie, who came back with a query as to how much longer Simmy was going to be.

'It'll be around half past two, I should think. Are you going to be all right till then?'

'No problem. But there's three new orders on the computer. One is for five o'clock this afternoon. I said we could do it.'

'Where is it?'

'It's somebody local, near the station.'

'And the others are when?'

'For Friday's funeral, as we expected.'

'Right. Good. Thanks.'

The girl started to say something about poisonous plants, when Simmy cut her short. 'I'm trying to have lunch,' she said. 'You can say all that when I get back.' And she finished the call. Conversation started again at neighbouring tables, and Christopher rolled his eyes at her.

* * *

Christopher drove her down to Troutbeck, where she transferred to her own car and he went home to Keswick, nearly twenty miles to the north. 'Will you go in to work?' she asked him.

'Not unless they shout for me. I might stay late tomorrow if it's busy, but there probably won't be a lot to do. People will be bringing things in for the next sale, and all I do is drift about looking at what's likely to make a good price, and get in their way. They ask my advice sometimes, but most people just drop the stuff and go. All there is to do is set it all out and compile the catalogue. Josephine cross-references them all on the computer. It's sheer genius. Janet can do it if she has to, but she's not nearly so competent. I'm hoping Josephine's back by Monday, so she can make sure it's all done properly.'

'Sounds like rather a lot of work to me. It must be exciting to see what turns up,' she said, as she always did. The romance of the auction, with the overlooked treasure and the general unpredictability, was showing no signs of wearing off. Added to that was admiration for Josephine's skill with the databases. She could trace vendors and hammer prices back through several years, and marry them up with a whole host of other statistics.

'Interesting, at least,' he said.

So they parted on a promise to make the most of the coming weekend, with Christopher driving down by coffee time and staying overnight. 'Next week will be fairly quiet,' he promised her. 'We can really focus on the house-hunting.'

Simmy found herself struggling to be optimistic about the search for a new home. It was the same emotion she felt concerning the baby – wanting something so much that it felt dangerous to entertain any real hope that all would be well. Because now, suddenly, she knew she really *really* did want to live in Patterdale. Sadly, the chances were they'd have to spend their early married life in a rented property – which didn't have to be such a bad thing, as her mother would remind her.

She was at the shop shortly before half past two, to find Bonnie deep in conversation with an elderly couple who seemed inclined to buy a large plant pot that Ninian Tripp had made over a year before. The girl's patience was admirable as the customers bickered and dithered over the decision. 'We only came for a bunch of freesias,' said the man. 'What do we want another vase for? Haven't we got at least a dozen already?'

'Not as lovely as this,' argued his wife.

'But it's far too *big*. Where are we going to put it?'

And so forth. Simmy went through to the room at the back, to check what blooms she had for the urgent new order. There would be a new delivery next morning, so it made sense to use up everything she could. When the people had gone, she'd ask Bonnie whether a specific colour scheme had been requested. While there, she made two mugs of tea and opened a packet of biscuits, assuming Bonnie would not have thought to have anything while there on her own. Bonnie's relationship with food was a lot better than it had been five years earlier, but it still wasn't very normal. Simmy did her best not to worry about it, but she never missed a chance to get some nourishment into her elfin employee.

At last the shop was empty, and the mugs were being drained. 'Thanks,' said Bonnie. 'Though you put too much milk in it again.'

'It's good for you,' said Simmy automatically. Then she asked about the order for flowers and any other business that had cropped up during the morning.

'Very dull, except for when Moxo came in. Detective Inspector Moxon, I mean. Must remember not to call him *Mr.*' She rapped herself on the forehead.

'I suppose you heard what he said.'

'Poisoned by seeds from a plant called datura. Devil's something.'

'Trumpet. The flowers look a bit like little trumpets.'

'He was actually a bit embarrassed.' Bonnie laughed. 'Especially when he thought you might have some of it here. He was so glad when I said I'd never heard of it, and was sure we'd never sold any. He had to check with you, though.'

'He's a good man,' said Simmy absently. Something had wriggled inside her, and she forgot what she'd been going to say. 'I felt it – the baby,' she said.

'Hey! Is that the first time?'

'Oh no. But it was stronger. The scan must have upset the poor thing. My mother says scans are probably nowhere near as harmless as they like you to think.'

'Well, people seem to survive them. Babies, I mean. When did they first start doing them? Those babies must be practically middle-aged by now.'

'My guess would be back in the eighties, but I don't really know. Long enough for anything serious to show up, anyway. Of course, my mother never had one with me. I'm not sure she ever had any real antenatal care at all.'

'She's great, your mother,' Bonnie enthused, as always. 'She really thinks for herself, doesn't she?'

'You could say that. But she's not at all her usual self at the moment. She's having ghastly dreams, and thinks she might have to take some sort of pill to make them stop.'

'Well, at least Moxon doesn't think you and she poisoned that man between you.'

That sentiment seemed to sum up the week so far, when Simmy stopped to think about it.

Chapter Ten

Simmy took the flowers to the house near the station and was suitably thanked, the composition of the bouquet admired and goodwill generally expressed. She then went home to Troutbeck, without first calling in on her parents. This was liable to be perceived as unkind under the circumstances, but she was too emotionally drained to be of any use to them. She would phone later on with the reassuring news that all was well with the baby.

Somewhere just below the surface was the notion that everybody was worrying about her. They thought it dangerous that she had witnessed the death of a man in her condition. They wanted her to remain serene. Already the difficulties over finding a house were causing anxiety, on top of running the shop and helping her mother. She had become aware, during the day, that Christopher, Moxon and Bonnie were all treating her like one of the auction house's rare porcelain lots. If she turned up at Beck View, Angie and Russell would no doubt behave in the same manner.

Cumulatively, it had the effect of making her worry about herself. She did have too much to think about, too many feelings to confront and process. The tears in the car were easy enough to understand, she supposed, but she owed it to this new baby to push Edith into the background. She thought she had successfully done just that, several months ago, but these things came back without warning – probably for the rest of one's life. The concern for her parents' well-being and that of their business was another insistent element that was not going to go away. The drift away from traditional bed and breakfast establishments towards Airbnb was ominous. Angie's comments that fewer people wanted the full morning meal were an indication of changing times. And it was impossible to ignore the implications. The timing was poor, but Simmy didn't think she was the only one to entertain the idea of pooling resources and setting up home together.

Thinking along these lines hurt her head even more. It introduced thorny questions about money, and worries about whether Christopher and Angie would end up hating each other if they lived in the same house.

And sitting in its own murky puddle of anxiety was the fact that a poisonous plant had been used to kill Grant Childers. This was horribly close to Simmy's line of work, as the police had instantly realised. This knowledge chafed inside her, as she thought of the likely reaction of local people when they heard about it. It might arouse hostility and suspicion, which would be bad for business. It made the whole thing feel even more personal than it did already. And that meant she was impelled, like it or not, to do whatever she could to identify the person responsible.

She made her call to Beck View, feeling dutiful and very slightly martyred. Angie sounded tired but resigned to whatever might come next. 'The police came round again this afternoon,' she said. 'A woman sergeant, I think she was, with a young constable. Said they needed to do a more thorough search of our kitchen.'

'Left that a bit late, didn't they?'

'That's what your father said. But to be honest, I expected them to be a lot more brainless about it than they turned out to be. You know, I suppose, that it was something called datura that killed him? Most likely in the form of a drink, so there must have been quite elaborate preparations made in advance. That meant the police quite sensibly ignored practically everything I've got in the larder. Rice and flour and sugar and pasta. But they took the gravy granules! And all the dried fruit, for some reason. They left the tins and unopened packets, but I can say goodbye to three jars of home-made chutney. It was rather fun watching them, actually. I think they knew the whole exercise was futile, which made the atmosphere surreal – especially with your father making his usual comments. You can probably guess the sort of thing. "That's right, check the pumpkin pickle for toxic seeds. It was made by that sinister Mrs Bundy in Oak Road. I dare say she's poisoned some husbands in her time." He really did say that.'

'They should have cautioned him about the laws of slander.'

'I know. But they just smiled about it. The boy was only about fifteen, by the look of him.'

'So they don't believe you when you told them you hadn't given the Childers man anything to eat or drink?'

'They have to be sceptical, I suppose. I mean, I would

say that, wouldn't I? But I wouldn't be daft enough to give him a cheese and pickle sandwich with poison in the pickle, and then leave the jar on the shelf – would I?'

'Probably not,' said Simmy, feeling better by the minute. 'So what happens next?'

'Don't ask me. Incidentally, we had a phone call from that Tristan Wilkins man just now. He wanted to make sure one or both of us were going to be at that meeting tomorrow about the Patterdale plan to build those chalets. Your father still thinks there's something peculiar about it, so he's decided to go along. You should go with him.'

'I might, I suppose, if he wants company. Christopher and I asked the pub lady if she'd heard about it, and she said she hadn't. That's odd, when you think about it.'

'It's not so much that he wants company, as the fact that it's Patterdale. If you're going to live there, you'll want to have as much information as you can get. You really don't want even more tourist traffic on those little roads.'

'I'm happy to go to the meeting, Mum, even though I can't see us ever actually finding somewhere to live there. There does seem to be a bit of a mystery to it all, whether or not we end up living in the middle of whatever it is.'

'Your father wouldn't like to hear you say that.'

'I know. I just think we're wasting our time even trying. We could have got something all sorted out in Keswick by now.'

'Hm,' said Angie, and went on to demand a full account of her daughter's day, starting with the scan. Simmy obliged, taking twenty minutes over it. When the conversation was finished, she felt much more relaxed than before. Her father had not lost his sense of humour, and her mother was almost enjoying being at the centre of a murder enquiry. That being so, Simmy was scarcely justified in agonising over them.

Thursday dawned crisp and clear, and Simmy's thoughts turned to funeral flowers. Bonnie had said nothing more about Miss Entwhistle. The short notice was unusual, especially on a Friday, but a burial in a churchyard was quite a different business from a cremation; if Miss E had been the organist or secretary to the vicar, she would receive preferential treatment. The undertaker would have to call in his reserve team of bearers and co-operate with whatever was required. Simmy might know the dead woman, at least by sight, given that the funeral was to be at her local church. There would be cars parked all along the sides of the road up to Kirkstone, and the whole village would feel the effects. And Simmy's flowers would be on very public display, so she would have to make a good job of them.

Ever since the mawkish little cremation of her own baby daughter, Simmy had given the matter of funerals quite a lot of thought. Edith's death had been so shocking that Simmy had not managed to pull herself together sufficiently to do the funeral properly. Nor had Russell or Angie. They went through the motions with undisguised reluctance and absolute ignorance as to what would be the most therapeutic way to do it. They had all learnt a lot about how *not* to do it in the process.

Which, she realised as she drove down to Windermere, was not a very wholesome line of thought, in the light of the new baby she was carrying. This one would not need a funeral, she assured herself fiercely. The next dead person she would have any personal involvement in would be her father, fifteen years into the future. Nobody she loved was going to die for a long, long time.

Nor would Simmy have to worry about Grant Childers' funeral, because his relatives were sure to take him back to the Midlands and deal with him there. Given the manner of his death, that was liable to be some weeks away yet. New theories could prompt new tests on the body, as the investigation was led down fresh avenues of enquiry.

Meanwhile, Miss Entwhistle would get a lovely send-off with a good display of beautiful flowers.

Bonnie looked wan, her smile of welcome very forced when Simmy got to the shop. 'Tanya phoned last night,' she said. 'She's coming in again after school today, if that's all right.'

'I've got to do all those funeral flowers. I won't have time to talk to her.'

The girl shrugged. 'She understands that. But I think Helen's worrying that Tanya's going to try to turn into another Ben, with this murder so close to home. She's told her to stay right out of it.'

'You can't blame her. Tanya's awfully young.'

'It's so *horrible* without him,' Bonnie burst out. 'It's almost as if he's dead, the way I keep wanting to talk to him and ask him things, and just hang out with him. It's like slamming into a wall, every time. Or falling into a deep hole. Everything seems so grey and empty. When we do FaceTime I can't say what I want to, because I daren't tell him about it. And that feels like telling him lies.'

'I know. I miss him as well. And there's no denying he'd love the whole poison thing. It's so unusual these days, I'm

117

still not entirely sure I believe that's what happened. I mean, would anybody really find the right plant, and then make some sort of infusion from it, and get him to drink it without noticing, and hope they did actually kill him? Wouldn't there be some sort of nasty taste? There seems to be such a lot that could go wrong. What if he didn't drink the tea, or whatever it was – or gave it to somebody else? What if it only made him sick? And *why*?' It always seemed to come back to the *Why?* question for Simmy. The reasons that people gave for committing murder never seemed quite enough, to her mind. The ultimate crime – the ultimate *sin* as well – surely must have a powerfully convincing motive behind it. And yet it so often felt as if it was little more than wounded pride or simple greed at the heart of the killing. People apparently valued their own public image so highly that they would take a life in order to protect it. Over the past year or two, Simmy had given this a great deal of thought, and finally been forced to accept the reality, however hard it was to understand.

'Tanya reckons it's to do with conservation, somehow. She thinks there's a conspiracy going on somewhere, and this Childers man got in the way. She says it could be several people all working together to make sure the murder worked as planned.' Again Bonnie's face fell. 'And Ben would say that's never a good idea, because somebody always gives the game away. It's terribly difficult to keep a secret when more than one person knows it.'

'Although there'd be a strong incentive in this case, wouldn't there?'

'That's true.'

Simmy put a halt to the conversation by diverting her attention to the computer, where it sat on the modest-sized table that served as shop counter. All the business had to be done on this barely adequate space, and it quickly became cluttered. The cash till was squashed in beside the laptop, along with a notepad, pen and landline phone. Orders came through online and by telephone, and had to be frequently monitored. There was a single high stool, meaning that only one person could sit down at a time. When business was slack, one of them would disappear into the back room, to tidy up, check stock or construct bouquets and wreaths. It was also Simmy's workroom when there were orders to fulfil – as there were this morning.

'That funeral,' she said. 'The one in Troutbeck tomorrow. Do you have any idea who Miss Entwhistle was?'

'Oh – I meant to tell you. Corinne's going. She's calling in to order some flowers, any minute now. Dorothea Entwhistle was her best friend at school, or so she says. I think she must have had at least eight best friends. Anyway, she was only fifty-five. Some sort of cancer, I think. She lived up at the top end of Troutbeck. I'd have thought you'd know her. *Everybody* knows her.'

'I might, by sight. Where did she work?'

'She did all sorts of things. Had her own little farm, with some sheep and things. Took walkers over the fells. Little groups at a time. Painted a bit, as well. You really should have known her.'

Simmy felt reproached for her lack of social involvement. 'My father probably did,' she said feebly. 'Gosh, look!' She was staring at her computer. 'Three more wreaths wanted. Honestly, this is terribly short notice.'

'The burial isn't till three tomorrow. They want the flowers by one. You've got loads of time.'

'Better get cracking, then. I'll need an extra delivery first thing in the morning. There's nothing like enough fresh flowers for all these.'

'It's good to be busy,' said Bonnie absently. 'Maybe Tanya can help a bit when she comes in.'

'That won't be necessary,' said Simmy stiffly. 'You're quite right – there is plenty of time. I've got to do six lots. Each one only takes twenty minutes or so. I was panicking for nothing.'

'Depends what else happens,' said Bonnie.

Chapter Eleven

Since nothing very much happened during the morning, Bonnie took the opportunity of researching everything she could find about the effects of the datura plant. As Simmy caught up with orders in the back room, Bonnie called the results of her Internet trawling through to Simmy, detail by detail. 'It doesn't say exactly how you prepare it,' she reported. 'No surprise there, I suppose. There are loads of different varieties, but they're all poisonous.'

'What does it taste like?' asked Simmy.

'Can't find that, either. Most poisonous things are very bitter, aren't they?'

'That would make sense. But a lot of lethal mushrooms taste quite nice, apparently.'

'And it's the season for them now. Why not use them, I wonder?'

'They wouldn't keep for long, unless you dried them. They'd go mushy . . .' Simmy trailed off, aware that she knew nothing about how to prepare a toxic drink from any kind of plant.

'Very funny,' laughed Bonnie. 'Mushy mushrooms. Yuk!'

Simmy emerged, drying her hands as she came. Since she'd been pregnant, she had made special efforts to avoid ingesting sap from the various blooms she worked with. All this talk of poison had made her even more careful. 'We ought to phone Ninian and tell him we sold his pot,' she said. 'I've only just remembered.'

'The money's here, in a special envelope.'

'I'll do it now, before I forget again.' Using the landline, she keyed the number that was still in her head, from when she and Ninian had been in frequent contact. There was no reply, so she left a message. 'Good news – we sold that big pot we've had for ages. The money's here, if you want to come and get it.'

'He phoned a few days ago, didn't he?' Bonnie said.

'Monday, I think. He's showing a surprising interest in that Patterdale planning application. Usually, he wouldn't care about a thing like that.'

'Maybe he's thinking of investing in tourist chalets. Probably a good idea, actually.'

'I don't think so.'

'Not for him, perhaps, but what about other people? Not everybody's going to think it's a terrible idea.'

'What does Helen think? Do you know?'

Bonnie gave her a blank look. 'How would I? I haven't seen Helen for weeks. I don't imagine she cares one way or the other.' Simmy had a profound admiration for Helen Harkness, Ben's mother, busy architect and capable parent to her five offspring.

'My father's going to a public meeting down at the Belsfield about it this evening. I thought I might go with him, seeing as how Chris and I want to live in Patterdale. It seems silly not to. It would be good to hear the arguments on both sides.'

'Is it a council meeting? Are they deciding whether to allow it?'

'No, no. That wouldn't be in Bowness – or in the evening. There might be a few council people there, I suppose. Actually, it still doesn't make sense to me that they're talking about it here, and not up there on the spot.'

'Maybe they don't want Patterdale people to know about it.'

Simmy opened her mouth to scoff at this suggestion, when it suddenly seemed less ridiculous. It *did* feel as if there was something underhand about the whole business, when she thought about it. It was odd that the landlady of the Patterdale pub was unaware of the proposed new buildings, and even when informed of them, she seemed much less concerned than she should be. Had the locals really heard nothing at all? Or had they been assured the thing would never happen? Did Tristan and the Proctor woman know better? What had really been going on during Sunday morning, down beside Lake Windermere, when Simmy and her father had been blithely walking the dog? There'd been leaflets and placards. It was likely to be covered by local news outlets, and featured on Facebook. Lots of local people had been assembled in protest – 'No, no,' she said. 'I'm sure it was intended to alert everybody from here to Patterdale and beyond.'

Bonnie was thinking, voicing her ideas as they occurred. 'I guess you can see the logic, sort of. Bowness is a centre for tourists, after all. It's a good place to attract a crowd.

And everybody's going to be thinking that if it's causing outrage down here, then it really must be important.'

'Right,' said Simmy. 'Although it's still peculiar. Why should Candy Proctor care what happens up there, for one thing?'

'It's not just her, though, is it?'

They went on to brainstorm all the conceivable conspiracies that might lie behind the Sunday protest. Was the planning proposal some sort of Trojan Horse? A thin end of a wedge, a sleight of hand, which was meant to divert attention away from something closer to home? And had Tristan Wilkins got wind of something sinister, that could not be confronted directly? What could be his reason for not proclaiming the whole story to the general public? Or did he intend to do so that evening?

All this took several minutes of quite enjoyable talk. Then Simmy tried to bring it back to earth. 'It'll all boil down to local politics,' she said. 'Wheels within wheels. Feelings running high in the committee rooms. Conflicts of personality.'

'I bet it'll be money at the bottom of it,' said Bonnie.

'Maybe there'll be some clues at the meeting. I'll be sure to watch everybody closely.'

'Can I come?'

Simmy entertained a vision of a roomful of self-important local dignitaries, all over sixty, interspersed with anxious property owners and bearded conservationists, with the fair-headed fairy creature that was Bonnie Lawson sitting in their midst. 'Of course you can. It's a public meeting,' she said.

'Who'll be there, I wonder? Who exactly is going to

be bothered enough about Patterdale to turn out for something like that?'

'We'll have to wait and see,' said Simmy. 'Won't we?'

It was half past eleven and Simmy was well ahead of schedule with the funeral flowers. They were keeping fresh in the cool back room, or so she hoped. They would have to wait for over twenty-four hours before being delivered. 'I made those wreaths a bit early,' she said ruefully. 'I panicked.'

'Not like you.'

'I suppose I thought there might be more orders still to come in. And there's still lots to do for the wedding, don't forget. This rushed funeral is a bit odd, when you think about it – if she was such a prominent person, wouldn't you think they'd make sure everyone had a chance to get the time off for the funeral? The end of next week would make more sense.'

'Corinne says there's some sort of maintenance work happening at the church for most of next week. They're going to be putting scaffolding up around the door, and that wouldn't do for a high-profile funeral. And all the mourners will be locals, so nobody's got to make travel plans.'

They were still chatting speculatively when the shop door opened to admit a large man with long orange hair and an eager expression. 'Blimey, it's Henry the Eighth,' murmured Bonnie, making Simmy giggle.

'Hello,' she said. 'It's Stuart, isn't it? Sorry I can't remember your surname.'

'Carstairs, for my sins,' he told her. 'Your dad must have mentioned me to you?'

'Yes, he did. You met him on Tuesday night and told

him about a place in Patterdale. And he saw you on Sunday as well.'

'Did he?' The man frowned. 'How come?'

'You were part of the protest in Bowness. That's where he saw you, holding a placard, in fact.'

'Oh – right. Just showing solidarity with some old mates,' he said vaguely, before briskly changing the subject. 'So – how's about that building plot idea, then? It's genuine, you know. You should snap it up quick before somebody else bags it. Look – I was hoping you'd come and have lunch with me somewhere and we can talk about it.'

Bonnie was performing her habitual little dance of frustrated curiosity, bobbing around Simmy in an unconvincing pretence at being busy, while clearly fixated on every word. Stuart Carstairs seemed entirely oblivious to her.

'Lunch?' faltered Simmy. 'Well . . .'

'Go on,' Bonnie urged treacherously. 'You're all up to date here.'

'The thing is,' Simmy began again, determinedly, 'Christopher and I went to Patterdale yesterday and talked over all our options, and we don't think we can take on a new-build. Not with everything else we've got to deal with.' She looked down at herself, wondering whether Stuart knew about the pregnancy.

'I dare say it seems a bit daunting,' he agreed. 'But you're young, and your dad says you've got plenty of flair for design and all that sort of thing. It would be a real legacy for the future – to pass down the family, so to speak.'

'New-build?' echoed Bonnie. 'What's this about, then?'

Simmy made no attempt to keep the story from her young employee. 'Mr Carstairs has a relative with a piece of land to sell. He thinks Chris and I could build a house on it. It's more or less in Patterdale.'

'Hartsop,' said Stuart. 'To be strictly accurate.'

'Oh!' cried the girl with rapturous enthusiasm. 'Helen could be your architect.' She paused. 'But would you get permission for it? Isn't that massively difficult?'

'Massively,' said Simmy.

'There are ways,' said Stuart, not quite putting a finger alongside his nose, but giving a quick wink instead. 'Local couple. Nothing pretentious or intrusive. Keep it in the vernacular. I can help you with the jargon.'

'So can Helen,' insisted Bonnie.

Simmy took a deep breath. 'I'm touched that you thought of me. But I won't take you up on lunch, all the same. Let me talk to my fiancé first. It's a huge decision, and we've got all sorts of things to consider. We did discuss it yesterday, as I said. And we really would find the timing impossible. Where would we live while it was being built? How long would all the paperwork take, before we could even begin? We don't know any builders, or how to supervise a job like that. Chris isn't particularly handy. We wouldn't be able to do any of the work ourselves. We'd have to get a bridging loan to cover the cost of it all.' She ran out of breath, aware that the others were regarding her with disapprobation.

'You've already talked yourselves out of it, then?' Stuart sighed. 'You'll regret it, you know. If you do find a place to buy up there, you'll drive past that new house, week after week, and wish you'd grabbed your chance when it was offered. Believe me – that's how it'll be.'

'We'll take the risk,' said Simmy, made ever more resistant by his words. 'At least, I think we will. I'll phone Chris this evening and tell him what you've said. I'm sorry if we're being disappointing.'

Stuart Carstairs gave a tight little smile. 'Just wanted to do your dad a favour, basically. And your mum. Good woman, your mum.'

Simmy recalled that her father had described this man as Angie's 'red-haired chum', implying that the real relationship was with her, and Russell much less so. Was all this essentially an attempt to ingratiate himself with a woman he held a fondness for? For all Simmy knew, he was single and intent on seducing the well-preserved and opinionated Mrs Straw by arranging a favour for her pregnant daughter.

She declined his rather lukewarm repeated invitation to lunch, and he went away with considerably less of a flourish than when he had arrived.

The afternoon saw the weather turn noticeably colder, and only one customer braved the sudden east wind to purchase a floral tribute for a female friend. Shortly after half past three, Tanya Harkness put in her promised appearance. Bonnie greeted her with a coolness that struck Simmy as uncalled for. Tanya herself did not seem to notice, being more than a little excited.

'I've found somebody who was on the lake cruiser on Sunday,' she burst out. 'My friend Letty was with her aunt, who's over from Australia, and it was the same boat as the man who got murdered was on.'

'How can you be sure?' Simmy demanded.

'Because the police put out a call for anybody who took the lake cruise on the midday boat from Bowness, so that must be the one he booked on. The aunt went to the police station yesterday, and they asked her all sorts of questions, and showed her a picture of the man. She didn't recognise him, though.'

'They must think somebody on the boat gave him the poison,' said Bonnie.

'Right!' said Tanya.

But Simmy was unpersuaded. 'Wouldn't that be very odd? Do they give out refreshments on the cruise? And how would they be sure it was him? It doesn't work. It's a daft idea.'

Tanya took up the argument. 'Okay – well, maybe they followed him when he got off, and got chatting, and took him to a cafe or somewhere, and bought it for him then. I mean, slipped him something they'd already prepared.' She drifted to a halt, hearing the several weaknesses in this scenario. 'No actual proof, though,' she sighed. 'Ben would say there's got to be proof, wouldn't he?'

'Yeah,' said Bonnie. 'But there obviously *is* something about the boat. The police must know that the Childers man was on it, and they think that's important.'

'We're doing what we always do,' Simmy complained. 'Just making wild guesses, with no idea what to *do* about any of them.'

'We have to discuss it, though – don't we?' Tanya looked confused. 'I mean – how else can we work anything out?'

'They need to know every detail of the man's last hours,' Bonnie announced. 'That's why the boat matters. It's obvious. They want to know everybody he spoke to, what he was doing, why he was here in the first place.'

'And for most of that, their main informant has to be Candy Proctor,' said Simmy. 'We have to assume she didn't tell us everything she told the police. After all, why would she?'

'To make herself feel important?' Bonnie suggested.

Tanya was leaning against the wall next to the door into the back room. It was a habit her brother was also prone to. 'She must be one of the suspects, don't you think?' she said slowly. 'She's the only person who actually *knew* him.'

Simmy looked at Bonnie, eyebrows raised.

'Yes, I told her all about it,' she confessed, without shame. 'Why not?'

'For all we know, he had loads of friends up here,' said Simmy, with the feeling that they were going round in circles. 'Haven't we said this already?' She got up from the stool, which she had taken as by right of seniority, proprietorship and pregnancy. 'There's work to be done. No more chatter.'

'And here's somebody come to see us,' said Bonnie, pointing through the big shop window to the street outside. A male face was peering in, waggling his fingers in a childish gesture of greeting.

Chapter Twelve

'That was quick,' laughed Simmy, as Ninian Tripp came delicately in, apparently wary of the female threesome. 'Amazing the effect money can have.'

He made a rueful face. 'It comes at rather an opportune moment, as it happens. I was wondering where my next cappuccino was coming from.'

She extracted the waiting envelope from its niche in the till and handed it to him. 'It went to an elderly couple who found it impossible to resist.'

'Nice to know,' he smiled. 'Can I bring you some more next week?'

'How many? I can't really take more than three.' They both cast their eyes around the shop, which was undeniably short of space. 'They have to go somewhere they won't get kicked over.'

'I'll bring two. There's a rather pleasing blue one I think might find favour.'

Tanya had been observing this exchange with interest,

evidently unfamiliar with the potter. 'This is Ninian,' Bonnie told her. 'He lives on Brant Fell and Corinne knows him. He makes pots. Simmy had a thing with him, a while ago.'

Ninian bowed. 'Pleased to meet you, young miss. At your service.' Tanya giggled.

'We're discussing murder as usual,' said Simmy. 'You know that man who was poisoned on Sunday? Well, it must have been almost exactly the same time as you were there, chatting to me and Candy Proctor. Apparently, the police think he was on the cruise boat. And then he died at my parents' house, while I was there. Can you believe that? It all seems to be a whole chain of coincidences.'

Ninian shrugged away the latter part. 'Nasty business. But I always did think murderers ought to consider poison more often. It's a highly effective method if you want to escape detection – and who doesn't? All the best crime novels feature poisoners, in my opinion.'

'Well, it's a bit near the bone if you sell plants for a living,' said Simmy sternly. 'Especially when the victim dies in your own mother's arms. It was very upsetting, I might tell you.'

'Undoubtedly,' nodded Ninian with an unconvincing attempt at sympathy. 'It must have been awful. But at least I assume you didn't know the chap? I mean – you had no personal investment in him, as it were?'

'That sounds a bit callous,' Tanya ventured, her face very serious. 'He was *somebody's* son or brother or partner. You have to look at the wider picture – don't you?' She turned to Bonnie for support.

'Absolutely. You do,' came the quick response.

'"No man is an island",' quoted Ninian languidly. 'Although I do think that's wrong. After all, I regard myself as a bit of an island, most of the time. Not many mourners at *my* funeral, I bet you.'

'We'll come,' said Simmy. 'Me and Bonnie. And Corinne. And all those shop women in Bowness who let you have things on credit.'

'They'll only be there to celebrate getting rid of such a nuisance.'

'Why – are you going to die?' Tanya seemed genuinely concerned, and Simmy remembered how young she was, and how confusing adult humour could sometimes be.

'Not today,' said Ninian lightly. 'But then – that's probably what the poor murder victim thought as well. We just never know, do we?'

'Stop it,' Simmy ordered. 'Go away. There's another order for the funeral. I've got to do it before I go home.'

'Dorothea Entwhistle,' nodded Ninian. 'Nice lady. She used to babysit me when I was a terrible two-year-old and she was about sixteen. We lived in Troutbeck then – did I tell you?'

'Probably,' sighed Simmy, fully aware that she was never going to get to grips with all the subterranean connections between the long-term residents of the area. It could easily be two centuries earlier, the way everybody knew their place in the pattern, taking it for granted and seldom explaining it to more recent incomers. Ninian's parents had both come from countless generations of Cumbrian folk, and although he had travelled briefly in his twenties, he was as much a native as Simmy's first employee in the shop, Melanie Todd or Bonnie's foster mother, Corinne.

'Will you go to the funeral?' asked Bonnie. 'Miss Entwhistle's, I mean.'

He put up his hands in mock horror. 'Who? Me? I don't do funerals. What would I *wear*?'

They all regarded his clay-smeared jeans and unravelling jumper and smiled. Nobody could imagine Ninian Tripp in a suit or properly polished shoes.

The arrival of a breathless customer, parked on yellow lines and needing to be somewhere else ten minutes ago threw everyone into a dither. Tanya and Ninian both made an exit, while Bonnie escaped to a corner of the shop until Simmy had constructed a hurried bunch of hothouse gladioli. When the woman had gone, it was time to focus on finishing up the day's tasks and preparing for the next morning. Simmy had a delivery to make to a house not far from Beck View, which was convenient. The plan was for her to share a quick supper with Angie and Russell, then to go with her father to the meeting in Bowness.

She was there by six, both parents looking reasonably relaxed. The final set of guests had left that morning and everybody else had cancelled.

'Really rather a relief,' said Angie. 'The police say I can use the back room again from Monday.'

'We're changing its name to The Murder Room,' joked Russell. 'And making people pay double to use it.'

Neither of his womenfolk laughed. Then, just as they were sitting down to their cold meat and salad, the doorbell rang. Russell, with much more animation than he had shown for a year or more, jumped up to answer it. Simmy and Angie heard the conversation from the other end of the hallway.

'Sorry to come at such a time, but there's never a perfect moment, is there?' came a female voice that Simmy recognised.

'Candy! Always nice to see you,' gushed Russell. 'Come in and have a slice of ham.'

'Oh dear – are you in the middle of eating?'

'Not a problem. Is there something in particular you want to talk about?' He had led her back to the kitchen, and ushered her in. 'Look who it is,' he said.

'Hi, Candy,' said Angie, with her mouth full. 'Sit down. Tea or something?'

'If you're making it. Thanks.' There was a tightness to her tone, which Simmy experienced as repressed hostility. She was thinking about Tuesday's encounter at the shop, in which Candy had been rather unpleasant. It appeared to her that the two of them were never going to be friends, and she wondered whether Angie and Russell felt the same. She waved a hand to make her own presence apparent, since nobody had bothered to draw the visitor's attention to her. Candy responded with a brief, 'Oh – hello.'

'What's your beeswax, then?' quipped Russell, still in a buoyant mood. 'Something to do with our murdered man, I'll be bound.'

'Has his family been yet? What's going to happen about his funeral? I *knew* him, you know. He was *my* guest, by rights. But nobody's told me anything. After I've been so forthcoming to the police, I'd have expected better treatment. Nobody's said a word since Tuesday –

and then it was just the bare minimum. I got very little more from you, Mrs Brown, in the shop. It's all been terribly frustrating.'

How does she know my name, Simmy wondered. The 'Brown' had acquired an oddly temporary aura, since she'd agreed to become Christopher's wife. It was beginning to feel like nothing more than a bridge between Straw and Henderson, soon to be forgotten.

'Nobody's told us very much either,' said Angie. 'They mostly don't, you know. After all, we must still be officially under suspicion, seeing that he died here. They're not going to spill the details of their investigations to any of us, are they?'

'Well *I'm* not under suspicion, am I? I've been extremely helpful, in fact. I've told them who he knew up here and what he generally did on his visits. If only I hadn't been so *busy* he would have been staying with me this time, as well.'

'And a great pity that he wasn't,' said Russell with feeling. 'You could have had all the fun instead of us.'

'Dad!' Simmy couldn't let him go on in the same flippant vein any longer.

Candy Proctor pursed her lips and said nothing. Angie had made a perfunctory mug of tea from the perpetually hot water on top of the Rayburn and now proffered it. 'Thanks,' muttered Candy.

'You'll be going to the meeting tonight?' Russell started on a different note. 'Shall we walk down together? We'll have to leave in about a quarter of an hour from now.'

'Oh, the meeting,' said Candy wearily. 'All right, then. You know, of course, that Grant was meant to be one of the main speakers? I mean – that's what he came up here for in the first place.'

All three members of the Straw family stared at her in amazement. 'No,' said Russell. 'Nobody told us that. Perhaps you could explain it to us.'

Candy briefly complied. Childers, it seemed, had originally been scheduled to spend his visit monitoring red squirrels. But then Candy had asked him to attend the protest rally and speak against the plans for the tourist park. 'He's good with words, you see,' she said.

'So you'd been in touch with him?' Simmy said. 'Before he came up here on Friday?'

'On and off, yes. I had to explain why he couldn't stay with me, for one thing.'

'But *why* couldn't he?' Angie frowned in bewilderment. 'If you knew all along when he'd be coming back, why didn't you keep a room for him? Doesn't he make the booking from one time to the next?'

Candy lifted her chin in resistance to Angie's tone. 'Because the dates were changed, and I was fully booked for the new date. He was originally going to come the first week of October, but the squirrel people wanted him to make it later. And Tristan was pleased because he'd get him as a speaker.' She sighed. 'It did all get rather complicated.'

'So this meeting's been planned for six weeks or more? That's when Childers booked with us. We had to check all that for the police,' said Russell.

'Does Tristan know him, then?' asked Simmy, trying to keep pace with what felt like a lot of new information. 'Did, I mean,' she amended.

'I think they emailed each other – but they'd never actually met.'

'And was he still intending to count squirrels? Nobody from the wildlife society or whatever it is has contacted us to ask where he is,' said Angie.

'Why would they? I don't suppose they knew – or cared – where he'd be staying. They'll have tried to get him on his mobile or computer, won't they?'

'I suppose so,' said Angie. 'Well, I hope they manage all right without him this evening.'

The three of them set out as soon as the scanty supper was finished. Angie had never actually said she wouldn't go to the meeting, but it had been assumed. She had always felt an obligation to be available for her guests during the evening, despite Simmy's insistence that there was really no need, and the habit had become established, even when there were no guests. Russell seldom went out after dark, either, but in his case it was more from inertia than a sense of responsibility. Even after his descent into a strange form of paranoia, where he might have been expected to suspect his guests of theft or arson, he seemed less worried than Angie about leaving them alone in the house. 'It's as if he only sees danger on the other side of the front door,' said Angie. But her own housebound evenings suddenly looked to her daughter as if they might stem from something rather more neurotic than first realised.

'Why don't you come as well?' Simmy urged her. 'You've got no reason to stay here on your own.'

'I don't feel like it,' was all Angie would say.

The walk down to the Belsfield Hotel was identical to the one Simmy and Russell had taken on Sunday with the dog. The hotel had a broad sloping garden that faced the lake. A path zigzagged up to the front entrance, but because the car park was at the back, most people went in that way. The meeting was to take place in a handsome room on the ground floor, with a capacity of eighty, according to Russell, who had swotted up on the hotel's many facilities, as part of his perceived role as local provider of hospitality.

'Eighty!' gasped Simmy. 'There won't be that many, will there?'

'We think there will,' said Candy. 'It's a very controversial issue. It's been simmering away for some time, until Tristan decided to do something about it.'

'Aren't you one of the organisers? Why aren't you there already, testing the sound system or something?' Russell asked. 'Is there a PowerPoint presentation? I love PowerPoint presentations.'

'Tristan's doing all that, with his little team of helpers. All I do is organise leaflets and posters. I'm not needed this evening, except to just put in an appearance. I've been doing my best to rally support for weeks now. It's an awful shame about Grant, of course. We've had to get some National Trust chap to come down from Carlisle, instead.'

'Was Mr Childers in the National Trust?' asked Simmy.

'I assume he was a member, but not a paid official or anything.'

'But he was against these new proposals? He was going to make a speech about how damaging they would be – something like that?'

'He was going to talk mostly about the implications from a planning perspective. The defects in the original application.'

'Sounds rather dry,' said Russell. 'Maybe we've been spared a pretty dull contribution.'

Candy Proctor turned on him in fury. 'This is *serious*,' she snarled. 'If this plan were to be passed, it would open the floodgates to countless others, all over the fells. It would be a *disaster*.'

'Steady on! You're getting a bit carried away, aren't you? These little battles are being fought all the time, right back to a century ago. There's no real risk to the fells – or the valleys, come to that. The whole area relies on the tourists, don't forget – you and me included. If somebody has the idea of providing a few more places for them to stay, where's the harm in that?'

'You're not in *favour* of them, are you?' Horror was plain on the woman's face.

'I've got an open mind,' said Russell piously.

Simmy found herself channelling Ben Harkness, as happened quite a lot. He would be asking himself whether this was the answer to why Grant Childers had been poisoned. Somebody wanted to prevent him from saying his piece about the chalet development. It seemed both obvious and mildly disappointing. But what exactly had the man intended to say? His role was still obscure. 'Would he have spoken against the plans, then?' she asked.

'Of *course* he would. Isn't that obvious?'

Simmy didn't respond to this rudeness. Russell spoke for her. 'We're novices at all this,' he said. 'You're saying that everybody at the meeting is going to be against the plans – right? No room for any arguments from the other side? Not so much a debate as a rabble-rousing exercise. But who are the rabble? The good people of Bowness, who are not terribly likely to care too much about events in Patterdale. You do know there's a perfectly good hotel there, which could provide you with a room like this, probably for a quarter of the price?'

'Whose manager can't see any reason to challenge the planning application,' Candy flashed back.

'Even Troutbeck or Ambleside would have been closer, though. Or Grasmere. You'd get a lot more concerned citizens in any of them than down here.'

'You're wrong. There are several good reasons why Bowness makes an excellent control centre. You might understand it better once the meeting starts.'

They had reached the meeting room, where Simmy immediately spotted Bonnie sitting in the second row with her foster mother. 'Look – Corinne's here,' she said. 'That's a surprise.'

'Keeping an eye on the girl, I presume,' said Candy Proctor, who evidently knew exactly who the pair were.

Simmy and Russell found seats in the row behind Bonnie and Corinne, while Candy made her way to the front row where a chair had been reserved for her. Bonnie turned round with a smile, but didn't speak. Simmy smiled back and then said to her father, 'Did she really say "control centre"?'

'Delusions of grandeur, or something very like it. They're all imagining themselves at the forefront of a vitally important campaign. Look at old Tristan Wilkins. Absolutely in his element. And those other two.' Russell indicated two men flanking Tristan at the table sitting at the front of the room. 'One of them's in the Friends of the Lake District, I believe. I heard him speak at a lunch I went

141

to ages ago, in Coniston or somewhere. That was when I was in the B&B group. Before you moved up here. I was quite sociable in those days. That's definitely the same man. You couldn't mistake that beard.'

'And who's the other one?'

'No idea.'

Simmy was still checking her observations against the few facts she knew about Grant Childers. It surprised her that her father was clearly not doing the same. There were leaflets on all the seats and she scanned through hers while they waited for people to settle down. It was a new one, taking everything a step further than the ones handed out the previous Sunday, with a tear-off section where people could pledge support and active assistance. There were impassioned pleas to 'Save the Lakes' along with assertions that the wildlife and ecology of the area could not withstand any more construction outside the strict boundaries already laid down. The proposed holiday chalets would breach this rule significantly. 'So why are they worried that permission might be granted?' Simmy muttered. 'It looks obvious that there isn't a chance they'll be allowed. What about the latest Local Plan? That's full of restrictions, isn't it?'

'I gather it leaves quite a lot of scope for development, actually,' said Russell. 'There've been arguments about it.'

Simmy, like every other resident of the Lake District, was aware, if only dimly, that the Local Plan was a document of vital significance, which was updated and debated fiercely every few years.

'So, what does that mean for this thing, then?' she asked.

'There must be more to it than they're telling us,' her father replied. 'There's politicking going on, if I'm not mistaken.'

142

'Enough to lead to murder?' She was whispering, but the woman in the seat in front of her must have caught the last word. She looked round in alarm.

Simmy smiled reassuringly, and was saved from having to explain herself by a sudden hush. Tristan Wilkins had rapped on the table, and everybody had instantly reacted. Simmy turned to check how full the room was, and realised there were a lot of empty chairs. A rapid count suggested there were between forty and fifty people. Still not a bad turnout, as Tristan was already bravely asserting.

There followed three lengthy speeches, two of which had Russell's hoped-for PowerPoint presentations. Maps, photographs of existing tourist parks, copies of the current planning laws came and went, most of them striking Simmy as only peripherally relevant. There was no detail at all about the actual proposal for Patterdale. Then the third man stood up, and talked in a soft voice about squirrels, water voles, newts, hawks and other shy upland creatures that would be hugely disadvantaged by the arrival of even one more galumphing tourist. Furthermore, there were rare plants to be protected from those same tramping feet. Or so Simmy summarised it to herself. He was a poor speaker, and without any pictures he was not making a good showing. But he seemed sincere, to the point of tears at one stage. He had begun by explaining that he was standing in for Grant Childers, who had tragically died only a few days earlier. He admitted he was a very inadequate substitute, and hoped the audience would bear with him. It seemed his line of work was in wildlife conservation, both flora and fauna, on National Trust property in the region.

At the end, Tristan stood up and drew everything to a heartfelt climax. 'So there you have it, ladies and gentlemen. You might be saying to yourselves that this is a very modest proposal, for a development that would go almost unnoticed. You might cite the tourist park at Troutbeck as a comparison, for example. It is several times larger than the one under consideration this evening. But does anybody seriously want a similar eyesore, however small, so close to the lovely slopes of Glenamara? Of course not. And so I beg you to sign the form you'll have found on your seat. Take spare ones home for your family and friends. We must all do whatever we can to conserve and protect this glorious part of rural England.'

'Eyesore?' murmured Simmy. She lived almost in sight of the said tourist park, and no longer even noticed it. It was, however, rather large and sometimes noisy. From the top of Wansfell it could fairly be described as intrusive, if not an actual eyesore.

Before Tristan could sit down, Bonnie Lawson's hand shot up. 'Can I ask a question?' she said in a ringing voice.

'What? Oh – absolutely you can. Of course. I meant to invite questions from the audience. Of course I did.'

'Liar,' muttered Russell.

'Why haven't you displayed the actual plans that have been put forward? Why haven't you told us who the application was made by? Why are you holding this meeting so far from Patterdale?'

Tristan Wilkins put up a hand, with a broad smile. 'I think you'll find that's *three* questions,' he said with a chuckle. When nobody in the room appeared to share his patronising humour, his smile quickly faded. 'Well, the answers are all quite simple. The fact is, we were made aware that this application was to be submitted shortly, and we – wisely, I think – decided to pre-empt the whole process by canvassing public opinion in advance. We all know how these projects can be slipped quietly through before the general public has even noticed. This time, we want to be prepared, with plenty of ammunition, gained from meetings like this. Does that answer your questions?'

'Who's the applicant?' called Russell, much to Simmy's surprise.

Wilkins took a deep breath. 'It would be invidious to name names at this stage, as I'm sure you can understand. We can agree to our response in principle without bringing individuals into the matter.'

'Nonsense,' said Russell loudly, but nobody spoke in his support. There were general mutterings and a degree of obvious confusion.

Simmy patted his arm reassuringly. 'Good question, Dad,' she whispered.

Tristan, however, evidently did not share this opinion. He was scanning the room with an expression that contained an odd element of defiance, beneath a determined attempt at sincerity and open-mindedness. 'Well, I think we've kept you all from your homes for long enough,' he said. 'I hereby declare this meeting concluded. Please take the leaflets away with you, unless you feel able to sign them here and now. I repeat – we only want to give you all the chance to express your views in general, at this stage.'

'Nonsense,' said Russell again, but went unheard. People were getting up, putting coats on and talking among themselves.

Bonnie was waiting in the hotel foyer for Simmy and Russell to emerge. Corinne was chatting to a woman Simmy didn't recognise. 'Are public meetings always like that?' the girl asked.

'I don't know. I've hardly ever been to one until now,' said Simmy.

'That was not a meeting, by any normal definition of the word,' said Russell, giving Bonnie a look of warm approval. 'Your questions were spot on.'

'I got them from Helen, actually. She didn't think she ought to come without knowing more details. She said there'd be reference numbers, and copies of the planning application and stuff like that. When they showed us those maps, I thought that must be it, but then I worked out they were just the ordinary ones that the walkers use. And those photos didn't really tell us anything, did they?'

Simmy looked round, with a vague sense that it might be better to go unheard by other people. 'Come outside,' she said. 'We can sit in the garden for a bit.'

Bonnie giggled. 'So the microphones and cameras can't pick up what we say? Do you think the hotel's bugged?'

'Just want the chance for a proper chat,' she said. 'It's going to be too busy tomorrow in the shop.'

'Do you need me?' Russell asked. 'Or can I go home?'

Simmy gave him a hug. 'Oh, Dad. I don't know where we'd be without you. But yes, you can go home. I'll head straight back to Troutbeck when I've talked to Bonnie. See you at the weekend, I expect. Go and tell Mum what a star you were. You and Bonnie.'

'Listen,' she said to Bonnie, as soon as they were seated on a bench overlooking the lake. 'Grant Childers must have

146

been killed to stop him from speaking at this meeting. I thought so before it even started, and now it's even more obvious. Something very weird is going on, don't you think?'

Bonnie rubbed her neck, thinking hard. 'Yeah – sort of. But we have to remember *how* he was killed. That whole poison thing is so complicated. It could easily have gone wrong. Somebody must have planned it days or weeks in advance. They must have known him pretty well, if they were able to give him something to eat or drink and be sure he'd really take it. I was thinking about that earlier on, and it's still bothering me. If there's somebody with so much to lose that they have to murder a man who was going to give a speech about planning regulations at a half-baked so-called meeting, wouldn't it be an easy matter for the police to work out who that was?'

'Moxon should have been at the meeting,' Simmy said.

'There were two people I think might have been part of his team,' said Bonnie. 'Didn't you notice?'

Simmy shook her head. 'It never occurred to me until now that the police might be there.'

'That's why I asked who was making the application. Because it seems to me that has to be the main suspect.' She paused. 'But after talking to Helen, and getting the brush-off from old Tristan, I wonder if we might be looking at the whole thing in entirely the wrong way.'

They were both too tired and confused to say any more. Simmy still had to walk back up to Windermere and find her car, while she presumed that Bonnie would go home to Corinne and her small foster brother. They were the last two of a long succession of children taken in by Corinne, for long and short stays, patched up and moved on to more permanent homes. Bonnie had clung on, enjoying the same home for several years, a perfect fit with a woman who treated her as half-daughter, half-sister, gentling the girl through her turbulent teens and offering a secure base for as long as Bonnie wished, even after she reached eighteen.

Chapter Thirteen

Simmy drove back to Troutbeck with her head full of devious local politics and cynical manipulation of local opinion. Even Helen Harkness's reluctance to show her face at a poorly defined meeting seemed significant. What was she afraid of? Presumably she saw risk in being identified with the wrong side of a controversy. But as Russell had pointed out, so far this controversy appeared to have only one side. And that side's arguments felt considerably weaker after the meeting than they had before. Which surely meant the whole thing had failed in its purpose? On her way out, Simmy had glimpsed Candy Proctor, standing by herself, frowning in apparent confusion. The man who had spoken about wildlife looked equally unsure of himself. She had not noticed anybody filling in the protest form and handing it to Tristan.

So what had the plain-clothes detectives made of it, assuming that Bonnie had rightly identified them? There had been no hint of dislike of Grant Childers, unless the lukewarm expressions of grief over his loss had a subtext. Perhaps nobody had much liked him, and barely missed him now he was gone. There was very probably a file on his laptop with the text of his undelivered speech. If so, the police would find it and draw their own conclusions.

Bonnie had speculated rather wildly about a widespread conspiracy to undermine any would-be property developments, not just in Patterdale but throughout the whole area. Simmy had had to bring her back to the central issue of Grant Childers' death. 'Why poison *him*?' she asked, more than once.

The girl hesitated. 'We need to find out more about him,' she agreed. 'We should ask your mother what the family told her. There could be lots of clues we don't know about.'

While Simmy had concurred in principle, she was reluctant to confront her mother with a string of questions, given the current state of things. 'Maybe at the weekend,' she suggested.

The weekend ahead was going to be entirely devoted to Christopher. She was quite determined about that. The past week had been fairly typical, in that she had only seen him once. The paucity of face-to-face contact was a constant frustration, with neither of them able to do anything decisive to change it. He could drive down to Troutbeck after work every evening, and then dash back to Keswick early each morning – they had actually tried that for a fortnight in September, only to find it created a whole new set of frustrations. There were the quiet days at the auction house, when he only had to show up for a few hours, which invariably coincided with busy times in Simmy's shop. She would leave him lying in her far-too-narrow-for-comfort bed, swallowing her frustration at the imbalance in their working lives – and usually feeling sick as well. The bed itself was a problem. She had offered to buy a new one, but never got round to doing so. The room would be swamped by a full-size double bed – which was what they definitely wanted when they finally had their own house to accommodate it. Christopher was restless in Troutbeck without all his things around him, and little to do in the evenings but go to the local pub, or stay in with Simmy. Neither of them was a great talker, and Simmy was an unenthusiastic board game player. 'This is awful,' she said once. 'We're not even married yet and we're bored with each other.'

'We'll factor in a whole lot of hi-tech entertainment, once we've got the house,' he promised. 'And make friends, and invite them round, and get a dog and redecorate the whole place. Then we'll have a noisy, demanding baby and we'll never be bored again.'

'I'm really not sure I want a dog,' said Simmy, fearing that she sounded marginally less definite every time she made this assertion.

'Cat, then?'

'I've never seen the point of cats. And they kill all the garden birds.'

'Funny – it's usually the other way round. The wife wants a houseful of pets and the husband flatly vetoes everything. In my experience, anyway,' he added.

'I like to keep things simple.'

'Simple Simmy,' he quipped, until silenced by the look she gave him.

Within five minutes of getting back to her cottage, she

phoned him. It was half past nine, and she visualised him in his bleak little Keswick flat, probably drinking beer and watching something mindless on Netflix. She was wrong. 'Robin's here,' he said, moments after taking the call.

'Who?'

'You know – Robin. The estate agent. He phoned me at work this afternoon and said he's heard about a place in Glenridding we might fancy. He brought the particulars round for me to see, and we got chatting.'

'What's it like? The place in Glenridding?'

'Small. Hardly any garden. Views. South-facing.'

'You don't sound too keen.'

'We'll have to see it before I commit myself. I'm being cautious, because I can see there might be some snags.'

'Did you ask him if he knows about those tourist chalets? I've just been to a very weird public meeting about them.'

'What? Oh no, I forgot all about that. Hang on, and I'll ask him now.'

She heard him talking to his friend, the words muffled. It was quite a short exchange, before he came back and said, 'He thinks it's all complete fantasy. There's no way such a development would ever get permission. Somebody's having a laugh. Did you say a public meeting?'

'Right. Forty or fifty people showed up, at the Belsfield.'

'That *is* weird. I'll tell Robin about it and see if he can come up with an explanation. He'll know some of the characters involved, probably.'

'Bonnie thinks it's a conspiracy.'

'Stranger things have happened. Anyway, what about you? What else is going on?'

There followed a five-minute exchange of trivia,

wrapped in an easy affection that was typical of their phone calls. It strengthened Simmy's confidence that she was right to be marrying this man. She had known him intimately as a child. They shared roots and history and formative experiences. However much of a cliché it might be, to go back to the start and marry your first sweetheart, there was something warm and familiar and *right* about it.

Before ending the call, she said, 'But Robin won't know people down in Bowness, surely? They're not councillors or anything, just ordinary business people.'

'I'll ask him anyway. I've always had the impression that my friend Robin knows everybody.'

She went to bed in a calm frame of mind that rather surprised her. She attributed it to being pregnant, the resulting hormones ensuring a level of serenity that scarcely fitted with the swirling events on all sides. None of them seemed to matter, just at that moment. Her primary duty was to get a decent night's sleep, and clear her mind of anything unpleasant. She was rewarded by a gentle twitching of her little passenger, as if to reassure her that everything was essentially all right.

The same could not be said of Angie and Russell Straw on that Thursday evening. He had got back to Beck View at about eight-forty-five, to find Detective Inspector Moxon talking seriously to his wife. They turned to greet him with a restraint that made him feel like an intruder in his own kitchen.

'Mr Straw,' said the policeman. 'How are you?'

'I'm perfectly all right, thank you. Just been to a most stimulating meeting. I asked a question,' he added proudly.

'You can tell us about that later,' said Angie. 'DI Moxon has been explaining more details to me about poor Mr Childers. The poison that killed him, to be exact. And things they found on his computer.'

'Oh? Am I permitted to hear it as well? Could you go over it again, do you think?'

'Briefly,' Moxon conceded. 'You'll remember that we quite quickly identified the toxin as being plant-based, probably datura. It would appear that it was either that or something very closely related. You have to ingest quite a lot of it to kill you – which is the case with Mr Childers. His bloodstream shows a significant quantity of it.'

'So why are you here again, telling us the same thing again?'

'That's a good question,' he said awkwardly. 'I'm sure you understand. I'm afraid I have to ask you one more time to confirm that you did not provide him with any food or drink at any point.'

'If Angie says she didn't, that should be good enough for you,' said Russell stiffly. 'I certainly didn't feed him anything.'

'Thank you. Then he must have got it somewhere else. I won't repeat all our thinking about that. His computer suggests that he was intending to give a speech while here—'

'Yes,' Russell said. 'At the meeting I've just been to.'

Moxon talked over the interruption. 'It's actually very well written. Quite powerfully expressed, too. You say you were there?'

'Yes. They told us that Childers had been scheduled to speak, but had unfortunately died. Nobody seemed especially sorry about it. They found some sap to replace him. Awful speaker. Not even very relevant.' He grew thoughtful. 'Although it's hard to say exactly what *would* have been relevant. It was a very peculiar excrcise.'

'In what way peculiar?'

'Well, they weren't at all keen to hear the views of the audience, for one thing. Little Bonnie Lawson was the first to put her hand up, and then I chipped in. Nobody else said a word. Bonnie thinks two of your colleagues were there at the back, which would have been a wise move, if she's right.'

Moxon said nothing to this, merely raising his eyebrows. Then he consulted a notebook. 'The meeting was in protest against a proposal for a number of new tourist chalets in Patterdale – am I right?'

'Apparently, yes. There were three speakers, going on about planning regulations, and wildlife, and density of construction. It was all fairly interesting in a vague sort of way, but by the end nobody seemed too sure how genuine the threat is anyhow.'

'Oh?'

'It would appear that no actual plans have been submitted. The whole thing could just be a silly rumour. Somebody getting the wrong end of the stick.'

'You know that Persimmon and Christopher want to find somewhere to live up there, don't you?' Angie interrupted. 'So there's a personal element to all this.' She looked pale and drawn. 'Although not as personal as the effects of a man dying in my arms have been.'

Moxon gave her a long, searching look. 'Not sleeping? Flashbacks?'

'A bit,' she admitted.

'There's help available for that, you know. Just to get you through the first part. I can recommend it.'

She gave him a watery smile. 'It's a whole lot of things at once, that's the trouble. The effect on the business is a worry. People have been cancelling. And then there's the baby . . . And it's getting more and more urgent that they find somewhere to live. Personally, I think it's daft to fixate on Patterdale. It wouldn't hurt Christopher to drive from Ambleside to Keswick, for example. I think he's being a bit selfish about it, to be perfectly honest.'

'Patterdale's lovely,' Russell argued. 'And the latest idea is that they might decide to build something from scratch.'

Moxon blew out his cheeks. 'They'd be very lucky to manage that.'

'Yes, well, we know of a little plot of land that might be available for the purpose,' said Russell.

'Wait a minute. Is this all connected somehow? You're telling me that there's some complicated rumour or early leak about a cluster of chalets, as well as a building plot – all in Patterdale, the whole thing arousing unusual levels of interest down here in Bowness? And somehow it links to a man who died here this week of apparently deliberate poisoning?'

'That seems to sum it up pretty well,' said Russell.

'Huh! Sounds a complete muddle to me,' said Angie. 'The only thing that would make sense is if there'd been some great big conspiracy from the start – right back to when Grant Childers booked the room here six weeks ago now. They told him then that they wanted him to speak at the meeting. Candy Proctor told him she was full, which is why we got landed with him. Some nonsense about changing the dates because of having to count red squirrels. It all sounded very fishy to me. How can they have taken *six weeks* to organise all this protest malarkey?'

Both men stared at her. Angie Straw had never been prone to theorising about the various crimes that her daughter had stumbled upon in her role as florist. She had impatiently instructed Simmy to stay out of anything of the sort, and to distance herself from young Ben Harkness, who revelled in such murder investigations.

'She really was full,' said Moxon. 'I've seen her bookings diary.'

'Oh, I don't doubt it. But that still doesn't explain anything, does it?'

Russell was looking puzzled. 'The timing is peculiar, though. Angie's right. Doesn't it feel to you as if there's some complicated plot going on, with carefully laid plans going right back to the end of August?'

'More likely it's just Persimmon's jinx at work again,' said Angie, who seemed mildly alarmed at her husband's support.

'She saw him die as well,' Moxon gently reminded her, always quick to defend Simmy.

'She did. But it appears to have had a lesser effect on her.'

'Hormones,' said Russell, with a look that boasted *See how enlightened I am.*

'She's probably worrying more about you than about

157

herself,' Moxon pressed his defence of a woman he was unmistakably fond of. He and Simmy understood each other in a way they both found special.

'Yes, she's quite a little saint,' snapped Angie. 'Everybody knows that.'

Russell seemed about to say *Hormones* again, before thinking better of it.

Angie had the grace to look chagrined at her own words, and hastily changed the subject. 'So – where did we get to? You accept that it was definitely murder, right?'

Moxon nodded. 'I agree with you that a suicide would be extremely unlikely to ask "Why?" in the way you say he did.'

'And you seem to be assuming it was somebody around here that did it, rather than someone back at home, giving him a specially prepared drink in a bottle to bring with him? We are sure it was drink, are we? As opposed to food.'

'That's what the pathologist tells us, yes.'

'That's a pity.'

'We did think of that,' Moxon said. 'I mean, the possibility that he brought it with him from home. But we couldn't find any signs of a container in his room or his car. Of course, if he did bring it with him, and drank it while he was out, there might well not be any evidence to that effect. The toxicology people think he must have taken it no more than an hour before he died. They say he must have felt ill almost immediately. I think I can be permitted to tell you we found a ticket in his wallet for the lake cruise Sunday lunchtime, and we've been trying to trace anybody who saw him then. It's been quite time-consuming, but given that most people book online, there is a list of about twenty-two people we know were on the boat with him. There are lots of others who booked on the day and didn't have to give their names.'

'And?' prompted Russell.

'Nothing conclusive. It's taken a lot of police hours, as you might imagine. And then there are the last-minute people, who just turn up and hope to get on. There was a dozen or so of them. Some paid cash, and there's no record of who they are. Not one of them can positively identify Mr Childers from the picture we showed them.'

'He was rather ordinary-looking,' said Angie.

'Presumably, if one of those passengers gave him the lethal drink, they'd lie about it,' said Russell.

'Isn't there any CCTV on the boat?'

'There is not,' Moxon said. 'But almost everybody made their own little films of the ride. We've watched them all, but can't see him. Mostly, of course, they've concentrated on the lake and the views, not the other passengers.'

'Perhaps we should focus on the plant poison,' Russell said thoughtfully. 'Do you think it was something home-grown? On an allotment or in a greenhouse – unless they just picked it from the hedge somewhere. Would that work for this datura stuff? I was always told that the only plant that grows wild in this country that we need worry about is deadly nightshade. That raises the question of premeditation, doesn't it? I mean – was the killer thinking years ahead, waiting for his seedpods or berries to ripen, or did the presence of poisonous plants in the garden give him the idea?'

'Or her,' said Angie.

Moxon merely sighed.

Russell was obviously enjoying himself. 'You can see why poisoning used to be so popular, can't you? There are so many gaps in the chain of evidence, it's almost impossible to gather real proof. Ben Harkness says there's no real proof against the Hay Poisoner, even though they hanged him.'

'You could say we're fortunate that most people don't know one plant from another, then,' said Moxon. 'They just think all berries are poisonous.'

'Which brings us back to Persimmon,' said Angie, with a quiet moan. 'She knows which plant is which.'

'But she doesn't sell the toxic ones,' Russell reminded her. 'Not even foxgloves, which I played with quite harmlessly as a child. I used to suck the nectar out of the flowers.'

'Foxgloves are wildflowers. She wouldn't sell them anyway.' Angie was drooping. 'Look, I'm half-asleep here. Is there anything else you want to tell us?'

'Or ask us?' added her husband.

'No, I don't think so.' Moxon's concern reasserted itself. 'I just wanted to update you, really. Oh – one more thing. Perhaps you could have a look at Mr Childers' speech, since you were at the meeting. I can email it to you.'

Russell nodded carelessly. 'Good idea,' he said. 'Let me give you the email address. We'll have a look at it tonight or tomorrow.'

'Thanks,' said Moxon.

Russell showed him out with a cheery goodbye and

went back to the kitchen with a bounce in his step.

'It's those pills they gave you,' Angie accused. 'They've made you quite unbearably chirpy.'

'You'd better start taking them as well, then,' he said.

Chapter Fourteen

Simmy's peaceful slide into sleep did not see her through the night. At three in the morning she woke with a gasp, fighting the tentacles of a deeply alarming dream. Her first husband Tony had been there, far more furiously angry than she had ever seen him in real life. His mother hovered behind him, the whole scene taking place among strange dead trees. There were berries hanging from the dry branches, which Tony was hacking down with a long knife. When he saw Simmy he brandished the weapon and told her everything was her fault.

Lying awake in the dark she forced herself to deconstruct the bizarre scene, remembering that she and Christopher had watched a peculiar film called *The Lobster* two Saturdays ago. The trees in the dream must have come from that. And Tony might be justifiably angry at her pregnancy, after losing the baby he expected to enjoy with her. Another man was going to have what he, Tony, deserved. So Simmy concluded that she felt guilty towards him. That made sense. And the berries – was he planning to poison her and the child? Or did that simply pop up because of the recent death by poisoning? Was there perhaps a clue trying to emerge from her subconscious mind?

If so, she couldn't see it. Tony Brown had been accused of harassment by a midwife who had been present at the stillbirth of baby Edith. She had subsequently attacked him with a knife, claiming extreme provocation. Simmy had been appalled at this unexpected alteration of character in a man she had thought she knew inside out. Now, in the dream, he held the knife and was apparently plotting to poison somebody.

With a sigh, she turned over and tried to get back to sleep. It took twenty minutes, but she got there eventually.

Friday morning was hectic from the start. The big Troutbeck funeral sent ripples down to Windermere and no doubt beyond. Dorothea Entwhistle had made the best possible use of her life, despite – or thanks to – being childless and unmarried. From her teenage years she had done good turns, pursued local causes, served on committees and made scores of friends. Simmy did the best job she could on the remaining floral tributes, and then drove all those ordered to the undertaker's in her van. One of the men she knew by sight came out to chat when he saw her.

'Big funeral,' she said, eyeing the long shelf of flowers, supplied by every florist in the region. The majority came from Ambleside, she noticed.

'You could say that,' he nodded. 'We'll have to run a special extra vehicle for the flowers. Kevin hates that.'

'Why?' There seemed to be an implied slight directed at flowers in general.

'It throws the system.' He shrugged. 'Though he doesn't have to make such a fuss over it. We've got it all under control.'

'It'll make a lovely display in the church.'

'It will,' he agreed. Then he added, 'Seems she was a nice lady.'

'Got the weather for it, too.' The sky was lightly overcast, the westerly breeze just enough to stir the autumn leaves, and no stronger. 'I always think it's wrong to have a funeral in the sunshine.'

'You're right there. Nothing worse than sweltering in these clothes, specially when it's a burial.'

She was still casting a professional eye over the tributes provided by her rivals. Her gaze was snagged by one with unusual white flowers that she did not recognise. On a closer inspection, she realised that it had been made by an individual mourner, not a florist. There was no ribbon, no discreet supporting wire. 'Go gently, old girl. It's been good to know you. Buzz.' said the card, which was larger than any a florist would supply. She barely glimpsed it before there was a flurry among the funeral vehicles in the yard just beyond the flower racks, and she realised her van was going to be in the way. There were strict parking rules, which all the florists regularly ignored.

'Move it,' hissed her friend. 'Bob's going to bawl you out if you don't shift it quick.' Bob was the conductor, senior man of the team, and a stickler for rules. She was out of the gate before the hearse could be impeded, already planning the remainder of the morning.

* * *

Bonnie was in much better spirits than she had been all week. 'Guess what!' she trilled, the moment Simmy was within earshot. 'Ben's coming home on Sunday. There's a broken pipe on his floor in halls, and they've told them they should try not to be there until it's fixed, because there won't be any water. He's staying tomorrow to finish an essay in the library, and then he'll get a bus first thing on Sunday.'

'All the way from Newcastle?'

'Um . . . there was something about staying tomorrow night with another student who lives near Carlisle.' She frowned. 'Is Carlisle on the way to Newcastle?'

'More or less. It'll save Mr Harkness a lot of driving, anyway. When's he going back?'

'Probably early Monday on the train. He'll miss a lecture, which is a worry, but nobody can take him, so there's not much choice.'

'When did he tell you all this?'

'Seven o'clock this morning,' the girl laughed. 'They'd been up half the night trying to sort the plumbing out. Three rooms are flooded, apparently.'

'Well, that's nice,' said Simmy, wondering whether she'd manage to see Ben herself. She had tried not to admit just how badly she missed him. Bonnie's deprivation was obviously much worse, but even so, his absence made quite a hole in Simmy's life as well.

'The trouble is,' Bonnie's face had drooped slightly, 'I don't know whether it'll be okay to mention the murder. Helen would tell me not to, if I asked her, but he's sure to find out eventually, and be cross with me if I don't say anything.'

'Maybe Moxon will have solved it by then,' said Simmy, with an optimism that felt wildly unwarranted. 'It would be all right to tell Ben, if that happened.'

There were wisps of her dream still floating around her head. The berries especially haunted her. She had hoped to share it with Bonnie, but other topics were taking priority. 'Christopher told me his friend Robin might have found us a house,' she began, in an attempt to distract the girl. 'He's given us a heads-up, before it's officially on the market.'

'Great,' mumbled Bonnie. 'That's you sorted, then.'

'Hardly. But it is getting urgent. We can't decide anything while it goes on like this.'

'Sell yours and rent somewhere bigger,' said Bonnie, as she had many times before. 'That's the simplest thing to do.'

'It's not actually much easier to rent than buy these days. Chris is going to have to move in with me in Troutbeck, and we'll drive each other mad.'

Two customers came in, jostling each other for first place through the door. Bonnie and Simmy smoothly attended to one each, supplying the requirements quickly, smiling patiently. 'That doesn't happen very often,' Simmy remarked, when they'd gone.

'It was fun. Do you think they knew each other?'

'That never occurred to me. What makes you think they might?'

Bonnie laughed. 'Bored housewives, playing silly games. Racing each other to the Zumba class, or whatever it is.'

'I don't think so. Why would they want flowers for a Zumba class?'

'A present for the teacher.'

It was a cheerful little interlude, born of Bonnie's good news, and Simmy was more than willing to participate. Her own worries were not of Bonnie's making, and she did her best not to bring them to work. Their discussions of sudden deaths and motives for murder could become intense at times, largely thanks to Ben Harkness and his avid interest in the whole subject. They would often argue, even taking opposing sides if there were suspects with equal claim to the role of killer, but on the whole Simmy felt confident that she was behaving in Bonnie's best interests. While much less fragile than she looked, the girl had known very hard times, and could still be badly affected by certain situations. Ben had been her mentor as well as her boyfriend, teaching her Latin, history, poetry, and much more, often wrapped up in a game, or a complicated project.

Thinking of Ben apparently conjured his mother, because ten minutes later Helen Harkness came into the shop, with a wary expression. 'Are you busy? Am I interrupting anything important?'

'I've got half an hour or so,' said Simmy. 'Then I'm popping up to Waterhead with a delivery. After that, I've got to do a room in a hotel for a wedding tomorrow.'

'If you've come to warn us not to talk to Ben about the murder, there's no need,' said Bonnie.

'I believe you. The fact is, I gather you two were at that peculiar meeting last night, and I wondered how it went. What were your impressions?'

'Who told you it was peculiar?' wondered Simmy.

'Three different people. Nobody seemed to understand what the actual point of it was. After going to so much

trouble and expense, there must have been a good reason –
but somehow it never got across.'

'That's what we thought – more or less – as well,' said
Simmy. 'Bonnie had an idea it was some sort of complicated
scheme to pre-empt the buildings before they've even put
the application in.'

Helen shook her head. 'That wouldn't be unusual. If
somebody in the council office had leaked the plan to Tristan,
he might have picked it up and run with it, calling the meeting
and handing out leaflets. That would make sense. But *why*?
Why should a semi-retired man who lives in Bowness, tending
his roses and minding other people's business, care about a
few new chalets all the way up in Patterdale?'

'There has to be more to it,' said Bonnie. 'Which is what
I said last night. There was no proper message, except for
wanting people to sign up to a protest group. He didn't
want to answer questions, either.'

'Maybe it's just his habit of minding other people's
business, as you say,' Simmy said.

'I don't think so. He's more about recycling and picking
up after dogs and banning bonfires. The nit-picky stuff.'

'What about Candy Proctor? She was handing out the
leaflets on Sunday, and is obviously working with Tristan.
She sat at the front last night. She keeps popping up,
actually. She knew the man who died at Beck View. And he
was supposed to speak at the meeting. Everything links up
through her, when you think about it.'

Helen looked from Simmy to Bonnie and back. 'I knew
you'd get onto the murder before long. Tanya won't shut
up about it. I'm terrified she won't be able to keep it from
Ben on Sunday. And that would be a disaster.'

'Yes, we know,' said Bonnie with a sigh.

'It's only because this is his first term, and he really does have to find his feet and keep focus. It's a very hands-on course, apparently. He's already got assignments and research projects that sound like overload to me. I didn't think it could get any worse, after all those A-levels, but this seems just as bad.'

'Yes, we know,' said Bonnie again.

'Of course you do. Sorry. It probably isn't as bad as I think. We'll find out more on Sunday.'

'I'm sure you don't need to worry about him,' said Simmy.

'I hope that's true. The thing is, I've got a friend with a son at Oxford. Just started his second year, and they found him last week almost dead from an overdose of something. The pressure got too much for him, apparently. It all feels so *scary*.' She shivered.

'Ben won't do that,' said Bonnie with total confidence. 'He *likes* pressure. If anybody can cope, it's him. But you'll have to warn Tanya not to talk. If he hears about it from her, he'll be furious with me for not saying anything.'

Simmy and Helen both laughed at this flash of selfishness. 'I'll tell her,' said Helen. 'But she's really full of it, you know. She thinks it all hinges on the lake cruiser. She's getting awfully like Ben,' she concluded woefully. 'I'm not sure I can manage another one.'

This time she was the butt of the laughter. Simmy was sitting where she could see the screen of her computer, and noticed that a new order had just come through. 'Um . . . I should look at this,' she said apologetically.

'That's okay. But I did want to ask you how the house-hunting's going. Have you got two more minutes?'

'Of course. Nothing's that urgent. Well, there are one or two hopeful developments. Do you know a man called Stuart Carstairs? Red hair. Runs a B&B down your way somewhere. Well, he's got a brother or something who wants to sell half his garden in Hartsop as a building plot. We were going to consult you about it, anyway. But then we decided the timing wouldn't work. We can't possibly build a house in time for the baby, and once it's born, I don't think we'll want to be bothered with builders and plumbers and council officials and all the rest of it. We found a lovely little place called Crookabeck, which would be absolutely perfect.'

'I know Stuart,' said Helen. 'And I wouldn't trust him with a dog kennel, let alone a relative trying to sell building land.'

'Ah,' said Simmy. 'That's a shame.'

The order was tagged *As soon as possible*. A last-minute bouquet for a couple who lived at Troutbeck Bridge. 'No problem,' muttered Simmy. 'I can take it when I go up to Waterhead.' She registered her acknowledgement on the computer and disappeared into the back room. Only when she had her gloves on and was deftly operating secateurs did she notice how hungry she was. She had her usual little lunch brought from home, comprising of a piece of cooked chicken, tomato, muesli bar, crisps and yoghurt. Randomly piled into a plastic box, it was only minimally appetising, but she bolted it all down as she worked.

It was just after one o'clock when she announced to Bonnie that she was making a second trip that day in the van, delivering flowers. 'Shouldn't be long,' she said.

But then her mobile summoned her, the message on the screen informing her that the caller was 'Chris'.

'Hey,' she said. 'I'm a bit busy. Can I call you back?'

'Not really. I've just spoken to Robin again. He insists we go up to Glenridding this evening to see this house. It officially goes on the market tomorrow and there'll be a rush, he reckons. We can't waste any time.'

'Oh.' She felt oddly lukewarm about this suddenly available house. 'Will it be worth the hassle, do you think? How many rooms are there?'

'Three bedrooms, two reception downstairs. Decent garden. Spectacular views. I told you last night.'

'How much is it? You didn't tell me that little detail.'

'The asking price is three ninety-five, but they might take less.'

'Not at this stage they won't. They'll wait to see what the interest is. If people start fighting over it, they'll probably put the price up, not down.'

'What's your problem, Sim? Why do you sound so negative about it? Robin's gone out on a limb for us here, and the least we can do is go and look at the place. It could be perfect for us. It'll be at least seven before I can get there, and then go for a meal somewhere afterwards.'

'I know. I sound awful, don't I? I just can't believe it can really happen. It would all be *so* perfect, it's too good to be true. That little Crookabeck place is like heaven. Imagine what it must look like in the spring.' She sighed. 'I daren't let myself dream, because I can't see how it could ever happen. Where exactly is this place Robin's found?'

'Not Crookabeck, I'm afraid. Further up towards the

lake, in Glenridding. On the left, I think. It must be very close to Ullswater.'

She said nothing, trying to juggle all her fears and hopes and telling herself that compromise was going to be inevitable.

'Sim? Are you still there?'

'Yes, I'm here. We've got to go and see it, of course. Robin's been wonderful. He's a good friend. It would be churlish not to go for a look.'

'Precisely. And we can go down to Crookabeck any time we want to, if we live there. It'd be a five-minute walk.'

Can. He said 'can' as if the whole thing was already settled. 'That's true,' she said, stifling a sigh.

She stowed the two bouquets carefully in the van and set out to make the deliveries. The road was so familiar she barely noticed it. Traffic was building up, as people began to arrive for a weekend in the Lakes. It often seemed that local workers knocked off halfway through a Friday in an effort to beat the rush. Ben Harkness had once remarked that the clever thing to do would be to stay on until six, by which time everyone would have gone.

The more recent order was for a guesthouse on the western side of the road, close to the junction with one of the roads up to Troutbeck. The lake came almost to the edge of the garden. Simmy drove down a short driveway between the house and its neighbour, and extracted the flowers from the back of the van. There were several beautiful Japanese acer trees displaying gorgeous autumn colours in the next-door garden, which also boasted a very large greenhouse. She paused to admire the trees and peer through the glass at what looked like a healthy crop of tomatoes. It made her feel hungry just to look at them.

A woman met her at the front door, with a familiarly harassed expression. 'Gosh, that was quick!' she said. 'They're for my sister. It's her anniversary and we're going round there later on. If I can ever get away, that is. We've just had a whole family turn up without a booking. Aren't people stupid! Four of them, thinking they could just find rooms without any warning.'

'Which it sounds as if they did,' said Simmy, with a sympathetic smile.

'Well, yes. Lucky for them. It would be a different matter next week, when nearly everybody's got half-term. But I've had to call in our part-time girls to cope with it all.'

'I know how it goes. My parents run a B&B.'

'Who doesn't?' said the woman, rather snappily. 'Whatever's happened to us all, that the only thing we can think about is providing beds and food for millions of tourists? When you stop to think about it, it's completely insane.'

In the road outside a car horn hooted. 'Look at them!' the woman went on. 'Crawling up to Ambleside, nose to tail. Like sheep. *Worse* than sheep.'

'They're looking for open spaces, rugged fells, somewhere they can get a sense of the natural world,' said Simmy.

'Oh yes, I know all that. And I admit there's space enough once they get onto the uplands. It's just such a nuisance that they all want somewhere to sleep when they come down again.' She laughed ruefully, and Simmy laughed with her.

Then the woman looked back at the road, as the horn tooted

again. 'My God, how crass! Look – he's hooting at a hearse.'

Simmy focused on the stationary cars, and realised it could only be the Entwhistle funeral. It had got entangled with the tourist traffic and would be late at the Troutbeck church if something wasn't done. 'I think it's the hearse that hooted,' she said. 'Somebody must be in the way.'

'Broken down, maybe.'

Simmy went closer for a better look. Two men were hurriedly pushing a white car to the side of the road, trying to clear a passage for the funeral entourage. The hearse was followed by two large black limousines, one of them filled with flowers on the back seat. It was two-fifteen and Kevin's schedule was looking to be in jeopardy.

She went back to her van, knowing she would have to wait until the blockage was cleared. The woman remained on her doorstep, watching the action in the road. Again Simmy caught sight of the big glasshouse. 'Lovely crop of tomatoes over there,' she said. 'Do you get any of them?'

'What? Oh no. I don't know what he does with them, but he's never offered us any. That's nothing to a few months back. He's got all sorts of exotic things in there, down the far end. Nice flowers as well. You should see if you can have some – be useful in your line of business.'

Simmy nodded, thinking she really ought to make more effort to buy locally. As it was, almost all her stock was bought in bulk from a large nursery in Lincolnshire. 'I'm afraid I'm not terribly responsible, environmentally speaking,' she admitted.

'We do what we can,' said the woman vaguely, and began to close the door.

* * *

Simmy eventually made the second delivery to a house on the eastern side of the road, just south of Waterhead. The fact that it was an actual family home, with no sign outside about tourism or vacant rooms, made her think again about the possibility of living in Patterdale. She and Christopher would be almost freakishly unusual, using the house neither as a second home nor as a holiday let. No guests, no direct involvement at all with the 'hospitality industry' as everyone persisted in calling it. When they had briefly contemplated looking for a home in the little town of Grasmere, the overwhelming presence of holiday visitors had been enough to deter them. Patterdale was at least both smaller and quieter than that.

Even this house, where she was delivering the flowers, was probably home to a tour guide or a hotel manager living off site. But she was never to find out, because a man wearing a vest and boxer shorts grabbed the flowers from her with a self-conscious grin and disappeared without a word.

She was back at the shop just after three, ready to tell Bonnie about the funeral and the numerous flowers, and the agreeable feeling of having contributed to a handsome send-off for Miss Entwhistle. Instead, she was met by her old friend DI Moxon, who wasn't looking very friendly.

Chapter Fifteen

'What's the matter?' she asked him. 'You don't look very happy.'

He grimaced. 'There are things you didn't tell me.'

'What? What things?'

'Last night's meeting, for one thing. Young Miss Harkness and her detective games for another. And now Dorothea Entwhistle.'

Simmy sank onto the stool beside the computer table. 'None of those things have anything to do with me. What do you think I've done?'

Bonnie was standing in the middle of the shop, close to Moxon. They both moved towards Simmy. 'Are you telling me you're unaware that Dorothea was a keen amateur plant breeder? That she had a whole row of glasshouses where she propagated just the sort of things we're convinced poisoned Mr Childers? As a florist, you would surely have known about that?'

She stared at him in bewilderment. 'I had no idea. I'd

never even heard of Dorothea Entwhistle until this week. Why would I?'

'Because she lived about a hundred yards from your cottage in Troutbeck, with a very obvious array of greenhouses behind her house. You can see them from almost anywhere in the village, as well as from up on the fells. *Everybody* knew about her. The funeral's the biggest Troutbeck's seen for decades.'

'Yes. I saw the traffic jam,' said Simmy slowly. 'And I saw another big greenhouse, on the main road. I don't normally take a lot of notice of greenhouses,' she finished, with some spirit. 'Most people with a garden of any size must have one.'

'Even Corinne's got one,' said Bonnie, clearly wanting to be included in the conversation.

'Okay,' said Moxon, scratching his cheek. 'I got it wrong, then.'

'So how do you know about Miss Entwhistle growing poisonous plants? Why would the police be interested in her?'

'We weren't, until somebody in the village asked us to keep an eye on the house during the funeral. You know, I expect, that there's a certain type of criminal who takes advantage of an empty house at such moments. Watching out for them is something we often get asked to do.'

'And the officer detailed to keep watch decided to have a snoop around her garden, did he?' It was Bonnie who spoke. 'Was it somebody who could identify every plant in her greenhouses?'

'We're all on alert for unusual plants at the moment. Obviously. And I was hoping you'd be helping us with that.'

'Sorry to disappoint you, then,' said Simmy stiffly. She was smarting under his unjustified accusations. 'And what's all this about Tanya?'

'She and some little friend of hers have been hanging around the jetty in Bowness, asking about the cruises and whether they provide food and where it comes from. They've annoyed quite a few people.'

'They think the man was poisoned on the boat, on Sunday, because you and your mates have been all over the waterfront there,' said Bonnie.

He exhaled, a long breath of exasperation. 'So I gather. It's what we might call jumping to conclusions. There is, I admit, reason to believe that Mr Childers did take the midday cruise, but if so, he must have made very good time to get back to Mr and Mrs Straw's by ten to two, which is the time your father made the 999 call. The timing is causing a lot of trouble.'

'So are there any other theories?' Bonnie asked, with her usual boldness.

'Plenty.' He was plainly uncomfortable and Simmy felt compelled to rescue him.

'That's enough,' she told Bonnie. 'You must know the police aren't going to share their investigation with you or me.' She turned to Moxon. 'So what's your beef about the meeting last night?'

'We'll come to that in a minute. Firstly, I need to ask whether you noticed anybody selling food or drink during the protest in Bowness. We've had a few reports of some unofficial activity of that sort. It wouldn't be unusual for someone to be handing out water or even snacks to people who'd travelled a distance to be there.'

Simmy frowned. 'I didn't see anything like that. They were just standing about with placards. But there easily could have been. We were busy talking to people, and might not have noticed. Those little green and white kiosks had people all round them. It was quite a crowd.'

'Hm,' he said. 'What time did you leave?'

'It must have been about half past twelve or a bit after. We stayed twenty minutes or so, then got back to Beck View for one.'

'The boat had gone, then, when you arrived there?'

'Oh yes. We saw it out on the lake, as we walked through Bowness. What time does it leave?'

'Midday. And the cruise is ninety minutes.'

They all contemplated the implications. 'So it came back to Bowness at one-thirty. He couldn't have been feeling ill, then, if he got back up the hill so fast,' said Simmy.

'He *must* have been given whatever-it-was on the boat,' Bonnie concluded. 'Don't you think?'

'There's no knowing,' sighed Moxon. 'There must be a dozen other ways it could have happened.'

'Don't you know yet exactly what the poison was, or how fast it works? Or if he took it all in one go, or a bit at a time? What would it have tasted like? Would he be able to walk after he'd drunk it?' Bonnie's questions poured out, all of them impressively relevant, to Simmy's mind.

'Still somewhat uncertain,' he said regretfully. 'The only thing we *can* say is that whoever gave it to him was extremely clever, and well prepared.'

'Assuming he was the intended victim, of course,' said Bonnie.

Both the adults blinked at her. 'Had you even thought of that?' Simmy asked the detective.

'We've thought of everything,' he said pompously, and unconvincingly.

Bonnie gave him a severe look. 'I still think you must know how quickly the poison works, and what the known rates of absorption are, and all that sort of thing.'

'Maybe in a television series that would be true. But the reality is that toxicology screening is slow and expensive. And there is still some disagreement at higher levels as to the expected benefit of doing that. Since we have found nothing in Mr Childers' possession to indicate what he took, how it was taken, *when* it was taken, or who gave it to him, the precise nature of the toxin's origin seems rather unlikely to answer those questions. We have of course kept samples, which can be sent to a laboratory if and when we decide it's necessary.'

Simmy got off her stool. 'Meanwhile, what happens?'

'We learn everything we possibly can about him – who he knew, why he came here, where he went. We still don't know what he did all day on Saturday.'

'Which doesn't matter much if he took the poison on Sunday,' Simmy remarked.

Moxon collected his thoughts. 'But it *does* matter that he was scheduled to address that meeting last night, and that a nice woman called Dorothea Entwhistle died a few days before Mr Childers, having been known to grow a number of toxic plants in her glasshouse. Those are facts that appear to have a considerable relevance to our investigation.'

'You think Grant Childers murdered Dorothea Entwhistle?' Bonnie stared at him excitedly.

'No, of course not. I never said anything like that. She wasn't murdered. But those glasshouses were unguarded for much of last week, while she was ill in hospital, and apart from you, it seems that almost everyone knew about them. An enterprising poisoner might well seize the chance to collect seeds or leaves or whatever and concoct his lethal cordial at home, with nobody any the wiser, and no direct link for us to follow.'

'I thought it was Tanya who was having the wild theories,' said Bonnie, with a smirk. 'Yours assumes an awful lot of detailed preparation – and then how did the poisoner persuade Mr Childers to drink it?'

'It does sound sort of possible, though,' said Simmy. 'In a mad kind of way. I take it nobody else around the area has reported any of the same symptoms – which would mean that Mr Childers was very cleverly targeted. It's sickening, though, that Candy Proctor palmed him off on my unsuspecting mother. Whoever turns out to have killed him, Candy's the one I really blame for the whole business.'

At which point, two people came into the shop. One was young Tanya Harkness, and the other was an unfamiliar woman who simply wanted to buy some lilies for a weekend dinner party.

Simmy dealt with the customer, while Moxon and Bonnie gathered round Tanya, talking to her in hushed voices at the back of the shop. Tanya appeared to be only mildly cowed by the policeman, defending herself with some very straight looks. The lilies were quickly provided, and Simmy smilingly sent the customer on her way. 'What did I miss?' she asked the others.

'No harm done,' said Moxon, in a rather false tone. 'But I

hope we're agreed that there is no further question of asking people about the lake cruise boat. That is not something a very young amateur detective is authorised to do. All right?'

Tanya and Bonnie both nodded compliantly. 'What, then?' Tanya went on to ask. 'Are you ever going to catch who did it?'

Simmy closed her eyes for a moment, suddenly tired of it all. 'I'm still wishing we could believe it was suicide all along. Why couldn't he have just picked a few berries in the hedge somewhere and turned them into a herbal tea or something – deadly nightshade berries are out at the moment, aren't they?'

'They are not, actually,' said Moxon heavily. 'It's at least two months too late.'

'Oh. I suppose I should know that. What about datura? Does it have berries?'

'Seedpods,' he said tightly. 'And you're clutching at straws if you still think it could have been self-inflicted. We've been over this already.'

She watched his expression and had no choice but to concede his point. 'You're going to tell me there's nothing else that grows wild in Cumbria that would have the same consequences. So whatever it was is almost certain to have been grown deliberately in a greenhouse.'

'Exactly.'

The two girls exchanged a look, before Bonnie said, 'Ben's coming home. He'll be here all day Sunday. It's going to be very hard to keep all this from him. He's going to want all the details.'

Tanya drew in a sharp breath. 'Mum's going to kill us if we tell Ben about this.'

'She won't kill me,' said Bonnie. 'And it's me he'll be furious with if he hears about it afterwards. I'm not sure I can risk it.'

'You make it sound like a threat,' Moxon said. 'A threat to me, I mean. Do you think I'm fearful of your boyfriend's interference?'

'He's only going to be here for one day,' Simmy reminded them. 'He's hardly going to solve it in a few hours, is he? If you ask me, it's never going to be solved. Somebody's going to get away with murder.'

'Not if I can help it,' said Moxon tightly.

'Somebody will say something, or the killer will give themselves away,' said Bonnie. 'Ben says that's what usually happens. Especially if the person thinks he's been amazingly clever. He just has to boast to somebody about it.'

'Or she,' said Simmy.

'Or she,' echoed Moxon with a nod. 'Poisoning was always seen as a woman's favoured method for killing.'

'Okay,' said Bonnie. 'Maybe it was a woman. Women are cleverer, after all. And maybe it was two people doing it together – a man *and* a woman. And you know who was best placed to follow Grant Childers' movements, because she already knew why he was here and what he was likely to be doing?'

She paused for effect and Tanya leant forward impatiently. 'Who?' she demanded.

'That Miss Proctor. The one who usually had him to stay. She knew why he was here and what his movements would be.'

Tanya blinked at her. 'How do you know that?'

'She said so when she came in on Tuesday. You'd think she was his mother, the way she was talking.'

'She turned up at Beck View yesterday,' said Simmy. 'I forgot to tell you.'

'She seems to be everywhere,' said Bonnie. 'That's suspicious in itself.'

Simmy was dubious. 'She's really quite upset about it. I think she liked the man and was very sorry he hadn't been staying with her as usual. I can't believe she was pretending. But she's got herself all entangled with this business in Patterdale, for some reason. I suppose it connects,' she finished vaguely.

'Of course it connects,' said Bonnie. 'If you ask me, it's the key to the whole thing.'

Moxon cleared his throat. 'Just because it appears that the meeting was the main reason for Mr Childers being here does not automatically imply that he was killed by somebody involved in the protest.' He spoke deliberately, as if giving dictation. 'I want you all to bear that in mind.'

'Yes, but . . .' Bonnie began, 'surely it's very likely that somebody wanted to stop him from speaking, because they were scared of what he might say?'

'Or could it be that his substitute was so keen to be heard that he bumped Childers off, so he could get a go?' It was Tanya, still excited, her eyes sparkling. 'Who took his place?'

'Some inarticulate nature conservancy person,' said Simmy. 'He didn't seem to be saying anything very important.'

'Enough,' barked Moxon. 'Why do I stand here letting you indulge in all this fanciful speculation? What sort of a detective am I, anyway? When I'm with you lot I seem to forget who I'm supposed to be. It's a disgrace.'

'You always say that, and you always end up glad that we helped you,' Bonnie reminded him. 'Anyway, it's Simmy's fault. She treats you like a normal human being, so you start to act like one. Disgusting behaviour when you're meant to be a robot.'

Ruefully, the man smiled. 'Well, you might have a point about the speech. It's really quite strongly worded against any new building in the Patterdale area. He must have done quite a bit of homework. The surprise is – now I think about it – that they didn't ask his replacement to simply read it, instead of producing his own material.'

'They probably would have done if they could have got hold of it. But they'd hardly be able to access his laptop, would they?' said Tanya.

'But what if he showed it to them first?' said Simmy. 'That would alert them, and make it even more likely that he was killed to stop him making the speech by somebody who wanted the development to go ahead.'

'A spy in their midst!' said Tanya, her eyes shining.

Moxon sighed and glanced at his watch; he then headed immediately for the door saying, 'I've been here much longer than I meant to be. I don't know where any of that has got us, but I apologise for any unwarranted accusations I might have made.' He was addressing Simmy. 'There has to be something we've all been missing, and I still think it has to do with plants. And you, Mrs B, are the go-to person in that department.'

'Thanks,' sighed Simmy. 'I'd better do a bit of homework, then.'

'Any help would be appreciated. I've got a very frustrated young sergeant tied to a computer, trying to find out every plant in the same family and how exactly to concoct a lethal infusion from them.'

The three females watched him go, each one with a smile on her face.

It was close to four o'clock, and Tanya was sent home with a reminder that she would be assisting Bonnie in the shop next morning, while Simmy took time off with her fiancé to give herself some breathing space. When she was gone, Bonnie and Simmy checked orders, tidied up and planned the next few days. 'I've got to go over to that hotel to do the wedding flowers in a minute. I'll be there until six. Can you close up, and then be here for opening tomorrow? You're okay about these Saturdays, are you? It's not too much for you?'

'Stop saying that. It's fine. I've been here a year or more now, after all. I might not know the names of all the flowers, but I can do everything I need to. If people want a weekend delivery, I just have to say that's not something we can provide, except for the big days like Mother's Day. Tanya's very handy, you know. She's better than me at the money. Why am I saying all this? You know it as well as I do.'

'I suppose I do. The thing is, I still don't know what I'm going to do next year. I'll need to be off for at least three months, right at the busiest time. Tanya's going to be doing her GCSEs, so she can't come much. I'll have to employ somebody else, on a short-term contract.'

'You probably will, but it's ages away yet. Let's get

Christmas over with first, and then you can make that sort of decision. You don't even know where you'll be living by then. If you're still in Troutbeck, you might find you can come down for odd days, with the baby – or leave it with your mother.'

'I won't still be in Troutbeck.' The flat statement, made with such certainty, gave her a pang. She liked her cottage, in a village that mostly escaped the worst of the tourist invasions, despite the very big holiday park. Or perhaps, she thought suddenly, *because* of it. People were self-contained down there in their lodges, with space to park their cars, and paths winding up into the fells with no need to come into the village centre at all. Perhaps the same would be true in Patterdale, if the proposed chalets were actually built. The visitors would be neatly corralled out of sight, and the handful of ordinary residents could pretend they didn't exist.

Bonnie said nothing. A moment later her phone jingled and she drifted to the front of the shop to talk to a caller that could only be Ben. Simmy caught odd words, but did her best not to listen as she went in and out of the room at the back. Loading the van with flowers for the next day's wedding took ten minutes, and for the next hour and a quarter she worked with practised efficiency to decorate the room. It was all finished on schedule, and by the time she had taken the van back and walked to Beck View for a quick check on her parents it was half past six.

The Straws were unnaturally idle when she let herself in and found them in the kitchen. 'What – no last-minute guests?' she said.

'Nary a one,' said Russell.

'Mixed blessing, then,' said Simmy. 'You get a rest, but lose out financially.'

'We're not very good at resting,' said Angie. 'And there'll be food going to waste. Eggs, for a start. I bought four dozen a few days ago. We'll be living on omelettes all next week.'

Simmy told them about Moxon's reproachful visit and how he didn't seem to have much idea about solving the murder. 'He thinks I should know more than he does about poisonous plants,' she concluded.

'And don't you?' asked Russell.

'Not really. I don't know any that have attractive flowers, and that's what I do. Flowers. Not seeds or berries, which are the poisonous bits.'

'Doesn't datura have nice flowers?' Angie said. 'White trumpety things. I've seen them somewhere. I thought the police had already decided they were the most likely poison? Wasn't that what Moxon said on Wednesday?'

'He seems to be less sure about it now. Bonnie was looking them up on her phone, days ago. She says they're called devil's trumpets, colloquially. But I think I've heard people talk about angel's trumpets. it's all in a muddle in my head. Every day somebody tells me something different.'

'That's because you're not concentrating,' said Angie. 'I'm the same. I feel as if my head's full of fog.'

'I shouldn't be so vague about flowers, though. Let me think.' Simmy searched her memory. 'The flowers aren't just white, I think. I can't remember ever seeing any in real life. Just pictures.' But something deep down stirred slightly. Where had she just seen unfamiliar white trumpety flowers?

'You realise we're sunk if we don't get some business soon?' Angie went on impatiently. 'The mortgage isn't going to pay itself.'

'Surely you've got *some* bookings in the diary?'

'Two next weekend, assuming they don't cancel as well. A scattering through November. People don't bother to book far ahead in the winter. They assume there'll always be vacancies.'

'We're tainted,' said Russell heavily. 'Word's got out, and we've been named and shamed. It's the kiss of death to have the word "poison" attached to anywhere that provides food. Stands to reason.'

'Shut up,' his wife told him.

'I'm right, though,' he insisted. 'And we're scuppered for any other career. Child-minding, pastry-making. I suppose we could turn ourselves into a brothel. One that doesn't provide refreshments.'

Simmy laughed, but Angie didn't even manage a smile.

Russell tried again. 'The mortgage can look after itself. There's a considerable equity in this property by now. There'll be a scheme where we tell the bank they can have it when we die, on condition we can live here till then.'

Again, something stirred in the depths of Simmy's mind. Possible arrangements, combined ownership, pooled assets – but they all involved the four of them living under one roof. Christopher had known the Straws all his life, but that didn't mean he would be happy to live with them. She had never dared to suggest it seriously, despite his occasional mentions of the existence of the big handsome Windermere house, which had to be worth a considerable sum. She wasn't even sure she could live with her mother full-time. Angie could be hard work, with her opinions and criticisms and sudden tempers.

'Are you eating here?' Angie asked Simmy. 'We've got plenty of sausages and bacon as well as eggs.'

'No thanks. I thought you'd have had supper by now. I'm meeting Christopher in Patterdale this evening. I'm going to be late, so I'm only here for a bit. His estate agent friend's got a new house to show us.'

'You don't look very excited about it,' observed Russell.

'I am, sort of. When we went there on Wednesday, I really fell in love with the place, like the first time I ever saw it. We went over a bridge to a tiny little place called Crookabeck. It's not on the way to anywhere. It would be so quiet and peaceful and safe there.'

'Perfect for a child, you mean,' said Angie, with an astute look. 'So is this house there – in Crookabeck?'

'No. It's further up, in Glenridding, I think. On the main road.'

Russell was scratching his head. 'Are you sure you've got it right? I've never heard of Crookabeck. I mean to say – I wouldn't forget a name like that, would I?'

'Hey, Dad! You're telling me there's somewhere in Cumbria you haven't heard of? That's terrible.'

'It is,' he said. 'I'm a failure.'

'It's probably just the name of the farm there, and when they converted all its barns and cottages, it turned into a little hamlet. It's completely gorgeous, even at this time of year. A river, and sheep, and birds, and—'

'There'll be walkers,' Russell said. 'There are always walkers.'

'That's no problem.'

'Horses and bikes, probably, as well,' said Angie. 'And dogs.'

'But none of those make noise or run you over. Except maybe the bikes. There's a path to Hartsop, which I want to explore as well.'

'I have heard of Hartsop,' said Russell, with an air of relief.

'Anyway, I need to get going in a minute. I'm sorry about all the cancellations. Can you use the time somehow? Go for a jaunt somewhere? You talk about all these little places you know, but I don't think you've been to any of them for years. Have you? When were you last in Hawkshead? Or even Coniston?'

'One gets out of the habit,' Russell admitted. 'And – do you know, I've never once been on that Lady of the Lake boat, or whatever they call it. I fancy a little cruise up and down Windermere.'

Simmy gave him a searching look. Someone had surely mentioned to him the fact that Grant Childers had apparently taken just such a cruise the day he died. Was her father turning amateur detective as well? In the early days, when Simmy had been involved with a killing in Ambleside, he had taken a lot of interest, but since then he had stepped back, increasingly alarmed by the dangers. 'Why would you do that?' she asked.

'Because it's there,' he said, with a disingenuous twinkle.

She met Christopher and Robin in the car park of the large white Patterdale Hotel, nearly half an hour late. She had phoned to warn them, giving them a chance to go to the bar for a drink while they waited. 'It takes ages to get here from Windermere,' she complained. 'I already hate the Kirkstone Pass. And it's going to be dark soon.'

'This is Robin,' said her fiancé. 'I don't think you two have met.'

Robin was about thirty, his hair dark and slightly greasy. He wore a suit that even Simmy realised was cheap, over a thin nylon shirt. Was property such a poor business these days, then, she wondered. 'Hello,' she said. 'Sorry to keep you waiting.'

'No problem. Shall we walk up for a look, then? The people are expecting us. It'll take us a bit less than ten minutes, if we're brisk. There's not really anywhere to leave a car up there now the weekend's upon us.'

As they walked on the narrow pavement, Simmy tried to engage the right frame of mind. This place could be her home within a few months. It was undeniably heavenly. To the left rose a series of bumpy fells with slopes in all directions. She could see a football pitch, and something that could be a farm further off. To the right was a neater landscape, with a uniform escarpment providing a long horizontal backdrop to the sweeping fall down to the little river that fed Ullswater. A white house drew the eye, giving a focal point and featuring on almost every postcard of Patterdale. Many of the most prominent buildings were painted white, including the White Lion pub and the big Patterdale Hotel. At the foot of that escarpment sat Crookabeck, and further south, little Hartsop. They nestled in age-old comfort, almost every usable patch of level ground already occupied by an old stone building. But in Patterdale there were still a few areas that might be available for development – a word that Russell would insist was a euphemism for desecration.

'Hang on,' she said suddenly. 'Isn't that where they want to put those tourist chalets?' She pointed towards the football pitch. 'Can we go for a quick look while we're here? We ought to have some idea of what it could mean for anybody living here.'

Robin glanced at his phone. 'We're already awfully late,' he demurred.

'Five minutes,' she insisted. 'It's not going to matter, is it?'

Taking the initiative, she crossed the road and followed a path that led westwards along a small valley that she thought had its far end at Grizedale. Crags towered above them to the south. The farm was nestled comfortably just ahead. 'Here,' she said. 'It must be, don't you think?' She swept her arm in an arc to indicate the imagined site. The ground was only relatively level, with knobby rocks and a muddy patch that would call for some intensive landscaping to transform into a holiday park. 'You could probably get a dozen or so of those lodges like they've got in Troutbeck on there, if you were clever.'

'I really don't think it's anybody's intention to build here,' said Robin. 'I've asked around, after Christopher mentioned it, and nobody's heard a thing.'

'There's quite a lot of hoo-ha about it in Bowness,' said Simmy. 'Which I know sounds weird, but it's true. It's taking neighbourhood watch to a whole new level, objecting to a proposal that hasn't even been formally made yet, in a place fifteen miles away.'

'Thirteen,' said Christopher. 'You told me it was thirteen.'

'Which takes half an hour or more to drive,' she said with some bitterness.

'They wouldn't get permission,' said Robin, with absolute confidence. 'It would be much too intrusive. You'd be able to see it from too many points. Look at the one in Hartsop – it's almost invisible. That's how they're meant to be. Even with the new Local Plan favouring economic development, this would be much too much to stomach. And I don't think it's the sort of thing they mean, anyway.'

'You can see the Troutbeck one from the top of Wansfell and Applethwaite,' Simmy said.

'That's an exception,' said Robin. 'Now, can we go back to the house?'

The house, which was another quarter-mile or so past the school, was bigger than she had expected, with a front door opening directly onto the very narrow pavement. Instantly she saw her toddler escaping her grasp and diving under the wheels of a passing car. There was no garage. The windows were small. It faced a cluster of trees and a stone wall. 'Lovely view from the back,' said Robin. 'But it's a bit too dark to see it properly now.'

The vendors showed them around, pointing out random features such as cupboards and curtain rails. The third bedroom was boxy, with a large tree keeping out much of the light. The owners of the house had clearly made enormous efforts to keep everything tidy, with the result that the rooms looked unnaturally bare. Upstairs they glimpsed a sullen teenaged boy in the third bedroom, and hastily maintained that they didn't need to disturb him. 'The baby can have the bigger one, next to ours,' said Christopher heartily. 'Visitors can go in here.'

There was sure to be a lovely view at the back in good light, with glimpses of Ullswater, perhaps, and maybe some lopping of the domineering trees. But the house possessed no direct access onto open ground. The garden was neglected, with a wall to keep sheep from stealing the beans, or whatever else was growing there. Simmy made no attempt to conceal her lack of enthusiasm, despite the valiant efforts of both men to excite her.

'I can't see how this could work,' she said at last, with an apologetic sigh. Her imagination had continued to accumulate reasons why she could not consider living there. The hall was narrow, the stairs steep. The area housing the washing machine and freezer was too small to accommodate baby equipment such as a buggy and car seat. There was a high step down into the kitchen. 'There's nowhere to *put* anything,' she objected, without bothering to lower her voice. She could feel herself channelling her mother.

Robin visibly flinched and Christopher groaned softly. 'But you do still like Patterdale in general, don't you?' he pleaded.

'I do. I think it's lovely. But you have to think of the practicalities. We need to be further from the road. There has to be somewhere we can put both our cars – really it should have a garage. The rooms here are all wrong for us.' She gave Christopher a pleading look. 'And I don't like the steep stairs. I'm really sorry, but that's what I think.'

'And you don't like the Kirkstone Pass, either,' her fiancé reminded her with an obvious struggle to be fair-minded. 'You'd have to use it every day, once you went back to work.'

'I expect I could get used to that, if everything else was right.' She chewed her lip, already feeling the strain and sadness of having to go back to work at all, once she had a child in need of her. 'If I had what I wanted up here, it would be worth it,' she added. She visualised the calm of Crookabeck, where there would be no hassles about parking, no traffic noise, and probably little risk of flooding. The buildings all appeared to have been placed on rising ground.

They were standing in the road a few yards away from the house, but marched quickly back to their cars when a sudden flurry of rain attacked them. Clouds covered the fells within moments and Simmy anticipated a murky drive home through the infamous pass. 'Is it wetter up here, do you think?' she muttered.

'Than what?'

'Windermere. Or Keswick. Or anywhere, really.'

'Probably not noticeably.'

'It floods, though, doesn't it? There was a big one just before I moved up here.'

'I missed it as well. But it was pretty dramatic, apparently, especially in Glenridding. They've improved the defences now, so we'll have to hope it doesn't happen again.'

Robin stood by his car looking uncertain. 'So . . . the house doesn't grab you, then?' he said.

Simmy grimaced. 'Oh dear, we must seem terribly ungrateful, when you've put yourself out for us. But—'

'That's okay. I'm used to it. It probably isn't really right for a family, when you think about it.'

'It'll sell quickly, don't worry,' said Christopher.

Robin sighed. 'Everyone still remembers the flood, that's the problem. There were pictures of the road all cracked and broken, and water rushing through half the houses. It's had quite an effect, which still hasn't gone away. Most of them are still online somewhere, and people always have to look before they commit to buying property.'

'I remember something about a landslide as well,' said Simmy.

'More than one, in fact. There were diversions and disruption for months.'

Christopher looked at his watch. 'I'm hungry,' he said. 'Shall we have something here?' He looked at the big white hotel. 'We'll get the car park money back if we do that.'

Simmy hesitated. 'Do you mind if we just go back to Troutbeck? I haven't been at home much this week, and there's food that needs eating. I'm not really in the mood for eating out.'

Her fiancé readily concurred. 'Suits me,' he said cheerfully. 'I'm all set for a lovely relaxing weekend, starting now.'

They drove back in separate cars, which gave Simmy more time for thinking than she really needed. Her thoughts were not the most optimistic or uplifting. Instead she flitted from near panic over where she and Christopher were going to live to what was going to happen to her parents, via DI Moxon's frustration and Bonnie's potential for disaster in the shop next morning. Nothing seemed smooth or encouraging. There were problems on all sides, some of them involving catching a poisoner before he or she could strike again. Because that, really, was the fear behind the failure to apprehend and convict a killer. If the original purpose behind killing Grant Childers had been something to do with the building of tourist lodges in Patterdale, and if it had not achieved its purpose, then there could be someone else in line for removal. Some other person obstructing the way of determined planners, perhaps.

But would a development company stoop so low? Would they really construct an elaborate conspiracy involving feeding the victim with something containing enough poison to kill him, in case he made such a convincing speech that their entire proposal would be dismissed before it was properly made? It felt wholly incredible. Ludicrous, even. How much more likely that a spurned girlfriend or jealous workmate had packed him some lethal substance in a bottle of corrupted orange squash for him to consume once in Windermere?

He could have carried his packed lunch outside with him, sitting on the lakeside in Bowness on Sunday morning and unwittingly killing himself. Why did the police not follow up that line of investigation? Childers could have neatly disposed of the packaging in a corporation litter bin, where it would never be found or analysed. The same went for the kitchens, gardens and dustbins of everyone who knew him back home in Halesowen. It was an impossible task – she had little hope that any real evidence was ever going to turn up against anybody who'd ever known poor Grant Childers.

The pessimistic mood persisted as she crawled up and around the snaking road that was the Kirkstone Pass. Visibility was very poor in the misty rain, and traffic uncomfortably heavy. A car behind her evidently judged her to be needlessly slow, driving right up to her bumper with lights on, trying to bully her into speeding up. Just as she began to do so, a white truck approached through the gloom at some speed, and she veered to the left to avoid it. Over the years she had learnt not to do this too violently, having once smashed a wing mirror against a stone wall and been appalled at the cost of replacing it. She missed the wall, settling onto the bumpy verge instead. Her wheels grated unpleasantly over stones at the foot of the wall and the car behind, in an effort to avoid a similar fate, found itself in the path of the oncoming truck. Almost at a standstill, Simmy heard the traumatising sound of metal on metal and breaking glass.

Chapter Sixteen

Not my fault, she muttered. *Definitely not my fault*. Both the other drivers had been behaving badly, while she had been a paragon of caution and good sense. Already there were other cars approaching from both directions. One of them might be Christopher, she realised, having left Patterdale ahead of him, while he had a few final words with Robin. In any case he would be delayed by the blocked road. Perhaps she should phone him and warn him, saying she'd go ahead and put some food on to cook while she waited. But the signal up there was poor, and he ought not to answer the phone while driving. On the other hand, he might worry that she had been hurt in the accident.

She opted to drive on while she still could, squeezing past two more stationary cars that had got caught up in the accident. She knew she ought to offer herself as a witness, but what would she say? That the tailgater deserved all he got for trying to bully her, and the truck likewise should have been going more slowly? The insurance people would make little of that, and the 'knock for knock' solution was the only fair one, in the circumstances. It was highly unlikely that anyone had been hurt, and her conscience was very nearly clear as she proceeded down into Troutbeck.

Her route passed the church, and natural curiosity caused her to slow down and try to locate Miss Entwhistle's grave, which ought to be piled high with flowers. There was space in the road outside and she stopped, thinking she could phone Christopher at the same time. She also realised that she was feeling shaky after the incident at Kirkstone Pass. The sound of the impact was still echoing in her ears, the violence of it reverberating. It would be good to hear her fiancé's voice.

He answered quickly, wanting to know where she was. 'In Troutbeck. Where are you?' was her reply.

'Standing beside a buckled pick-up truck with about six other people, seeing if we can move it out of the way. One of the wheels won't work, which is causing some problems.'

'I saw it happen. I was right there.'

'I hope it wasn't your fault? Why didn't you stay to help?'

'No way was it my fault, and I didn't think there was anything useful I could do. Somebody must have called out a tow truck by now, surely?'

'Yes, but the traffic's backed up about half a mile in each direction already. The trouble is, it's so misty, someone's going to rear-end something if we don't do what we can to get it clear.'

'It's not anybody we know, is it?' The thought had not occurred to her until that moment.

'The car belongs to a man from Yorkshire who was coming here with his wife for a romantic weekend, using the scenic route, which added too much time to the journey. He knows he was driving badly. The truck's from Kendal or somewhere. The driver's Polish and scared stiff he's going to lose his job.'

'He was going much too fast.'

'So I gather. He's very remorseful about it as well as the Yorkshire chap.'

'Maybe it'll teach them a lesson.' She could find no charitable words for the two men, who might easily have damaged her and her car in the process of hitting each other. In fact, with hindsight it looked quite miraculous that she had gone unscathed.

'Huh,' said Christopher.

'Anyway, I'll be home in a few minutes and get started on some supper. It sounds as if you might be some time.'

'I thought you said you were at home already?'

'I'm at the church. I'm going for a quick look at a grave. It's flower business.'

'But it's dark. It's been dark for hours.'

'I can see enough. There's a light on in the church and the door's open. It's a bit mad, I know, but I want to get out of the car for a minute.' There was the sound of men's raised voices coming through Christopher's phone. 'You'd better go,' she said. 'See you soon.'

She found the new grave in the feeble evening light, helped by a beam from the church door, but was disappointed to see only three floral tributes adorning it. She could see that none of them had come from Persimmon Petals. There was a man pottering about close by, picking up stray scraps of litter. 'Where did all the flowers go?' she asked him.

'Undertaker's men took them away. Gave them to nursing homes, I dare say. Isn't that the usual thing?'

'After a cremation, maybe. It seems a shame not to leave them on the grave, even if just for a couple of days.'

The man shrugged. He was probably a church warden or lay preacher, she supposed. The vicar was barely recognised by her, but she was pretty sure this was not him. She had not once been to a service in her local church. 'They get messy,' the man muttered. 'Especially in weather like this.'

There was still a mizzly rain, covering everything with a damp autumnal frosting that was a long way from the sparkle of winter ice. Her head was bare and she could feel her hair getting wet. A large mound of funeral flowers would soon have gone sad and soggy, she conceded. She went back to her car with a sense of something unresolved. Only as she parked outside her cottage did it strike her that she had been unconsciously searching for a hand-made tribute containing white trumpet-shaped flowers.

Christopher arrived twenty-five minutes later, which was quicker than she'd expected. It was nearly nine o'clock and they were both seriously hungry. She found peanuts to stave off the worst pangs while a large ready-made fish pie heated through in the oven, and peas were boiled on the hob. 'I wish I could have some alcohol,' she whined.

'What's stopping you? Mindless propaganda by a health and safety society gone mad.' He looked at her with a smile. 'I'm just channelling your mother, you realise. But I really don't think a glass or two is going to do any damage. Probably the opposite. Moderation in all things – isn't that what they say? It's not moderation to give something up altogether.'

'I might have a beer then,' she said, with a pang of guilt. 'I'm sure you're right. When did I become such a conformist?' How could these social taboos gain such a hold over everybody, she wondered. When her mother was pregnant, it was apparently quite normal for expectant mothers to knock back half a bottle of wine every day, at the very least. They smoked like chimneys too. And as far as Simmy could see, the resulting babies of her generation were more or less healthy. It was the current cohort of toddlers and infants that had rotten teeth and endless allergies, if reports could be believed.

'It's the times we live in. Go on – be a devil,' said Christopher, going to the fridge. 'My mum always said we thrived on the Guinness she drank all the time she was expecting.'

'Just what I was thinking,' said Simmy.

They ate together in the kitchen, chatting amicably about work and families and changing seasons. The quest for a house had been shelved for the time being, as had the fact of a murder under Simmy's very nose. She encouraged Chris to describe recent items sold in his auction house, never tiring of his tales of naughty postcards tucked in among views of Torquay, and a gold coin lodged in the middle drawer of a small cabinet. The best story was of a diamond necklace wrapped in tissue paper and taped to the back of a high shelf in a big mahogany wardrobe. 'About ten people must have missed it,' he said. 'The buyer found it, and was entirely within her rights to keep it. She wore it a few times before selling it for three grand.'

The glamour of the whole business mixed intriguingly with the grubby reality of house clearances and unwashed dealers. The past two days had been spent receiving items for sale at the next weekend's auction, the tasks of sorting, listing, valuing, photographing and presenting it all more than enough to keep the whole team busy for the coming week. 'But at least we've all got the weekend free,' said Christopher. 'And I won't have to go in until after lunch on Monday.'

'I still don't like leaving Bonnie and Tanya to cope on Saturday mornings,' she worried. 'Not since Tanya cut herself that time.'

'It taught her to be more careful. We learn by experience.'

'I know,' she sighed, 'and I don't expect it'll be very busy. Ben's coming home on Sunday – did I tell you?'

They went on to discuss the boy wonder, with his prodigious intelligence and dedicated studies. Christopher could never entirely bring himself to approve of Ben, despite all Simmy's efforts to proclaim his virtues. 'His mother doesn't want us to mention the murder,' she said. 'Bonnie isn't sure she can manage that. She thinks he'll be furious when he eventually gets to hear about it.'

Christopher was deeply uneasy about references to deliberate killing. His association with Simmy had been rekindled over the murder of his own father, much to his dismay. Her role in identifying the perpetrator had left Christopher speechlessly wrestling with a host of conflicting emotions. Then again, a friend of his had died in Grasmere, dragging Chris into far too close an encounter with police investigations and suspicions about his auction house. The fact that it had happened a third time was even more unsettling. Aware of this, Simmy had done her best to avoid talking about it. She had pushed it onto her parents, maintaining that it was largely their problem, and all she had to do was offer soothing words every day or two.

Ben Harkness, however, had shown no hesitation in involving Christopher in the Grasmere incident. His questions were direct and his theorising tenacious. It was evident to Simmy that her fiancé was never going to really like or trust the young man again after that.

The evening drifted on, imbued with the relaxed knowledge that there would be two further evenings to come, where they could eat and chat and cuddle and watch a movie or play a game and let the world outside do its worst. The urgency of finding a new home would not go away, and there was every chance they would be back in Patterdale at some point over the weekend, but their evenings would be sacrosanct. 'We'll have to go to Beck View on Sunday, though,' she warned him. 'You haven't seen my parents for weeks.'

'No problem,' he agreed languidly. 'Do you think your mum might manage one of her wonderful roast pork lunches, if we ask her nicely?'

'She might,' said Simmy. 'If I remember to ask her tomorrow.'

By arrangement with some kindly guardian angel, neither of their phones rang even once the entire evening. Nobody came to the door demanding attention and action. Darkness fell quickly while they were still eating, and few vehicles passed outside. The baby stirred gently inside Simmy, apparently grateful for the long overdue meal, or perhaps enjoying the forbidden alcohol.

But a spirit of perversity was lurking somewhere, overcoming the good offices of the angel. 'I hope Robin isn't too disappointed,' said Simmy, entirely against her better judgement. 'Or you, come to that.'

He hesitated to speak, still leaning back on the sofa cushions, one arm round Simmy's shoulders. 'I can see it isn't going to be easy,' he finally agreed. 'But I don't want to make many compromises, either. Chances are, we'll stay for thirty years or more, once we find the perfect place.'

'So you wouldn't really have accepted that house, if I hadn't objected to it?'

'I might, but I'm sure I would have regretted it pretty soon. It seemed fine to me until you pointed out all its defects. And you were absolutely right to do so. I'm obviously too unimaginative to make a sensible decision. We should probably have a look at the building plot in Hartsop, after all. It was foolish of us not to when we had the chance.'

'I want to live in Crookabeck,' she said childishly.

'I looked at a map today – a really large-scale one. It's an easy walk from Hartsop to Crookabeck, along a quiet path. It goes through a farmyard, and follows the little river. They're practically the same place, in a way.'

'That sign we saw said it was two miles from one to the other. That's a long walk, there and back.'

'My point is, it's all really quiet and unspoilt in both places. No roads or shops or pubs. Just sheep and walkers.'

'I know. That's what I've been saying. Although my imagination isn't much better than yours. What would it be like in the snow, or when that river floods, or even when it's really hot? Would there be midges? Are there loads of horse riders? How are we supposed to decide, when there's so much we can't predict?'

'We use blind faith. As long as we're together, and Junior is fit and well, the rest doesn't really matter. Though I might insist on a dog. Something slow and dim, that doesn't chase sheep.'

'It obviously has to be a Patterdale terrier,' she said lightly. 'And I'd force it to live outside.'

'Terriers chase sheep. And they're nothing much to look at. It would have to be a Labrador, or a golden retriever. And I would want it on the bed every night to keep my feet warm.'

'Over my dead body,' she said, rather too sharply. Having been witness to the mess that people's dogs could make on a bed, thanks to her mother's lax rules at Beck View, she knew she could never contemplate a dog in a bedroom; even the thought of it on the sofa made her feel itchy. 'They leave hair and fleas everywhere, not to mention the mud.'

'Sim, we shouldn't stop each other from doing what we want. And don't say everybody has to compromise, because it's not really a compromise, is it, if I want something and you veto it? I grew up desperately wanting a dog and my parents would never allow it. Then I was travelling for years and it was completely out of the question. Now I'm in a flat and the poor thing would never get any exercise. But if I've got a wife and a baby and a garden and a million acres of fells outside the back door, then I think I should have a dog to complete the picture. What would you do if I just came home with a puppy one evening?'

'I'd say you were a selfish pig, I expect.'

'But would you slam the door in our faces? Mine and Fido's?'

'I might.' She pulled a helpless face, indicating her confused feelings. 'I don't want to stop you doing what you want. That would be horrible.'

'Hm. I can see this marriage thing isn't going to be plain sailing. How do other people manage? How do they stay happy, when sharing one's life with someone else seems so terribly fraught?'

'They come to some sort of truce, I suppose. I must admit, I quite like golden retrievers.'

'Hm,' he said again. 'You didn't used to be like this, you know. You were wonderfully soft and sweet and shy when I knew you before. Now you've got all decisive and opinionated.'

'I was sixteen. You were awkward and irritable and rude to your parents.'

'You're saying I've improved, but you've changed for the worse.'

'I'm saying we've both grown up. But bizarrely, I still love you. And I'm having your baby. As the song says, that's one way of saying I love you. We're stuck with each other now, whether you like it or not. I'm definitely not going to do this on my own.'

'Then stop picking fights with me, you daft thing. The world's doing its best to get between us as it is. Let's just try and stay on the same side, okay?'

'Okay,' she said, leaning over to kiss him.

Chapter Seventeen

At Beck View, Angie and Russell were having a less peaceful evening. Simmy's abrupt departure, after a bare twenty minutes' stay, left them both with a sense of being short-changed. The absence of any guests was almost unprecedented, leaving them with nothing urgent to do but worry about money and what the future might hold.

'She's never going to find anywhere in Patterdale,' said Russell, for the twentieth time. 'The place is just too small. And most of the properties are too big. Some of them were built as guesthouses, with seven or eight bedrooms.'

'Well, there's nothing we can do about it, is there?'

'There could be, actually. If we sold this, and went in with them, we could afford to buy one of the big places jointly, and there'd be enough space for us to keep out of each other's way.'

Angie shook her head vigorously. 'That would be fatal. There'd be rows every morning in the kitchen, and she'd expect me to turn childminder while she went back to work. Besides, what makes you think anyone's selling a seven-bedroom house there? I thought they'd only managed to come up with a building plot until now. I suppose there's some hope that the one they're seeing this evening will turn out to be ideal.'

Her husband sighed. 'Well, we've got to do *something*. We can't just sit here for the next umpteen weeks or months, until everybody forgets we had a murder here.'

'You mean we should turn into detectives and somehow solve the mystery? You think we've been missing some clues?'

'We should have paid more attention to the bloke. I barely even looked at him.'

'Neither did I until he was thrashing about on the landing. If only he hadn't said he'd been poisoned, there might never have been a suspicion that it was foul play at all.'

'I expect there would. There'd have to be a post-mortem, and they'd have found whatever it was then.'

'Yes, but they could have put it down to suicide. That would be far less damaging to our reputation.'

'We should have thought of that before telling the cops what he said, then. We were much too honest for our own good.'

'Persimmon would have said something. You know how matey she is with that detective.'

Russell gave himself a mock slap. 'And there was me thinking we'd brought her up right, telling her she should never utter a lie and always be helpful to the police.'

'I never told her that,' said Angie. 'I've never had very much time for the police, as you very well know.'

'She's just naturally honest, then. We can't take any of the credit – or blame. And I dare say the Childers family would have argued with a verdict of suicide. Families generally do, after all. It makes them feel guilty if a relative kills himself. As if they've failed him somehow.'

'Which in this case, I dare say they have. He sounded to be quite a lonely person – coming up here every few months all by himself.'

'Well, I blame Candy Proctor when it comes right down to it. She should have made space for him, instead of foisting him off on us.'

Angie got up from her chair, too restless to keep still any longer. 'I think she's a bit jealous of us for having all this attention over Childers, funnily enough. Even though she must know how awful it is for business. She's a funny woman.'

'I think she might have a thing for old Tristan, you know. She was gazing at him raptly through most of that meeting last night. She was in the front row and he was at the top table, chairing it all. I still don't know what he thought he was doing. It was all rather a shambles, really.'

'Grant Childers dying like that must have come as a tremendous shock to him and his fellow organisers. Scrambling for a replacement speaker and so forth.'

'Who turned out to be a right wally. Which reminds me – we should have a look at the speech Childers was intending to give. Moxon will have sent it by now.' He opened up his laptop, which was often left undisturbed for days on end, and started carefully tapping the keys. 'An attachment,' he said. 'Now . . . let's see . . .'

Angie leant over his shoulder, unsure how much interest she really felt. When Russell successfully brought the text up on the screen, she could barely read it. 'Can you make it bigger?' she asked.

This too was accomplished, and for a minute or two they read in silence. Then Angie repeated the first lines aloud. '"As a regular visitor to Cumbria, I would like to begin by appealing to everyone's finer human feelings. I would like to remind you of the sheer spiritual uplift that can be created by the simple expedient of standing on a fellside and letting nature envelop you. The birds, the running water and the unadulterated light all speak directly to the visitor's soul." Blimey! The man was a poet.'

'Not only that. He's quoting precedent, where tourism has blighted communities, look. Then he's got a whole lot of factual stuff about traffic, flood plains, even wind farms. He must have spent weeks on it. Anyone hearing this would be in no doubt about letting that proposal go ahead. They'd have marched to Patterdale there and then.'

'Yes,' said Angie slowly. 'I think you're right. He would have been the star of that meeting. Tristan must have been absolutely sick when he realised he wasn't going to be able to use this stuff.'

They read to the end and then closed down the computer. 'Well,' sighed Russell. 'The police must have found that a prime piece of evidence. It gives them a motive, as well.'

'All they need to do is identify whoever it is who wants to build the tourist park,' said Angie. 'Sounds simple.'

'I have a feeling there's a bit more to it than we understand. We should have told Simmy to have a look at the site where these new chalets are supposed to go. It was marked on the map on that leaflet they gave us, though not down to the nearest yard, admittedly.'

Angie had another thought. 'I wonder how they'll manage this sort of thing without Dorothea Entwhistle. She'd have been a prominent supporter of the cause.'

'Tristan's certainly going to miss the old girl. I always thought she did most of his thinking for him. Not so much about local politics, but she did help him with his roses.'

'How do you know about that?'

'Don't you remember his greenhouse blowing down in that storm a few years ago? She let him put the delicate things in hers, up in Troutbeck, and they've been pals ever since.'

Angie shrugged, as if she had no interest in such matters. Instead she went into the larder and opened the big fridge. 'I'll have to freeze all this bacon – and it never really tastes right when it's been defrosted. The dog will probably end up eating it.'

'He'll get fat,' said Russell, patting the faithful Lakeland terrier sitting beside him. 'There's a good boy. Simmy should get a dog, you know. I can't think what she's got against them. This little fellow has never done anything to annoy her.'

Angie's restlessness was increasing. The prospect of the coming weekend with no guests, no plans to go out, no way of knowing what might happen next, all added up to a highly disagreeable set of emotions. 'Did she say whether they were coming here on Sunday?' she asked Russell.

'I think they are. Do you want me to phone her and ask?'

'In the morning. Christopher likes pork, doesn't he? Maybe he'd settle for bacon and sausages instead.'

'In your dreams,' said Russell.

Nothing more was said for several minutes. Russell found himself wishing he smoked a pipe, if only to give himself something to do with at least one hand. Sitting by the Rayburn, legs stretched out, he felt shamefully lazy. It was nearly twenty years since he and Angie had moved north and set themselves up in the hospitality industry – which he refused to call it. The time had hurtled by. He had thrown himself into the role of jovial host, as well as exploring every corner of the region. He swotted up on local history, advised on the best walks and the lesser-known attractions, and predicted the weather with uncanny accuracy. His previous career had never been remotely as satisfying and absorbing as this new life turned out to be. With Angie firmly in charge, all he had to do was make people welcome and keep Beck View's approval rating high. The money they earned was plenty for their modest needs. Angie seldom went out, other than to call in on Simmy in the shop or have coffee with her handful of friends. Once in a long while there would be meetings with other B&B proprietors, where they exchanged ideas about soap and duvet covers and black pudding. There seemed little need for a busy social life when there was such a constant stream of people coming through their front door and lingering over long conversational breakfasts.

And now, all of a sudden, everything had changed. It started with Simmy getting pregnant again and needing to find a new place to live, because the existing house was not big enough. Or so the youngsters insisted. To Russell's mind, the cottage in Troutbeck was perfectly adequate for a small family. And the much-deplored commute from Troutbeck to Keswick was nothing compared to what countless thousands of people managed right across the country. The idea of them living in Patterdale was distasteful to Russell, who did not like driving on narrow roads with hundreds of tourists who did not appreciate the hazards. If necessary, he could walk to Troutbeck, even if it took all morning, No way could he walk the thirteen miles to Patterdale, although admittedly there was quite a good bus service, which he was determined to make full use of.

And all that faded into the shadows in the face of this confounded murder. This was going to force much more urgent change onto him and Angie, if the current spate of cancellations was anything to go by. The news had spread like a galloping horse through Facebook and Twitter and Lord knew what else. The local TV station had filmed in the street outside, making Beck View all too recognisable. 'All publicity is good publicity,' Russell had said optimistically a few days ago, but it turned out he was wrong about that.

Several things had to be achieved if the situation were to be saved. Firstly, any tiny hint that the Straws had provided the lethal poison must be firmly suppressed. Secondly, it would help if the whole story could somehow be given a romantic slant. Something about a jilted lover or tragic misunderstanding would be good. Thirdly, the stalwarts of Windermere had to stand beside them in full support. This was a lot to ask, given Angie's persistent refusal to follow many of the guidelines about hygiene and good order. Her attitude to visiting dogs alone put her outside civilised public opinion. Fourthly, the solution, when it finally came, to the mystery of who supplied the poison should be made very public and be very dramatic. For that, they would need young Ben Harkness, and sadly, he was not available.

He got up and went looking for his wife, who had gone upstairs some minutes before. 'We should be making a bigger effort to find out what happened,' he blurted, seeing her in their bedroom. 'We can't just sit about doing nothing, can we?'

Only then did he observe that the stalwart Angie, the woman everyone listened to and obeyed, was in tears.

Russell Straw was no braver than any other man when it came to weeping females. His first impulse was to call Simmy and get her to come and put things right. But he couldn't do that. It was half past nine, and she might already have gone to bed. And what a pathetic course of action that would be. 'Hey!' he said softly. 'What's all this?'

There was no immediate reply. When it came he supposed it would be about the business, and reputation and feeling helpless. Instead, she burst into louder sobs, her face blotching and her voice thick. The words came out loud and uncontrolled. 'I keep seeing that man's *face*. It's in front of my eyes all the time. It's worse since I read that speech. It makes him more of a real person. When's it going to stop? I can't carry on like this. I'll go mad. Oh, Russ, I think I really might be going mad.'

This, he realised, was serious. She never called him Russ.

* * *

They spent a desperate night, Angie too distraught to sleep, and neither of them tired after an unprecedentedly idle day. They kept the light on between the hours of two and four, first talking, then trying to read. They had not spent such a night since their daughter's baby had been stillborn and the world turned black. Angie's tendency to exaggeration led to an obsessive listing of everything that could go wrong from this point on. Simmy's new baby would die, there would be another world war, the roof of the house would blow off in the next big gale. Nothing was safe.

Russell was dumbfounded in the face of all this. In recent times, he had been the anxious one, verging on paranoia at times. But his fears centred around burglars and other vaguely defined invasions of his property. His own declining powers were at the root of it, as he sometimes recognised. He would forget something crucial, lose something precious, fail to fulfil a promise. It made him neurotic, endlessly worrying about his own mental state. Angie, on the other hand, had never doubted herself. The sudden apparent terror that her own mind was failing shook Russell's world as nothing had done before.

And all because some swine had fed poison to one of their guests, with never a thought for the consequences.

He knew it was futile to offer empty reassurances in the face of such distress. Better to confront the fears and tackle them realistically. But the small hours were not conducive to rational discussion. Everything was out of proportion, values distorted by the silence outside and the cold, dark sky. Finally, they switched out the light and sank into muffled sleep that neither one expected to be restorative. Their pillows were hot and crumpled from the wakeful hours, the duvet heavy on their clammy skin. *It'll be better in the morning*, Russell insisted to himself as he finally dropped into sleep.

It was almost nine o'clock when they woke. 'What day is it?' Angie mumbled. 'Were we really awake half the night?'

'I fear so. It's Saturday, I think. We need to phone Simmy and see what she's proposing to do tomorrow.'

'You do it. I'm staying in bed this morning. You can bring me some tea and toast.'

'I can do that. That will not be difficult. But are you sure?' He examined her uneasily. 'You're not exactly *ill*, are you? Just overstressed and panicked. I realise I'm no expert, but it does strike me that it would be more therapeutic to get dressed and find something to do.' At the back of his mind the word *depression* floated alarmingly. The very last person in the entire British Isles likely to succumb to such a state was his wife, Angie Straw. He was not prepared to allow such a thing to happen.

'Therapeutic?' she echoed.

'Exactly. It looks to me as if it's that or go on some despised medication. Like me,' he added. His own tendency to anxiety had led to him resorting to chemical assistance, albeit at a low and diminishing level. 'You wouldn't want that.'

'No,' said Angie softly. She was fully aware that she'd boxed herself into an uncomfortable corner where she might be forced to contradict herself. 'Although you must admit these are extraordinary times, where several assumptions are under attack.'

This was more like it, he thought. She was using long sentences, with long words, her mind evidently clear. Any hint of incipient insanity had gone. Perhaps his feeble arguments at three in the morning had worked better than he could ever have expected. He couldn't recall exactly what he'd said, but it had been along the lines of 'while fear of madness is frightening and self-perpetuating, the evidence suggests that you are in fact entirely rational'. Perhaps that was all she had needed to hear.

'I admit it unreservedly,' he said. 'But I still think you ought to get dressed and take your place in the world.'

'Whatever that might be,' she muttered.

'We could make the most of our freedom and go out somewhere. Coniston, perhaps? Or Hawkshead. It's lovely there.'

'The only sensible place to go would be Patterdale,' she said. 'I can barely remember what it looks like, and if Persimmon is going to live there, I should make an effort to get to know it.'

'Good thinking,' he applauded, with a vast inner relief. 'We'll do that, then.'

'Just give me ten more minutes,' she insisted, pulling the duvet over her head.

Telephone calls kept Russell busy for the next half-hour. He was on his mobile to Simmy when the landline summoned him. 'Angie!' he called up the stairs. 'Come down and talk to your daughter.' He left the mobile on the stairs and answered the house phone.

It was Suzy Gorringe, who for a shameful few seconds Russell could not place. 'Oh yes, hello,' he said, stalling for time. Then it came to him that it was the dead man's sister, who should be treated with immense sensitivity. 'What can I do for you?'

She was, it seemed, deeply unsatisfied with the lack of progress in the police investigation. 'He was *poisoned*,' she said shrilly. 'Why can't they use some of these hi-tech forensic tricks to find out who did it? All they have to do is work out exactly what the poison was, and trace it back to the killer. How many ordinary people know how to make a lethal dose of atropine or whatever it was?'

'It's sure to be on the Internet,' Russell suggested.

'Well, that's where you're wrong. I've spent *hours* researching every known poisonous plant, and nowhere does it tell you exactly what to do with them. You have to have special professional approval before you can learn anything in detail. Like the police – they, if anybody, must be able to get at the facts.'

'I suppose all the hedge witches are long gone,' he said, unwisely. 'They'd have known precisely what to do.'

'What? Who? Are you taking this terrible thing seriously, or not?'

He bit his lips, literally catching both upper and lower between his teeth to stop himself from describing the night he and his wife had just spent, thanks to the seriously terrible thing that had happened under his roof. 'I believe I am,' he said, after a pause.

'Sorry, sorry,' she groaned. 'I shouldn't take it out on you. I was only phoning to see whether you'd heard any more. It's very frustrating having to stay down here, miles from where it happened. And they haven't released Grant's body yet. We're stuck in limbo and it's driving us all mad.'

'It must be dreadful,' he said, as warmly as he could. 'But I'm afraid we're none the wiser than you are. All we know is that your brother was popular in this area, with everyone saying how shocked they are.'

'Huh!' she scoffed. 'I'm afraid you've got that altogether wrong. As far as I can see, nobody liked poor Grant one little bit.'

Chapter Eighteen

Three minutes after the call from Mrs Gorringe, the landline pealed again. Russell assumed it was the same woman having remembered more she wanted to say. But it was Tristan Wilkins, of all people. 'Russ, old friend,' came the excessively hearty greeting, 'how's things?'

'Not great,' said Russell, who was never much good at prevarication.

'No, I dare say not. Now listen, I've been chatting to dear old Stuart about this and that, including this Patterdale nonsense. He put me straight about your girl wanting to find a place to live up there, and how impossible it's likely to be, unless she takes him up on this building plot suggestion. Not easy, timing-wise, I can see that – but surely good sense in the long run? That's what Stu thinks, anyway. She's obviously concerned about the planning thing, as we all are.'

'I don't think she is, actually. Even if it did happen, it's small enough not to make a lot of difference to anything.'

'Dangerous words, my friend. Anyway, Stu and I thought it would be constructive to have a proper talk about that, and a few other things, with Candy for good measure. You must be dying for some distraction from the ghastly Childers business. Why don't you and Angie come down to mine for some lunch today? Say twelve-ish. Nothing fancy – just a cold collation as my mother used to say. Daphne's a dab hand at that sort of thing.'

'Oh!' This was highly unusual, and Russell could not guess at Angie's reaction. 'Let me go and ask her. Hold on a minute.'

Angie had gone back upstairs with the mobile, but was not speaking into it. 'She says we should go there for roast pork tomorrow,' she reported. 'She thinks it would do us good to get out of this place.'

'Must be a conspiracy. Guess who's just asked us to lunch today? At this rate, we'll never need to cook again.'

'Who?'

'Tristan. Apparently Stuart and Candy are going to be there as well. Cold collation, he says. Sounds rather nice. Are we up for it?'

She frowned. 'They'll talk about the Childers man. It'll be awful.'

'So you want me to say no?'

She didn't answer directly, still agonising about it. 'They'll try to make me describe exactly how he died, and I really don't relish the thought of that.'

'We'll tell them the police asked you not to. And they might have interesting things to tell us. I think, you know, that we ought to be trying harder to figure out exactly who did the deed. If we combine forces with

225

the others, we might make a bit of headway. This is so peculiar, being invited at such short notice, I think we really have to go along with it. He's hanging on, waiting for an answer.'

'I don't know . . .' Angie dithered.

'Well, I've got to tell him one way or the other.'

'Tell him yes,' said Angie wearily. 'I don't want to turn into one of those women who can't face social gatherings, do I?' She was half-dressed, and started to pull on the final layer.

'You do not,' said her husband, and went to give Tristan the good news.

Angie finished dressing and joined Russell in the kitchen. 'Don't you think it's highly likely to have been one of them?' she said, as if this had been obvious for days.

'Um . . . Er . . .' said Russell blankly. 'One of who?'

'Candy or Stuart or Tristan – who poisoned our guest. Or all three of them together.'

Russell spoke cautiously. 'Do you really think so? If I've got the logic right, having seen that speech, it strikes me they'd be the last people to do it. They needed him alive, surely? Far more likely to be the faceless developers wanting to build that park.'

'I know that would make more sense. But you and Bonnie seem to think there are no such people, and it's all some kind of smokescreen.'

'Hm. That's getting a bit deep for my simple mind. Tristan said they want to talk about Patterdale and Simmy wanting to live there. And Tristan's always keen for people to admire his roses, isn't he? He'll probably take us on a guided tour of his garden.'

Eating scrambled eggs and drinking tea, ten minutes later, she said, 'What was that about a hedge witch? Who were you talking to?'

He had forgotten Suzy Gorringe. 'The sister. She thinks the police should have worked out the killer by now. I said we needed a hedge witch to talk us through likely poisons. We don't know one, do we?'

She pondered this. 'I always thought Simmy's Ninian might have a bit of that about him. If a hedge witch can be male.'

'Why not? Though I must say I've never thought of him in that sort of light.'

'He's a potter – he digs clay out of ditches. He experiments with chemicals, colours and so forth. It's not a million miles from brewing up deadly nightshade concoctions, is it?'

'Good God, woman! Ninian has no reason to murder anybody. He's practically a hermit. He doesn't *know* anybody.'

'He knows Corinne, and us, and Dorothea Entwhistle.'

'Does he? Who told you that?'

'Persimmon said something about it last night. She was talking about the funeral, remember?'

'I missed that part.'

'There must be plenty of people around who know how to use wild plants. People who added hogweed and ransoms and nettles to their stews to bulk them out when times were hard. They'd have to know about hemlock and nightshades and yew and whatever else might kill you.'

'Toadstools and henbane,' he added.

'Exactly. It's a big subject, but we all know a bit about

it, if we live in the country. Anyone over sixty, at least.'

'What about Dorothea, then? She was the ultimate plant person.'

Angie sighed. 'We can't accuse *her* of murder. She was dead at the time.'

'Not quite. I gather she died on Sunday night.'

'Are we going to say all this at Tristan's lunch? Flinging wild accusations about, based on what we think people might know about plants? A good way to win friends, I don't think.'

'Might be fun, though.' He yawned. 'Roll on bedtime, I say. We got less than four hours' sleep.'

'First we've got to go and be sociable, heaven help us. I feel as if a steamroller just ran over me.'

'A bit of fresh air will put you right,' he said with forced confidence.

Ten o'clock came and went, and once again they were left with nothing to do. 'We ought to make some sort of effort to attract visitors,' said Angie, with scant enthusiasm. 'I suppose I could have another go at Facebook.' Several years ago, she had allowed herself to be persuaded by Simmy that it would be a good idea to establish a 'presence' on the Internet. But her Facebook page had always been a pathetic shadow of what Simmy had envisaged, and Angie had not updated it for at least eighteen months. Instead she relied on Booking.com and word of mouth. She was vaguely aware that Twitter existed, and that numerous guests recommended Beck View via that medium, but provided no input of her own. The demand for accommodation in Windermere was such that she rarely saw any need to advertise.

Now there was still a scattering of bookings over the coming weeks, at least. There was no real cause for panic in the long term. Memories were short and habit a powerful force. At least half of her guests were repeaters, coming back year after year, as Grant Childers had been with Candy Proctor.

That thought gave her sudden pause. 'You know what,' she said, 'I can't help thinking it's odd that Candy hadn't got Childers safely booked in ages ago? I mean, if he came up here two or three times a year, wouldn't he book ahead, from one time to the next? That's what people do, when they know how busy it gets. What if she deliberately shunted him onto us for some reason?'

Russell blinked. 'Why would she?'

'I don't know, do I? Maybe she disliked him and couldn't stand another visit from him. Maybe it's more sinister than that. If there was a careful plan to kill him, it would throw suspicion off her if he was staying somewhere else. It could be that this has all been thought through for months, in every detail.'

'Candy's no murderer,' said Russell. 'And what possible motive could she have? What's more,' he went on with increasing energy, 'if this has got something to do with that new holiday park, it couldn't have been planned far in advance.'

'That's what I mean. You forget that it was six weeks ago that Childers booked with us, and they'd planned the meeting then. That's *ages* ago.'

'I did forget that, I admit. It's not really so strange, though, is it? Planning business moves incredibly slowly. It might have been sitting on somebody's desk for months.'

'You're back to believing there really are some plans, then?'

He scratched his head. 'I don't know. Bonnie asked about it and got an extremely vague reply. She thinks it's nothing more than a rumour, with no basis in fact at all.'

'But they called that meeting. Why would they do that? They must have something to go on.'

'I intend to ask them about it over the cold collation, actually. We can ask Candy about the booking as well. All the main players are going to be there. The topic is sure to arise. In fact, I suspect that's the whole point of the exercise. They'll want to ram home to us the point that they only stood to lose by Childers dying.'

Angie drooped. 'I just know it's going to be awful. I hope they'll give us somewhere to sit. My legs are all wobbly.'

'I prescribe a gentle walk down the hill, along with the fresh air. And of course there'll be somewhere to sit. It's not a garden party.'

'Isn't it?'

'Even if it is, there'll be seats.'

'It's at least a mile from here,' she complained.

'Downhill.'

'What about coming back?'

'We can catch the bus. Somebody might drive us. We can get nicely tipsy and leave that in the lap of the gods.'

'You've got an answer for everything,' she accused him.

They washed up the few breakfast plates, and Russell went outside with his dog for half an hour. Only five years earlier, the animal would have been dashing himself against the trees at the bottom of the garden in an effort to catch a grey squirrel. It had been an ideal way of exercising, with Russell urging him on. Now the squirrels had almost gone, exterminated by purists who insisted the red version should be given its rightful land back. Russell had regularly remarked on the politics of wildlife conservation, and how it seemed to involve as much destruction as it did protection. 'I like grey squirrels,' he would say, until such a statement became too dangerous to utter aloud.

Back indoors, he found Angie on the sofa, doing nothing.

'I'm thinking,' she defended. 'I still don't understand what this lunch thing is all about.'

'I was thinking as well. I suppose it's just that they all feel under a cloud, with the murder investigation going on all around them. So they want to show solidarity with us, and make us see what fine fellows they all are.'

'Hm.'

'They might even be feeling sorry for us, being landed with a murder victim and having all the bookings cancelled. Perhaps they've got our daughter's interests at heart and they want to help with finding a place in Patterdale. After all, these people are our *friends*. Especially Stuart. He's got quite a thing for you, remember.'

Angie smiled. 'I am quite fond of Stuart, actually. I do hope he doesn't turn out to be a murderer. Like you with Candy. But that leaves Tristan and he's far too bombastic to kill anybody. He'd be much too worried about being caught and losing his reputation.'

'That's true of everybody, really. The prospect of being

arrested for murder is more than enough to stop us all from committing the act.'

'With a few notable exceptions,' said Angie. 'I'm referring to the various killers Persimmon has run into since she's come to live up here.'

'They all expected to get away with it.'

'Well, I just hope nothing awful happens during lunch. I can't cope with anything else. If it were up to me, I'd insist we only talk about roses and babies. And Patterdale, if we stick to the chances of Persimmon and Christopher finding somewhere to live there.' She sighed. 'But it won't be up to me, will it?'

'It's hard to imagine them staying off the subject of Childers, I must admit. But we can try, if that's what you want. Or at least keep things vague. We can say the police have asked us not to discuss details. A bit of a fib, but it will serve the purpose. That's always a useful line to take with anyone who gets too inquisitive.' He grinned and rubbed his hands together. 'I don't know about you, but I'm rather looking forward to it. It'll make a very nice change.'

'It feels like an awful effort, to be honest. If it gets too much for me, I'll pretend to be having a panic attack, shall I? Nobody's going to be very surprised by that.'

He gave her a sceptical look. 'Since when has anything been too much for you?'

'Since about two o'clock this morning, if you remember. You practically had to talk me down from the ceiling.'

'Oh pooh!' he scoffed. 'That was all just a bad dream. Put it out of your mind. That's what I'm going to do.'

'Hm,' was all Angie said to that.

Only then did Russell catch up with the conversation between Angie and Simmy. 'Are we really not providing lunch for the young people tomorrow?' he asked.

'What? Oh – no, we're definitely going to them. She's going to cook a piece of pork, by all accounts. Has that ever happened before?'

'Once or twice when she was married to Tony. And she did that little housewarming do, when she first moved up here. But I don't remember an actual Sunday lunch with a roast. I'm looking forward to it already.'

'And she didn't like the house.'

'Ah. That's a shame. What's wrong with it?'

'Dark, apparently, and not enough garden. She's thinking of the child, of course. I wonder whether they'll manage more than one,' Angie mused, with a faraway look. 'Hard to imagine after all this time.'

'Not for me. I can see the whole thing. You hear of women having their first at forty and ending up with three. If that happens—'

'Stop it. I suppose you think we'll be doing the school run and helping with homework when we're eighty.'

'I really can't see why not,' said Russell stubbornly. They both knew he was envisaging a belated revenge on his wife for vetoing any further babies after Simmy. If he'd had his way, there'd have been five, to match the Henderson family. Russell had always envied the Hendersons.

'She went to see the spot where that holiday park might be – as far as she could work out the exact location. There's a fairly level field close to the football pitch that looks ripe for development, given a hefty dose of imagination. We could mention that to Tristan over lunch.'

'Indeed,' said Russell, wondering whether he really had the stamina for a lot of conversation and social interaction, not just today, but tomorrow as well.

Chapter Nineteen

In sharp contrast to her parents, Simmy woke at dawn, with a stiff neck from the awkward position she'd been forced into to accommodate Christopher in her inadequate bed. Many more months of this, and the bulk of the unborn baby would ensure that one of them would have to decamp to the spare room. In point of fact, the bed had never been big enough to provide a good night's sleep for two people, however intimately entwined they might be.

'Urghh,' she said. 'We can't go on like this.'

Christopher was still asleep and made no response. She poked him to rectify this imbalance. He made a noise like a Herdwick sheep shaking its wet fleece, a sort of flurrying flight into wakefulness from some distant realm. Simmy felt remorseful. 'Sorry,' she said. 'I didn't realise you were so deeply asleep.'

'What's the matter?'

'Nothing, really. I've got a stiff neck. It's morning.'

'I don't believe you. It looks dark to me.'

'It's half past seven. I want a mug of tea. And we have to plan the day. I can't justify asking Bonnie and Tanya to run the shop if I'm just going to slob about doing nothing.'

'You've got a very outdated work ethic,' he grumbled. 'And surely the girls aren't going to be at the shop for ages yet. What – half past nine? You needn't start worrying about them until then.'

'Stop being so logical. There's a whole lot we've got to do.' She rubbed his bare shoulder affectionately. 'Am I being awful? I'm hungry, for one thing, and I just feel we ought to get up and start doing some jobs.'

'Only a bit awful. You might be right about the jobs, although I can't imagine what they are. As far as I can see, we've got an entire weekend free of obligations. We could even drop in on one of my sisters this afternoon. And tomorrow we could go to a car boot sale. The season's only got a week or two left. I never get to go to as many as I'd like.'

'That sounds fine,' said Simmy, unable to come up with any objections, apart from a vague reluctance to follow either of these suggestions. Whatever she and Christopher decided to do was going to feel self-indulgent and irrelevant to the central issue. An issue that her fiancé seemed intent on ignoring. He had made it very clear that he was not going to discuss murder, nor share in the brainstorming and hypothesising that Simmy, Bonnie and Ben had become so accustomed to. This time there was no Ben; instead Russell and Angie Straw were directly affected, and that inevitably meant that Simmy was too. DI Moxon evidently thought the same. 'Although we'll both have to spend some time with my parents tomorrow. They're beginning to think you're avoiding them.'

'Hardly. When have I had a chance to see them? Everything's always so hectic.'

This did not strike Simmy as an entirely accurate statement. Once the fortnightly Saturday auction was over, Christopher usually had to make an appearance on the Sunday, with people coming to collect large purchases and argue over mislaid items. Then he would meet up with Simmy later in the day. None of this justified the word *hectic* to Simmy's mind. The intervening weekends, like this one, were admittedly busier, with shopping and eating and walking and house-hunting to be fitted in. But even they were hardly hectic.

'I'll phone them in a bit. Without any guests, they might not be up yet. I'm not sure how we left it last night – I was in rather a rush.'

It was half past eight before Christopher joined her for a modest breakfast. Her early morning hunger had been partly assuaged by some toast, but now she had some more, with orange juice and yoghurt for good measure. The growing baby seemed to be stealing more than its share of the calories she consumed, and various cravings were assailing her. Sausage rolls, avocados and anything containing large chunks of meat were her particular favourites. There was a growing shopping list awaiting execution. 'First job is a shopping trip,' she announced. 'There's hardly any food in the house after last night. I'm surprised I didn't get indigestion, eating so much so late. I was ravenous.'

'Where do people go to shop from Patterdale, I wonder?' he said. 'It's a long way from anywhere with a supermarket.'

'They probably do it online. I keep meaning to set that up here, actually. It's even quite a trek from Troutbeck.'

'We could do it now. You can have all the sausage rolls you can eat, without having to carry them into the house. And it's always bedlam in the supermarket at weekends.'

She could think of no reason to resist and was content to let him loose on her computer, only providing occasional suggestions as he activated the delivery service. It turned out they could not be provided with a delivery that day, which left the original plan of doing their own shopping the only option. This, Simmy reminded herself, was how being a couple was meant to go. Sharing, bickering, dreaming and wasting time in deciding the next course of action. Being quiet together sometimes, before girding up to go out into the world side by side. It was all soothingly normal. Why then did she still feel that they were being inefficient? More than that – they were guilty of selfishness and neglect of what really mattered. Somewhere there was a murderer who very probably felt he or she had got away with the ultimate crime. Unless Moxon had been very economical with what he told her, it seemed that the police were at a loss. There were too many variables, too many unknowns. Where, when, how, why – the questions were legion. The 'Why?' one stood out as the most important. Why on earth should poor Grant Childers, meek-mannered Midlands bachelor who loved the Lake District, find himself innocently consuming poison on an ordinary Sunday morning in Windermere? Hadn't he asked the very same question himself, seconds before he died? *Why* was he dead? What possible reason could there be?

Finally, it was time to call Beck View. Russell answered, but before they'd managed to say much, he was summoned to the landline. Simmy was handed over to her mother, who admitted she had only just got out of bed. The Sunday pork roast occupied much of the conversation, with the unusual decision to eat in the Troutbeck cottage causing some amusement on both sides. 'Don't forget the apple sauce,' said Angie. 'I'll bring you some bacon and sausages, to compensate.'

It occurred to Simmy that she had not purchased an actual joint of meat in a shop since the early years of her marriage to Tony. Christmas turkey didn't count, and there had been a one-off arrangement with a group of Troutbeck residents, whereby a whole sheep had been shared. Its owner specialised in old-fashioned mutton, persuading his neighbours to take various cuts at discount prices. Simmy had ended up with a shoulder, which she had undercooked and found remarkably tough. The enterprise had faded away before the procedure could be repeated.

The day was decidedly autumnal. While the trees still retained their leaves, the colours were changing daily, and there was a bite in the air. Simmy's thin jeans were not adequate for the temperature outside and she went upstairs to find a thicker pair, forgetting that her new shape would require some adaptation of her usual wardrobe. 'I can't find any trousers to fit me,' she wailed, after frantically rooting through the drawers. 'Even the stretchy ones are too tight.'

Christopher came for a look. 'Better go and buy some more, then,' he said. 'Unless you want to borrow something from Hannah or Lynn. They might still have a few maternity things.'

The idea was not appealing. Her baby would have

numerous cousins on its father's side, and that was a good thing. There would be toys and equipment to spare. But clothes were different. 'Surely they'll have thrown everything out by now? Lynn's youngest is four, and it doesn't look as if she's planning any more. Hannah's are a lot older.'

'Well, it was just a thought. They're really excited about this new baby, you know. They love being aunties.'

'They've had plenty of practice. I'd have thought one more would seem fairly mundane.'

'You don't understand about families,' he said, with a whiff of regret. 'You never really did. All those years ago, on the seaside holidays, you couldn't quite grasp how it worked.'

'I know. And this poor child is likely to be almost as deprived, unless we can manage a sibling.'

'One step at a time,' said Christopher, with a look of alarm. 'Things are complicated enough as it is.'

'There are lots of positives to being an only,' she went on, hardly hearing him. 'Life is wonderfully peaceful, for a start. And you get all that top-quality attention.'

'We're not going to be helicopter parents,' he warned her. 'This kid is going to climb trees and fall into freezing becks and get chased by angry rams. And I'm not paying for violin lessons. I hate violins.'

'We'll have the social services after us.'

'No, we'll have that Corinne woman cheering us on.' He had only met Corinne once for a few minutes, but had recognised a kindred spirit within seconds. 'We can go to her for moral support.'

Simmy had changed back into her summer jeans, with

a pair of tights underneath. The tights only came up to her hips and were uncomfortable. 'I hate clothes,' she grumbled.

Christopher laughed, relentlessly mocking her sour temper, refusing to take it personally. 'You need a big sheepskin cape to huddle into. With the woolly side in. Very *Game of Thrones*, that would be.'

She smiled, grateful for his forbearance, but still feeling jaded. 'Maybe there'll be one in the next auction.'

'Sadly, I don't think they exist, but there's often a full-length mink coat going for ten quid. Come and bid for one of those instead.'

Banter was something Christopher did well. His ironic wit always cheered her, reminding her that he had lived a full and unconventional life thus far, and regarded rules as something to be taken lightly. The more she got to know him, the more similarities to her mother she discovered. She could see that her own tendency to conformity needed just such a balance. There was a permanent subtle challenge just below the surface of his words, urging her to take more risks, broaden her horizons. She hoped it wouldn't eventually exhaust him and turn him bitter, if she failed to respond as he wanted.

'I'm still feeling sorry about the house,' she said. 'Rejecting it so quickly. You probably think we could have made enough alterations for it to be perfectly all right for us.'

'I told you – I would have taken it if you'd liked it, but I can't say I fell in love with it. I'd like a bit more character, and higher ceilings.'

'Maybe we should try harder to make the building plot work. You could have your high ceilings, and I could have my big windows. But there must be pages of restrictions and requirements, to fit with the local vernacular. Real stone, for a start, which must cost a fortune.'

'"Local vernacular",' he repeated. 'Get you.'

'No, get my dad. He loves words like that. He'd probably want to design the house for us, based on Brantwood or somewhere.'

'He'd have to find the million quid to pay for it, then. Besides, it would never work in Hartsop. Brantwood would be nothing without the lake to reflect itself in.'

'Ben would say we've missed the moment. Born in the wrong century. All those huge houses that middle-class entrepreneurs built for themselves. You could have made a vast empire out of the auctions, selling oil paintings and porcelain or something, and we'd end up living in somewhere like Storrs. With columns and porticoes and fabulous dormer windows in the attic.'

'Storrs?'

'Just south of Bowness. It's a hotel now. And I'm not sure about the windows. I think the money to build it came from the slave trade.'

'There's always a catch, even in the nineteenth century. And the Victorians weren't very keen on antiques. They wanted new stuff, imported from Japan and India.'

'You could have done that, then. I'm sure it was all so much easier in those days.'

'Hey – it's nearly half past ten. We're wasting the day, which I thought you were determined not to do.'

'At least I haven't been agonising about Bonnie coping with the shop.'

'True. So, this is the plan. Shopping first, then lunch

242

somewhere, then up to see Lynn, then home for a movie. Right?'

She blinked at this sudden onset of efficiency and authority. Something snagged. 'Does Lynn know we're coming? Have you said something to her, without telling me?'

'Nothing definite, but she wants to talk to you about babies and indigestion. Heartburn. Cravings. That sort of thing.'

Lynn was the youngest in the Henderson family, and had two little girls. She and her sister, Hannah, had been adopted as small children by Christopher's parents, who already had three boys. To her own subsequent disbelief and embarrassment, Simmy had unquestioningly accepted the sudden appearance of these young sisters as entirely straightforward natural acquisitions. They had appeared suddenly on one of the annual joint seaside holidays when she was about eight, and it never occurred to her to wonder how it had happened. The whole complicated history that existed between the Straws and the Hendersons centred around Simmy and Christopher, born on the same day, but who had spent more than half their lives apart, scarcely even thinking of each other. His parents were now dead, under extremely painful circumstances. The facts around his father's demise were still causing unease.

'I don't get heartburn,' she said. 'And I don't really want to talk about babies.'

'Don't be stuffy. She wants to be friends, that's all. The whole family's thrilled about the baby.'

Simmy had forbidden him from revealing the news to his siblings until she was well past three months in the pregnancy, something he thought unfair since Angie and Russell had known from the start. Now he was eager to make up for the lost time and ensure that the new

Henderson would be fully embraced by one and all.

'I know. It's just . . . there seem to be more important things to think about at the moment. Houses, for a start. And money, my parents, the shop.' She grimaced. 'We can't just dither about, not getting anything settled.'

'Money?' He cocked an eyebrow at her. 'What about money?'

'I keep telling you – if I put the shop in mothballs, or whatever they call it, while the baby's small, I won't have any income. You'd have to pay for everything. And until you sit down with pen and paper to do the sums with me, I'm not convinced we can manage.'

He sighed. 'You don't have to worry. Worst case scenario is I move in here and the three of us can live as cheaply as one. We've *got* a house, after all, it's just not terribly convenient. Other people survive in much worse situations than this. I could easily pay your mortgage here, for as long as you like. It's hardly any more than the rent I'm paying now.'

She was saved by the telephone from going round the same old circle yet again. 'It's Bonnie,' she said, with an alarming sense of relief. To be summoned to the shop to deal with some sort of minor crisis would rescue her from the sense of being stuck in a loop with Christopher where nothing was ever decided and time passed while they went round and round, getting nowhere.

'Hey, Bonnie. Everything all right?'

'Don't panic. There's no problem. Just that we can't find that box of oasis. Tanya's doing a little display for the window and she needs it. I told her to improvise, but she says that won't work. It's looking nice, actually. You'll like it.'

'I used it all up on the wedding thing yesterday. I had to pack masses of it in to keep those hollyhocks upright. I forgot to order any more.'

'Oh. Pity. I've heard from Ben, by the way. It's all going to plan. I can spend all tomorrow with him.'

This, Simmy suspected, was the real reason for the call. Bonnie's excitement was spilling over, and she had to share it. Tanya, as Ben's sister, would be unlikely to appreciate the depth of the older girl's emotion. And Bonnie had no real friends of her own age.

'That'll be lovely,' said Simmy 'Just don't talk to him about murder.'

Bonnie laughed. 'Tanya's determined to have it all solved by the end of today, though I can't imagine how. She keeps having crazy ideas about it, something different every time. Her latest is all about infusing the seeds of the datura plant, and making such a concentrated poison out of it that just a few drops would be enough to kill someone. She's good at chemistry, would you believe? So she understands about stuff like distillation. Doesn't make much sense to me.'

'It all sounds very clever,' said Simmy doubtfully. 'Unless she actually tries it for herself. That might turn dangerous. Does she know where to get the seeds?'

'Luckily, no. It's all theory at the moment. She has found a few more snippets on the Internet, but not enough to worry anybody.'

'That's a relief. If it's not busy you can go home a bit early, you know. You must want to—' She bit back the rest of the sentence, but Bonnie heard it anyway.

'You were going to say I must want to get myself ready

for seeing Ben,' she accused. 'Like what? Wash my hair? Paint my toenails?'

'Sorry. I forgot who I was talking to for a minute. I don't do any of that stuff for Christopher, so I have no idea why I should think it appropriate for you.'

'Right.' Bonnie laughed cheerily and changed the subject. 'It would be great, though, wouldn't it, if the murder was all sorted today, and then we could tell Ben the whole story and he wouldn't be distracted by thinking he had to be a detective again, and he wouldn't be cross that I hadn't told him about it.' The girl was evidently regretting the drastic change from earlier times when she and Ben had thrown themselves into murder investigations to the exclusion of almost all else.

'Tanya would be off the hook as well,' said Simmy.

'That's the thing. She's hogging all the research to herself. All that stuff Ben and I always did together. She hasn't explained it very well to me, even though she keeps showing me pictures on her phone. The datura flowers look nice. But I'll never understand all the science side of it. I mean – what's distillation anyway?'

'Don't ask me. It sounds like what they do to make whisky in illegal stills.'

'That's exactly it,' said Bonnie. 'And she keeps talking about *Breaking Bad*. I think she's too young to watch that, don't you?'

'I have no idea,' said Simmy, feeling too old for such issues. Then she remembered that she would one day have her own teenager who would watch unsuitable material and have to be monitored by parents who were in their fifties and struggling to maintain a footing in a world she could not at that moment even imagine. She tried to focus on what Bonnie had been saying, something niggling at her. Suddenly she got it. 'You know – I've seen a datura flower just recently. Devil's trumpet. It was in one of Miss Entwhistle's funeral tributes.'

'Sorry. Gotta go,' said the girl. 'There's a customer.'

Chapter Twenty

'What was all that about?' Christopher wanted to know. 'Whisky and devil's trumpets? Sounds like a film by that Spanish chap.'

'You don't want to know. It's about murder and poison, and things you prefer not to think about.'

He flushed. 'That makes me sound awful. If it concerns you, it concerns me. Isn't that the way it works? I was hoping the cops would have solved it all by now. It's a week ago, isn't it? Every contact leaves a trace, and all that stuff. Of course, without Ben Harkness, they must be very handicapped.'

'Don't start on Ben. It'll be a week tomorrow since it happened. And there isn't any contact when the killer uses poison, is there? That's the main point, I assume. It's much easier to get away with it, because there won't be any forensic evidence. It's probably a good thing Ben isn't here. He'd find it very frustrating.'

'Right. Except the actual toxin used must be traceable, surely? That's evidence.'

She looked at him in surprise. 'You sound as if you've thought about it.'

'Not really. I used to read a lot of Jeffery Deaver. His detective could tell you where the poisonous plant had been grown, and how it had been delivered. Believe it or not, I used to find all that stuff quite exciting. But then it all got too close for comfort when my dad died and I lost my appetite for it. And poison seems weirdly old-fashioned now. Which is odd, when you think about it. Maybe nobody has the brains any more to plan a really good murder. They just stab and slash and shoot.'

'This one certainly must have been well planned,' she agreed. 'Last I heard, they still didn't know how he was actually persuaded to take whatever it was. Bonnie and Tanya have been trying to find out how poisonous berries or seeds can be processed to make them effective. The Internet is very shy about going into detail, apparently.'

'There's a surprise,' said Christopher, not entirely sarcastically. 'I would have thought you could get complete instructions on how to make a lethal concoction, if you search hard enough.'

This sudden interest from him made Simmy ridiculously happy. She had resigned herself to shouldering the trauma and worry arising from the murder all by herself. She would have to deal with her parents and Moxon and all the unpredictable variety of people who dropped into the shop to talk about it. Now, perhaps, she could dump at least some of it into her fiancé's lap and let him try to sift through it. 'I've never heard of Jeffery Deaver,' she said.

'You have. I was there once when Ben mentioned his books. You just don't remember names very well.'

'Don't I?' This felt like an unfair accusation. 'I remember the names of my customers, and your sisters' children. And your brothers', come to that.'

He laughed at her. 'Stick to the point, woman. What was that about devil's trumpets?'

'It's a plant called datura. Moxon mentioned it right at the start as a likely source of the poison. There's a family of plants that all produce similar toxins, but I think the police are sure now that it was datura. I still don't know exactly what it does to a person – what it is that actually kills you. We don't know where Mr Childers went, or when, the day before he died. He knew lots of people up here and was scheduled to speak at a meeting on Thursday. He seems to have gone on the lake cruise from Bowness on Sunday. Rightly or wrongly, there's an assumption that whoever killed him did it to stop him delivering his speech. Last I heard, anyway. The police have shown the speech to my dad, apparently. I ought to ask him what it says.'

'Stop, stop,' begged Christopher. 'I realise I've got a lot of catching up to do, but don't blind me with details. Do you sell these trumpet things in the shop?'

'No, I don't. But I've seen some recently. It came back to me when I was driving back from Patterdale last night, which is why I went to the churchyard to see if I could find them on the grave. I saw them at the undertaker's in the morning, but didn't have time for a proper look. It was one of the wreaths for Dorothea Entwhistle. There were masses of them. They had to use a second car for them.'

He flapped a hand at her. 'Slow down,' he said.

But she couldn't stop, now the full significance was

getting through to her. 'It had been nagging at me since yesterday morning. There was so much else to think about, I never made the connection properly. Not that it gets us anywhere, I suppose.'

'It might. If you could find out where they came from, you might at least help the police make a comparison – or something.'

She was enchanted by his sudden involvement. Until now, it had always been a struggle to get him to accept Ben and Bonnie as part of a package with her. Even when he discovered a body in Grasmere, finding himself under close police scrutiny, he resisted the youngsters' efforts to share in the experience. It was that, Simmy guessed, that had made him so slow to admit that this was something that might well occur again, and that he had little choice but to take an interest. His automatic inclination to look away and pretend it wasn't happening was never going to work. Perhaps at least he had come to understand that.

'I don't know where they came from,' she sighed. 'I remember noticing the bouquet was home-made, and signed by someone just with a nickname, which I can't now remember. It was just a couple of seconds, and I was looking at all the wreaths, not just that one. A whole shelf ful, or more. Bob made me move before I could have a really good look.'

'So did you find it on the grave?'

'No – there were only a handful of wreaths left, and it was very dark, as you said. The rest were all taken to nursing homes and places like that. The vicar must have said he didn't want a great mound of them slowly rotting away in his nice tidy churchyard.'

'But they're *poisonous*,' he protested.

She smiled. 'I doubt if anybody's going to eat them. If I remember rightly, they wilt quite quickly. They'll just go into a compost bin somewhere and never be seen again.'

'It's only yesterday,' he said, suddenly urgent. 'You should tell your policeman chum and he can track them down. What do they look like?'

'White. Not as trumpety as daffodils. More like big convolvulus, really. You know – bindweed. They're rather lovely, although they grow bigger and better in hotter countries.' She paused. 'I didn't know I knew all that.'

'They'd grow all right in a greenhouse, I suppose?'

She stared at him. 'That's right. You're sparking off all sorts of murky ideas that I've had floating around my head all week, and I never linked them together. I've been such a ditz lately.'

He clearly knew better than to comment on this. 'So – are we going shopping, then?'

'We've got no choice, as we're catering for visitors. Joint of pork, vegetables, drink. I've forgotten how to do it.'

'I like being hospitable. I'm already looking forward to our housewarming party in Patterdale.'

Wary of being called *stuffy* again, she smiled. 'You think it'll really happen then, do you?'

'How can it not? I've always believed in autonomy and willpower and all that. Making your own destiny, and taking charge.'

'Not like me,' she said, on a sudden insight. 'I just let it all happen around me. I'm being a drag on you, aren't I? If it was up to you, you'd be knocking on every door up there and offering to buy the house whether or not it was for sale.'

'It might yet come to that,' he warned. 'You're not a drag – just a useful counterbalance. Now, unless you want to rush off and share your thoughts with the Moxon man, I suggest we get on with our programme.'

She wrinkled her brow. 'I ought to phone him,' she worried. 'But I suppose it can wait a little while. Maybe I can do it in the car, on the way to the shops.'

Christopher drove them northwards, without consultation. The biggest shopping centre was Keswick, about sixteen miles distant, the route not only running through Patterdale, but also passing via the 'other' Troutbeck. The fact there were two settlements carrying the same name, both on the A5091 had caused Simmy and her friends great confusion when she had first moved to the Lakes. Her cottage was in the larger version, which was the default destination of satnavs and anyone living in the southern reaches of the area. Driving through the smaller one always gave her a shock. *How did we get here?* she would wonder, on seeing the name on the sign.

She tried to phone Moxon once they were on the A66, but could only get voicemail. She left a message saying she had something to tell him, but didn't expect it was of any great importance. 'Well, I've done my civic duty,' she said, putting the phone away.

The shop was busy, but they made a game of it, blithely throwing cakes and soups into the trolley as if feeding ten people rather than four. 'We don't do it very often – we have to give them a feast,' said Christopher. Simmy laughed and hoped he was intending to pay for it all.

It felt inefficient to be going all the way up to Keswick –
a town Simmy had still not properly explored. 'Where are
we going from here?' she asked. They had not stopped in
Patterdale, which struck her as strange. 'No time,' Christopher
had said, quite rightly. But they had slowed down when
passing the house they had looked at the previous evening. 'It
is very dark,' he conceded. 'On the outside as well as in.' The
grey stonework was quite usual for the area, but somehow
this particular house had an extra level of shadow. The two
Patterdale pubs were painted white, and many buildings
had decoration around the windows. In contrast, this was a
gloomy-looking building.

'It's dour,' said Simmy, giving the word two long syllables.

The road meandered up to the dramatic modern
slash of the A66, and Simmy found herself trying to give
Christopher a more comprehensive résumé of the story
concerning Tristan Wilkins and his fellow protesters. She
reminded him of the bumpy little field, which was said to
be earmarked for development. He shook his head. 'As
Robin said last night, there's no way they would allow a
load of new chalets. The idea's ludicrous.'

'Well, in that case, there's something extremely odd
about the whole thing. There has been from the start.'

'Are you thinking it's connected with the murder of
your parents' B&B guest?'

'I think it must be,' she said.

Having accomplished their shopping, Christopher
announced that they were going to return by the A591,
lunching at one of his favourite pubs just north of Grasmere.
'The Traveller's Rest is calling me,' he joked.

She was quite content to let him have his way. The day was still rose-tinted with everything between them so harmonious that nothing seemed to matter very much. 'But aren't we going to see Lynn?' she remembered. 'That's back the other way, isn't it?' His sister lived a little way east of Penrith. 'We'll be driving round in circles at this rate.'

'We've got to get this meat and stuff put away first,' he pointed out. 'Lucky we didn't buy anything frozen, but we still can't carry it round in the car all day.'

She sat back and let him take charge, despite a suspicion that his itinerary was clumsy if not downright inefficient. The food would have to sit in the car while they had lunch, after all – which was not something she felt should worry them. 'Okay,' she said, with a small shake of her head. 'I'm sure you know what you're doing.'

To her surprise, he bridled. 'Why? Have I got it wrong?'

'No, no. Forget I spoke. It's lovely to have such a nice, relaxed day with you. Everything so ordinary and domestic – it makes a very pleasant change.'

'Except it doesn't, does it? Not really. You're thinking about poison and where on earth we're going to be living this time next year, and I'm wondering whether Josephine is going to be back at work next week and how much the reserve should be on a pair of Japanese vases. Neither of us can focus for long on roast pork or maternity trousers.'

'It won't hurt us to try,' she persisted. 'And it's all part of the same picture, really. Except the poison,' she added sadly. 'That doesn't fit at all. That's the thing about murder, isn't it? The way it chops through normal life, and overturns everything you were taking for granted. That poor man, who nobody seemed to be very bothered about when he was alive, just a very quiet, normal chap, with his routines and his hobbies. Why in the world would anybody go to such lengths to kill him? It's frightening because it seems so senseless.' She paused. 'Oh dear – that wasn't supposed to come out today, was it? Sorry about that.'

Christopher laughed. 'We're almost at the pub. Let's see if we can at least concentrate on something that's about *us*. Like finding a house, or choosing baby names. Just for a little while?'

'We can try,' she said.

It came as a relief to find that there was nobody they knew in The Traveller's Rest. Grasmere had initially been their favoured location to live, being neatly situated between their places of work, but they quickly discovered that it was not only a dauntingly popular spot for tourists, rendering daily life for anybody not involved in 'hospitality' somewhat peculiar, it was also expensive. The handful of properties not already modified for the use of visitors were quickly snatched up the moment they became available. Simmy and Christopher had almost immediately dismissed it as unviable. The fact that he had also found himself much too close to a murder there clinched the decision.

The pub was not in the village itself, but on the main road. It had obviously been a coaching inn, offering a change of horses and a much-needed rest for anyone travelling long distances on bumpy roads, two or three centuries ago. There were fields behind it, scattered with shaggy Herdwick ewes. Simmy remembered stopping here several years ago with her father, when she had still lived in Worcester and had come for a visit.

Making a game of it, she and Christopher carefully chose their food and drink, discussing calorific values and optimum balance of protein and vitamins. 'The real joke,' said Chris, 'is that neither of us actually cares very much about food.'

'Well, perhaps we should,' she said primly. 'After all, everybody else in the country seems to.'

'It's decadent,' he stated flatly. 'When you've seen people living on the same narrow range of choices, most of it stuff they've grown themselves, with meat a rare luxury, you feel a bit sick in a supermarket. I'm not pretending I feel like that all the time, but it comes over me now and then. And nobody would willingly opt to exist on the incredibly dreary diet they've got in places like Rajasthan, but I definitely think you and I have got it right. Eat to live, not live to eat.'

'I always get that one confused,' she laughed. 'But I know what you mean.'

The mood lasted a delicious fifteen minutes, before Simmy's treacherous mind began to draw connections between the lavish salad she had ordered, containing avocados, prawns, nuts, rocket and pulses and the toxic plant material that the wretched Grant Childers had unwittingly swallowed. She looked down at her plate, focusing on the scattering of seeds covering everything. She ran through one more time the way everyone had been so instantly certain that his death had really been murder. It had been that single word *Why?* that had clinched it. As Angie had said, nobody who was intent on self-destruction would utter that particular word. However much they might all wish it had been an allergy or an accident, neither theory could be made to work.

Christopher was watching her face. 'You're thinking about poison again, aren't you?' he accused.

'A bit,' she admitted. 'I was thinking maybe it had been an allergic reaction all along. But I can see that won't work. Sorry.'

'Don't apologise. We did our best to ignore it, and we've failed miserably. But I can't see how we can do anything about it, however much we might want to. You can tell Moxon about seeing those funeral flowers. That might be a brilliant clue – but *you* can't follow it up, can you? That's down to him.'

She grimaced. 'I doubt if Ben would agree with you.'

'So what do you think he would do about it?'

She gave it some thought. 'Good question. He'd probably try to get a list of all the people who sent flowers for Miss Entwhistle. Except the undertaker wouldn't tell him. The police would have to do that.'

'What else?'

'He'd go back to the start and find out all he could about Grant Childers. Not just who knew him and what his family think about him being murdered, but what sort of person he was.'

'How would he manage that?'

'I don't suppose he would.' She sighed. 'Thanks. You're being very patient with me.'

'Not at all. I'm only now starting to understand why this matters so much.'

'Oh?' She ate a large, succulent prawn, followed by two leaves of rocket that she picked up in her fingers. 'Isn't that obvious? I was there when the man died. So was my mother.'

'Yes, I know. I mean, in general. All those other murders, most of them tangled up with your flowers in one way or another. You take it personally. And that Moxon man exploits you because of it. Even without Ben, you're useful to him. And with the police showing such dreadful success levels, they need all the help they can get.'

'We're not doing as badly as all that,' came a female voice from behind Simmy.

Chapter Twenty-One

There was a woman sitting alone at a table in the window. She was in her early thirties and had straight light-brown hair tied back from her face, which was long and narrow. Her eyes were a shade of blue-grey that matched the baggy jumper she was wearing. Simmy knew she had seen her before, and concluded from her words that she was a police officer. Probably a detective. 'I know!' she crowed, after fifteen seconds. 'You came to Beck View last Sunday. I only spoke to you for a minute, didn't I? I can't remember your name.'

'Emily Gibson. Detective Sergeant. I'm impressed you remember me at all.'

Simmy nodded. 'I don't expect I'll forget that day for quite a while. This is Christopher, my fiancé. He lives in Keswick.'

DS Gibson acknowledged the introduction with a brief flicker. 'I'm sorry I listened to what you were saying. It wasn't until I heard the name "Moxon" that I really took any notice. You had your back to me – I didn't realise who you were until then.'

Simmy waved away the apology with a smile. 'It's nice to see you,' she said, in all sincerity. Even the soft snort from Christopher did nothing to change how she felt. 'I left a message for Inspector Moxon just now.'

'So I gather. Was it something important?'

Simmy looked around at the other customers. Nobody seemed to be listening, but she was hesitant about discussing a police investigation in public. Why didn't this Gibson person feel the same? 'Come and sit with us,' she said.

Christopher snorted again, more loudly. 'That's all right, isn't it?' Simmy asked him. 'Just for a few minutes?'

'Be my guest,' he said, with a flap of his hand. 'I'll just finish my delicious steak and let you two talk about poison.'

With a sinking heart, Simmy recognised the man of earlier times, resistant to her involvement with the forces of the law and the unpredictable violence of those who committed murder. Had his apparent interest all been an act, then? Was he merely humouring her? She saw Gibson observing them both with those blue-grey eyes. They were her best feature by a long way. Her nose was too thin and her chin too prominent for anything approaching beauty – but her eyes were lovely. Full of intelligence and good temper, they would earn anybody's trust.

The change of seat was smoothly accomplished, and the conversation resumed. 'Well, the thing is,' Simmy began, 'I remembered seeing a rather odd home-made wreath for Miss Entwhistle's funeral yesterday, made from datura flowers. At least, I'm reasonably sure that's what they were.

I was delivering tributes at the undertaker's, and had a look at all the others. Professional curiosity, if you like. There was this home-made one that caught my eye. The flowers must have been grown under glass, I think. There were six or eight of them on a bed of moss. It was nicely done, but obviously not by any florist.'

'Who were they from?'

'That's where I get stuck. It was a nickname that I'd never come across before. And I can't remember what it was. Must have been a close friend, I suppose. Datura is poisonous, you know,' she finished, superfluously.

'Yes, I know. And the toxin that killed Mr Childers was definitely from the datura family. Most probably from that exact plant, but not in its natural form. No trace of seeds or leaves or flowers in his system. They've got to have steeped it and extracted the toxin that way. Easily done if you know the technicalities. Makes the pathology a lot more difficult to identify.'

'I expect it's just a coincidence. After all, it would be very foolhardy to publicly reveal that you had access to a highly toxic plant, just when there was an investigation going on into a deliberate poisoning.'

'It's entirely possible that there's no connection. You could argue that it's purely innocent, and that the person sending those particular flowers must be a long way down the list of suspects, or off it altogether.'

Simmy sat back to have a think. This woman was Moxon's new sidekick, presumably. She would have quickly learnt how special he was, how undamaged by his work he remained and how contented he and his wife were together. Simmy found herself experiencing a rare stab of jealousy.

'How do you get along with the inspector?' she asked.

'What? You mean DI Moxon? He's all right. A bit slow sometimes. A bit soft. But he's brilliant at all the local knowledge. Knows everybody and how they all connect. If you could just remember that nickname, he's sure to know who it is.'

'I tried to find those flowers again, after the funeral, but they'd nearly all been taken off to nursing homes. That's really why I phoned him. I thought he could check with the undertaker, and see if he can track them down.'

'Probably worth a try. Thanks. But as I say, it's more likely to be completely innocent.'

They both looked at Christopher, who had been giving his full attention to his food. He glanced up, aware of their scrutiny, and shrugged defensively. 'What?' he said.

Neither woman answered. Simmy was aware of the most subtle of power struggles going on. He had tried to dominate her with his snorting and his sniffy remark. And she had done as she wished, despite him. He had lost nothing by it, while making his feelings plain. This was all good, she told herself. They all knew where they stood.

'I wish I could remember that name,' she said. 'I expect it'll come to me. I keep thinking "Jazz", but it wasn't that.'

'That suggests he's called James,' said Christopher diffidently. 'Don't you think?'

'Possibly – except it *wasn't* Jazz. It was a bit like it, that's all. I know I'm being dim. It's hormones, probably.'

For the first time, DS Gibson glanced at Simmy's middle. 'Oh! I didn't notice. You're not very far on, are you?'

'Twenty-two weeks. More than halfway. It seems to be going rather slowly at the moment.'

'Is it your first?'

Simmy took a deep breath. She had known this question would arise, but apart from the hospital people, nobody had yet asked it. She unfairly blamed Moxon for not warning his colleague in advance. Why should he? demanded the voice of reason. He would probably feel he was guilty of an outrageous intrusion on her privacy if he mentioned it to anyone.

'I lost my first one, before I came to live here,' she said. 'She was stillborn.'

'Oh Lord. How terrible! You must be feeling pretty nervous about this one, then?'

Simmy relaxed. 'You could say that. They'll be keeping a close eye on me, of course. But it's not a very rational business. You lose trust in the whole process.'

'I can imagine.'

Simmy believed her and was grateful. She looked to Christopher, trying to include him, aware that he could not be comfortable with the direction the conversation had taken. He gave her a bracing smile, which said, *I'm here for you*, and which she found quite irritating. This wasn't going to be easy, she realised, over the coming months. Pitfalls were appearing on all sides. Characteristically she blamed herself for her fiancé's discomfort, and took refuge in the presence of the police detective. Solving a murder was an excellent method of distracting oneself from personal issues, after all.

'Thanks,' she said. 'So – you haven't got very far with the investigation, then?'

Gibson leant back slightly. 'Whoa!' she warned. 'That's a bit strong. We're following up on a whole lot of leads, asking for witnesses who might have seen Mr Childers in the hours before he died. The usual stuff.' She narrowed her pretty eyes. 'How much does DI Moxon generally share with you, then?'

Simmy smiled. 'That depends. You can't really generalise. A few times I've been a key witness and he's told me quite a lot. Other times I've been out on the edge and it's been Ben or Bonnie that's most involved.'

'Or me,' said Christopher. 'A couple of times, anyway.'

'I see.' She regarded him with a steady look. 'What's your line of work, Mr . . . ?'

'Henderson. I'm a partner at the Keswick auction house. Been there a couple of years now. Finally found my vocation, you might say.'

'Nice,' she said vaguely. 'Antiques and flowers, then. Both liable to arouse strong feelings, when you think about it. I mean – some of those collectors can get tremendously protective and competitive, can't they? And so can gardeners, cherishing their precious dahlias or whatever.'

'It's not so much that,' said Simmy, 'as people's reaction when receiving flowers on special occasions. That can spark off all sorts of deep emotion. I never understood before how flowers can be used maliciously. As a reminder of something awful, or sent by a stalker, or even a subtle kind of sarcasm. The possibilities are endless. And all I do is fulfil people's orders, asking no questions.' She remembered the woman in the pub in Patterdale, who she had first met in a farmyard, her carefully made bouquet flying over her head, hurled by the enraged recipient. 'They can be a catalyst, bringing things to a head in a bad marriage. It's scary to think of what I might walk into without any sort of warning.'

'But no flowers involved where Mr Childers was concerned?'

'Well . . .' Simmy began to doubt the quality of this young woman's intelligence, 'haven't we just been saying he must have *consumed* some, which killed him?'

'Oh!' Gibson put a hand to her mouth. 'So we have. But nothing to do with you, of course. That's all I meant.'

'I hope not,' said Simmy. 'Except that I was there when he died.'

That effectively finished the conversation. Christopher's steak was all gone, and time was passing. He wiped his mouth with a flourish and plonked the napkin down beside his plate. Simmy got the message.

'We'd better be going,' she said. 'We've got to unload the shopping before it starts to go off.'

'It was nice to talk to you,' said the detective. 'And thanks for the hint about the funeral flowers. We'll get back to you if there are any questions. And if you remember that name . . .'

'It'll come to me,' she said confidently. 'Although I don't suppose it'll be much help when it does. And you know the undertaker removes all the cards before taking the flowers to nursing homes. They give them back to the family. Except Miss Entwhistle didn't really have any family, as far as I know.' She heard herself prattling. 'Well, you'll know better than me about that sort of thing. I never even met the woman.'

'You did, though,' said Christopher, to her amazement. 'She was that old girl we used to see in The Mortal Man

266

sometimes. The one with the Patterdale terrier. I thought you knew that.'

She stared at him. 'How did *you* know?'

'She buys stuff at the sales sometimes. Used to, I should say. Garden things, mostly. And she often did the car boot sales, selling her surplus plants.' He shook his head. 'I thought you knew all that.'

She blinked at him. 'I never made the connection. How could I, when I never even knew her name?'

'She lived about two hundred yards from you, you idiot. People are probably wondering why you weren't at her funeral.'

Simmy had nothing to say to that. So the somewhat unkempt woman with the little black dog who would sometimes have a brief chat with her and Christopher in the pub was the one who'd died, apparently to universal sorrow. The fact that she had never known the woman's name struck her now as a great omission. And yet she hardly knew the names of anyone in Troutbeck. People didn't go around introducing themselves, or if they did, it was mostly just a first name they provided. Simmy had not joined any local societies, did not go to church, had done no door-to-door canvassing. How was she supposed to know who everybody was?

Yet her fiancé evidently did. 'Who else do you know, then?' she asked foolishly. 'Do you think you could tell me everyone's name in future?'

He took it lightly. 'I'll try,' he said. 'Now get your things and let's be off.'

He drove them back to Troutbeck without saying much. Their route took them through Ambleside, where the one-way system forced them through the centre of the town, which was a slow process. 'Oh, there's Stuart!' Simmy said suddenly. 'I keep seeing that man. He's the one whose friend has got the building plot. We ought to stop and talk to him, really.'

'Impossible,' said Christopher. 'There's nowhere to stop along here.'

Stuart had not seen them, and soon disappeared into the estate agent's on the main street. 'Did you see him?' she asked Chris. 'You said you know him, didn't you?' She was in a constant haze as to who her fiancé knew, especially after his revelation about Dorothea Entwhistle. His parents had lived in Bowness for decades, and although their eldest son visited infrequently, he must have met at least some local residents over the years. His mother had been averagely sociable, and would doubtless have enjoyed showing off her adventurous offspring. All the other Hendersons remained stolidly in place, barely going anywhere.

'Did I? When? I don't think I did, you know. What does he do?'

'He's got quite pally with my mum for some reason. He's about fifty, with ginger hair. He's big and looks like Henry the Eighth. He's got a B&B near Beck View, and a wife who does practically all the work. He's quite nice, I think. Seems very keen for us to look at that building plot.'

'We should, I guess. It's all swirling round, not getting any closer to a decision. I keep wondering which of us is holding things up.'

'It doesn't work like that. It's more that neither of

us is very good at this big stuff. When I moved up here, my dad did most of the work. He found the cottage and talked me through the finances. I brought some furniture with me, and my mum got some things as well. All I did was choose curtains and carpets. I was a baby – I see that now.'

'Well, I might know your man by sight, but I can't think of a Stuart, offhand. Who's this friend of his, with the plot? He's the one we should talk to.'

'It's his brother-in-law, actually. He must think I'm dreadfully ungrateful. Are you saying we should think again about building from scratch, then?'

'Not really. The mere idea makes me feel weak. But people seem to think it would make sense.'

She knew what was really going on. Christopher could see no convincing reason why he couldn't simply move into her Troutbeck cottage and save themselves a whole lot of hassle and expense. His nomadic early life had persuaded him that he could live in a shoebox with perfect ease. All that was needed, to his mind, was a bigger bed. He pretended to understand when Simmy insisted that this was not a viable option, but she knew he was humouring her. As a result, his efforts to find a new home were muted. Yet when she voiced some of these observations, he strenuously denied it. 'I'm just as keen as you are,' he insisted. 'But you can see for yourself that it isn't going to be easy.'

And being Simmy, she blamed herself for being awkward. The cottage had two bedrooms, a garden, lovely views and a sound roof. A lot more than most small families had to put up with these days. But there was only space for one car outside, only one room downstairs, apart from the kitchen. As an only child, she had taken solitude and silence for granted all her life. When married to Tony, she had arranged things so that they each had their own area of the house to escape to. Christopher came from a big, untidy family, and had no concept of privacy or the desire for a room of one's own.

'Nearly there now,' he said superfluously. 'We'll grab a quick cup of tea then head off to Lynn's, shall we?'

'Okay,' she said, still wondering at the wasteful route they had taken so far that day, carving a wide circle through most of the southern part of the Lake District. But experience had taught her that men habitually used the long way, if it meant avoiding small, winding country lanes. Only her father diverged from this stereotype, choosing tiny dead-end tracks for his explorations, charting his progress on a map and adding yet another discovery to his collection. But that had been a while ago now. Russell Straw was a lot less adventurous than he once had been.

'Have you ever been up the Struggle?' she asked Christopher now. 'If we live in Patterdale, we might be using it quite often.'

'Once. It was a nightmare. I must have met six different vehicles, all on narrow bends. Not to mention the bikes. It's only there to get the tourists excited. Half of them have no idea what they're letting themselves in for when they decide to use it.'

The Struggle linked Ambleside to the Kirkstone Pass, and was famously steep and winding. In icy conditions, it was unthinkable. The gradient was one in four, which numerous cyclists saw as a challenge. 'I don't think my little car would manage it,' said Simmy. 'Maybe I'll have to get a Land Rover.'

'Huh,' was all he said to that.

Chapter Twenty-Two

While Simmy was being driven all around the area, Angie and Russell were walking down the hill to Bowness, setting out early in order to give themselves time to savour the unusual situation. 'We hardly ever do this,' she observed. 'I feel as if I should take your arm and carry a parasol.'

'Why a parasol?'

'I don't know. There's something weirdly Edwardian about me today.'

'I know what you mean,' he said, to her surprise. 'I've felt that way myself a few times. We live in a town that had its heyday a century ago, after all. There must be hundreds of appalled Edwardian ghosts crowding the streets, if we could but see them.'

It took them both back to their early years together, when they would banter and fantasise for hours on end. Angie had taken reluctantly to marriage, fearing it would stifle her ambitions and limit her freedom. Aware of this, Russell had done his best to at least liberate her imagination. Forty years later, he was sorely afraid that he had failed. His wife had never found her rightful place in the world, never concentrated on nurturing any particular talent. Before establishing their bed and breakfast business, she had worked in a day centre run by Social Services, before migrating to a hostel for the homeless. The pattern of offering support to other people was the only discernible theme. Although she had a degree (in English and geography) she had no actual qualifications. Her earnings had accordingly been minimal.

Russell, ever optimistic, had thought that parenthood might become a vocation in itself, but that too had brought disappointment. Angie found the business of raising a child slow and frustrating. 'You can't begin to imagine how long a day with a two-year-old can be,' she moaned. 'There's about twenty minutes of enjoyment and the rest is sheer tedium.'

She had, however, been thrilled at the prospect of becoming a grandmother. She could have those twenty minutes and then pass the child back to its mother. A perfect arrangement, to her way of thinking. When little Edith had died, Angie's world had tottered as much as anyone else's. Now there was a second chance, and everybody was holding their breath.

'I'll be glad when this year is over,' she said now. 'It's not been one of the best, has it? That complaint about us didn't help. And all that business with the Hendersons was pretty grim. And I can't stand the suspense over Persimmon's house. Not to mention the baby.'

'I know. And I can't help feeling we're letting her down. If we sold up and retired, we could let her have enough equity to buy something rather splendid. I don't think she realises how much we've got salted away.'

The income from Beck View had regularly exceeded a thousand pounds a week, and the Straws had spent very little of it. There had been no time for holidays, no taste for expensive cars or fancy toys. Their savings, ostensibly destined for their care in extreme old age, were very substantial as a result.

'She wouldn't take it,' Angie objected. 'She thinks we'll need it in our dotage.'

'I dare say she could be persuaded,' he said mildly.

And then they were at the Wilkinses' residence, in Kendal Road, a short distance south of Helm Road, where the Harkness family lived. It had taken twenty minutes or so to walk there from Beck View. Walking back, uphill, would probably take longer. The house was detached, with a large, well-kept garden and a view of Brant Fell. 'Must be worth well over half a million,' murmured Russell.

'Closer to three-quarters, I'd guess,' said Angie. 'The wife has some kind of business, hasn't she?'

'Search me,' said Russell.

They were greeted by Tristan, who ushered them into a large conservatory at the back of the house. It looked out onto half an acre of shrubs, vegetables and a big greenhouse. There were also four wooden boxy objects, which turned out to be beehives. A small lawn provided rest for the eye, but no space for any running about. The Wilkinses did not have a dog and there was no sign of grandchildren.

Candy Proctor was sitting in a cane chair with a glass in her hand. A low table with a mosaic design on its top held bowls of nibbles. She smiled feebly at the newcomers. To

Russell's eye, she looked even more wan and melancholy than she had two days before. 'No Stuart?' he said.

'He's cried off,' said Tristan, with a frown. 'Something urgent up in Ambleside, apparently. Daphne's not happy about it. She likes an even number.'

Daphne Wilkins then put in an appearance, wearing a long blue skirt and a string of pearls that reached almost to her waist. She moved smoothly to a trolley and asked the Straws what they'd like to drink. 'There's gin, Campari, Martini, sherry . . .' she offered.

'A nice, straightforward G&T for me, please,' said Russell. 'Don't bother with lemon. I always find it makes no difference at all to the taste – don't you?'

Nobody answered at first. Then Candy said, 'It does if you squeeze it.'

'But that's bad manners. You'd have to do it with your fingers, and they'd get sticky, so you'd have to lick them, and that way lies the end of civilisation.'

'Oh, Russell,' sighed Angie, but there was a twinkle of fun in her eye. 'Trust you.'

'Angie?' Daphne prompted.

'Oh – the same as Russell, thanks. We never seem to have any gin at home. It'll be quite a treat.'

The atmosphere was redolent with social effort. Tristan appeared to be at a loss, with his wife so efficient and brisk that there was nothing for him to do. He hovered close to Candy, who kept shooting looks at him that seemed to be saying *I understand how you're feeling*. Angie found herself trying to decide whether the two of them were having an affair, finally concluding that there was no way Candy would be so obvious if that were the case. Instead, the poor woman was demonstrating her frustrated adoration with very little inhibition.

'Pity about Stuart,' she said. 'He's a good friend of ours.'

'Yours,' said Russell. 'I don't think he likes me very much.'

Sipping her gin, Angie imagined how the pairings would have worked if there'd been an even number. Tristan and Candy, herself and Stuart, leaving Russell to schmooze the intimidating Daphne. He would probably quite enjoy that, she thought. Instead, both the Straws undertook to learn what they could about the woman they had barely met before. The cold collation was evidently looking after itself in the kitchen, because the hostess showed no sign of needing to be elsewhere. 'I gather you run your own business,' Angie ventured. 'Is that right?'

'Don't we all?' said Candy Proctor, who seemed anxious to talk to someone. 'Daphne's the same as the rest of us, basically.'

'What? You're not running a B&B somewhere, are you?' said Russell.

'Self-catering, actually. I've got a couple of barn conversions that I use as holiday lets. Long-term, mostly. Less work that way.'

'Well, blow me,' said Russell. 'Why didn't we know that? You've kept it very quiet.' He gave Tristan a reproachful look.

'Nothing to do with me,' said the host. 'I've got enough to do here. As Daffers says, it's not a great deal of work, and she's quite capable of running the whole show on her own.'

'Have the police been to see you again?' Candy suddenly blurted. 'Are they any closer to finding who killed poor

Grant? It's such a shame, you know. He was so inoffensive. I keep asking myself *why* anybody would want to kill the poor man. What possible harm could he have done anybody, to deserve something so awful?'

'Hey, Candy,' Tristan gently chided her. 'I thought we agreed we wouldn't bring that subject up. Poor Angie won't want to be reminded of it, will she?'

'It seems so long ago already,' said Angie slowly. 'And it's not even a week yet. As far as we can tell, the police aren't making much progress. They're probably missing young Ben Harkness, although they'd never admit it. Mind you, my daughter tells me there's a sister who's almost as clever. She's helping Bonnie at the shop today.'

'They shouldn't allow those youngsters to have anything to do with it. They could get themselves into real danger. It's irresponsible.' Tristan Wilkins was harrumphing like any good Edwardian, much to Russell's amusement.

'I don't think they can stop them,' he said. 'And with police resources so stretched, they might be glad of the help.'

'He sounds like such a nonentity,' said Daphne. 'The murdered man, I mean. As if he must have just been a pawn in a bigger game. Don't you think?' She looked round the little group. 'Not that I know anything about it, really.'

'Just what I was going to say,' her husband told her, rather rudely. 'The only person here who'd even met the man before is Candy – apart from Russ and Angie, obviously. I'm not sure Candy thinks he was a nonentity.'

Candy shook her head. 'It's too complicated for me. However did somebody even manage to get him to take the poison? How would you *do* that, unless you lived in the same house? It could so easily go terribly wrong.'

'Maybe it did,' said Russell. 'Maybe the lethal dose of whatever it was, was meant for somebody else.'

Nobody made any response to that idea. Daphne tittered slightly, a sound that struck Angie and Russell as wildly incongruous in such a dignified woman. Russell pressed on. 'Or perhaps one of his relatives packed him a nice lunch to bring here with him, and he ate it on Saturday afternoon. It doesn't have to be anybody up here, does it?'

Eyebrows wavered up and down, but still nobody joined in with the speculations. 'We met his father and sister, and sister's husband. They all seemed fairly upset, I suppose. But not exactly shattered.'

Never would Russell Straw utter the word *devastated* unless he was referring to a patch of land ravaged by locusts or earthquake. The source of his objection was not so much inaccuracy as over-usage and cliché.

'Come on, mate,' urged Tristan. 'Give it a break. We didn't invite you here to talk about poison, did we?'

'Didn't you?'

'I told you. It's this abomination in Patterdale we're most concerned with. We think we might well have stopped it in its tracks, after the fuss we've been making. For a little while, at least. My contact at the council assures me there'll be short shrift when the application goes in formally.'

'Isn't that a bit . . . undemocratic?' wondered Angie. 'I mean, it's not the right procedure, is it, to raise objections before there's even an application? You only knew about it because you've got spies everywhere.'

'Spies? Me?' The protestation seemed deliberately melodramatic, displaying layers of insincerity, sarcasm, false modesty, bombast and a dash of anger. 'What makes you think that?'

'The way you talk, for a start. You said yourself you'd got a contact on the council. That sounds like a spy to me.' Angie faced him steadily, totally unintimidated. 'You're playing some game, with your leaflets and meetings, probably all designed to feather your own nest.'

Candy and Daphne both gasped at this sudden accusation, while Russell silently applauded. Tristan seemed almost glad to have a worthy adversary. His broad chest swelled and he grinned cheerfully at her. 'We all do what we can to survive,' he agreed. 'But I'm at a loss to see how objecting to a parkful of new tourist lodges can be of any benefit to my own activities. After all, my attentions are mainly devoted to the garden these days. You really must come and see my roses, by the way. We thought that could be a postprandial treat for you.'

'So why do it? Why worry about Patterdale at all? That's what nobody can understand.'

'Candy,' said Tristan, adopting a weary air, 'you explain it, will you? Again. I thought we'd dealt with that one weeks ago.'

'Not now,' said Daphne firmly. 'Lunch is ready. It's nearly half past one. We've been talking when we should have been eating. Come through, will you?' Brooking no interruptions, she led the little party into a large square dining room, decorated in shades of brown, with solid oak furniture and a handsome Chinese carpet. Dishes and bowls containing salads, cooked meats, relishes and crusty bread were arranged on a Victorian sideboard. 'Help yourselves, and take a seat,' she instructed.

'It's like being at a conference,' murmured Russell, who had at one time attended more than his share of weekend conferences.

The food was lavish in quantity and quality. Daphne must have worked hard all morning, cutting tomatoes into fancy shapes, making her own coleslaw and arranging meats in patterns on the big central charger. Four bottles of wine also awaited them. 'Nobody's driving, are they?' said Tristan. 'Help yourselves.'

'Lovely!' said Candy. 'It all looks too good to eat.'

Everyone laughed, and Angie grabbed the top plate, not hesitating to be first in line.

They sat at the handsome table and ate quietly for a while. Russell and Angie had both expected to feel unequal to a big meal, after eating more of their surplus breakfast stocks, but they proved themselves wrong. 'Looks as if Stuart won't be missed,' said Tristan, eyeing the wreckage. 'I said we should get another chicken,' he told his wife.

'It's just so delicious,' Candy said apologetically.

'You needed feeding up,' Tristan smiled at her. 'You've been looking very peaky lately.'

'It's always the same after a busy summer. I never seem to have a minute to sit down and eat a proper meal.'

'Victim of your own success,' the man laughed. Which inevitably brought more thoughts of Grant Childers to the surface. Nobody had forgotten that Candy's success had led to Angie Straw being the one holding the dying man. The unfairness of it was still rankling, as was the impression that Candy somehow held Angie to blame for what had happened to her pet visitor. The cancellations at Beck View added considerable insult to the injury.

'Well, we're not busy at all,' said Russell. 'Those who assumed that the scene of a murder would carry added value were altogether wrong.'

'It's just that it's too soon,' said Daphne, who was contentedly working through a large plateful of her own food. 'Give them a few months for the dust to settle and they'll be flocking back to you.'

'I'd better start composing a new page for the website, then,' said Angie. 'House of Death. Or should it be Doom? See the spot where an innocent guest was foully poisoned, in Windermere's own quiet streets. Enjoy a few nights in the very room where he drank the lethal mixture . . .'

'Hush, woman,' said Russell, watching the three horrified faces. 'You're forgetting yourself.'

Candy was frowning, her face pink. 'You think it was something he *drank*?' she whispered, fiddling with her wine glass.

'That's the general idea. I just got carried away for a minute. Sorry if I upset anybody.'

'Huh!' said Candy.

'Exactly what is so important that Stuart couldn't come?' Angie asked, in a clumsy effort to change the subject. 'I always enjoy a chat with him. He's had an interesting life.'

'He's what they used to call a "wide boy",' said Tristan. 'Finger in every pie. Always knows what's going on before anyone else. Don't know how he does it.'

'Because he's so interested, that's why. And people like him, even when they know he's probably not totally to be trusted. He's funny and clever, and there's no malice in him.'

'Okay, Angie,' said her husband. 'We all know you're

in love with him. It's a cross I try to bear with dignity.'

Again Candy flinched and flushed. 'Oh dear,' she said.

'Ignore him,' Angie advised. 'He's had too much wine.'

For dessert there was a huge bowl of chopped fruit in a juice made from sweet white wine and spices. Banana, pineapple, kiwi, figs, mango, apple, strawberries, pear and more. 'What a lot of work!' moaned Candy. 'It looks fantastic.'

'It was a pleasure,' said Daphne, as if she meant it.

It was half past two, and Russell was looking purposeful. 'We haven't really talked about Simmy's chances of finding a house in Patterdale,' he said, looking at Tristan. 'We'd appreciate any help you can offer.'

'Ah. Yes,' said Tristan. 'The thing is, that was more Stuart's territory than mine. All I know is that he's got some interests up there and he's a bit concerned that you're going to let the chance slip through your fingers. That's the main message, as I understand it.'

'I see,' said Russell doubtfully. 'It's not really up to us, you know. Our daughter's a mature adult with a fiancé. It's entirely up to them.'

'Obviously. But Stu seemed to think there was rather a lot of dithering. Don't quote me – it's not my business, except as a go-between.'

'If they don't want to build something from scratch, I could maybe find them a barn with permission for conversion,' said Daphne, from a point behind Russell's shoulder. She spoke quietly, as if mentioning a small, casual detail that wasn't really of any importance.

Russell turned. 'In Patterdale?'

'Hartsop, actually. Just a thought.' She shrugged.

'Permission's applied for and pending. Shouldn't be a problem.'

Russell met his wife's gaze, a question passing between them. 'All right,' he said. 'We'll tell them.'

Then the house phone began to peal and Daphne went to answer it. 'Yes, hang on,' she said, before holding the receiver out to Angie. 'Your daughter,' she said.

Chapter Twenty-Three

'Hey, Mum,' came Simmy's voice. 'Glad I found you.'

'What's the matter?'

'Nothing really. It's just that Bonnie and Tanya are in a tizz about something, and want us all to meet at Beck View. What time will you be home?'

'I don't know. Not too much longer, I suppose. We've had a marvellous lunch.'

'Good. I'm in Troutbeck, with Christopher, and we can come and collect you if you like. Did you walk to the Wilkinses'?'

'We did. It takes at least twenty minutes. Is this urgent?'

'It might be,' said Simmy obscurely. 'Are people listening?'

'Very much so.'

'I won't say any more, then. I don't know exactly what it's about, anyway, but apparently Tanya's found something out. It sounds fairly important. Oh – and I assume you left your mobile at home?'

'I did. So did your father. You know how we feel about phones.'

'Well, I remembered where you said you'd be, so no harm done.'

Angie sighed. 'There's no escape, it seems.'

Simmy laughed. 'I'll come for you, then. Give me fifteen minutes. Oh – and tell me the exact address.'

The Wilkinses and Candy Proctor all thought there was something strange about this conversation. 'Is she all right?' Candy asked.

'Oh yes. Some nonsense about the shop, apparently. They just want us to provide a place in Windermere for everybody to get together to talk about it. She's coming here to collect us and drive us home. She and Christopher are always busy at the weekend. They'll want to get on with it.' They began to gather themselves for departure, strenuously enthusing about the wonderful lunch.

'But I wanted to show you my roses,' protested Tristan. 'If I'm lucky they'll still be flowering in December.'

'The garden's a marvel,' Angie assured him. 'We're hopelessly jealous.'

It was just after three when everyone assembled at Beck View, sitting around the kitchen table. Christopher was irritable and restless, showing signs of having lost an argument. 'We were supposed to be visiting Lynn,' whispered Simmy to her mother. 'She's not too pleased about it and has given Chris a bit of an earful.'

Angie knew Lynn from childhood, but had seldom seen her since then. 'She always did like her own way,' she said.

Tanya and Bonnie were sitting very straight, like much younger children finding themselves in formal adult company. Simmy was opposite them, interested and encouraging, but at the same time nervous. The atmosphere was brittle, nobody quite knowing what to expect, or what the script was going to be.

'Why didn't you just call the police if you've got something important to report?' Christopher demanded. 'Why go through this silly pantomime?'

Bonnie faced him squarely. 'Because we can't decide whether it's really evidence or just guesswork.'

'Not guesswork,' Tanya corrected her. 'Observation.'

'Okay,' Bonnie conceded.

'So tell us, for heaven's sake,' Angie ordered.

Bonnie waved at the younger girl, who took a deep breath and then plunged in. 'Right. Yes. Well – on Sunday morning I was sitting on the waterfront where they were doing that protest, watching what was going on, and taking a few pictures and a video on my phone. Mainly I wanted the swans, but I caught some of the people as well. There were people from school and then Ninian Tripp showed up and was talking to a woman.'

'What time was this?' asked Simmy.

'About half past eleven until I had to go home for dinner. Once the cruise boat had left, I just pottered about taking random shots as I went.'

'We must have just missed you, then.'

'I guess so. What time were you there?'

'A bit later than that. So, get on with it – what exactly did you see?'

'Okay. So – there was a sort of stall, giving out drinks to people who were protesting. There was a sign saying "Home-made ginger cordial – no charge". It was being poured into paper cups. I thought it was a bit unusual, so I filmed it for a minute or so. I kept on seeing people I knew. That red-haired man from Ambleside – he's called Stuart, I think. He came to our house a few times to see my mother a year or so ago, when he had some building done.'

Simmy and Russell both found this of interest, eyes widening. 'Was *he* giving out the drinks?' asked Angie.

'No. As far as I could see, there wasn't really anybody in charge of the stall. Nobody was standing behind it all the time, but it looked as if there was a woman keeping an eye on it, and then I realised there was a man who was topping up the cups from a cool box under the table, every few minutes. When I was filming, they were talking together. I don't know who they are, but Bonnie thinks you might.'

'Just show us,' said Christopher wearily. 'Cut to the chase.'

'Right. I've put it on the laptop, so you can see better.' She produced a slim computer and set it on the table facing Russell. Simmy got up so she could see it clearly over her father's shoulder, and Angie leant sideways for a better look.

'There's Ninian,' said Simmy. 'Oh, and that's Candy Proctor, by the table.'

Russell watched quietly for a few seconds, before saying, 'There's old Tristan, see. Chatting to Candy. They must be the two you mean. Tristan must have been the man topping up the drinks. Can't see Stuart anywhere.'

'We did see him holding a placard, early on,' said Simmy. 'There were so many people, you can't hope to have got them all in one little video.'

'Nothing's happening,' Angie complained. 'Just people drifting about with placards, and some tourists – probably waiting for the lake cruise boat to dock.'

'Right!' said Tanya, with a surprising tone of triumph. 'That's the point, you see. Look – there it is.' The film showed the prow of the cruiser appearing on the right-hand side of the screen. All the people on the screen turned to look the same way, drawn by the appearance of the boat. Then it finished abruptly.

'That's it?' asked Christopher. 'I can't see anything remotely suspicious in any of that.'

'It sets the scene,' said Tanya stubbornly. 'I took some still pictures of people waiting to get on the boat, mainly because they were casting some good shadows. The sun came out for a minute, and the water was all sparkly. And there's a final bit of video, a few minutes later. Let me show you.'

She clicked through five or six pictures, most of them featuring swans walking among human legs. 'That's Grant Childers,' said Angie suddenly. 'Oh God – it's Grant Childers.'

Simmy crouched over Russell's shoulder, peering closely. She had never seen the man alive. 'Is it?' she said. 'Doesn't he look *ordinary*?'

It was true. A man of medium height, indeterminate age, holding a paper cup was standing with a faraway look on his face. 'What happened next?' asked Simmy, her imagination hard at work.

'I'm not quite sure, but I have a feeling he didn't get on the boat. Let's look at the last bit.'

She tapped her keyboard and another scene came up. Tanya had scanned the street in front of the Belsfield Hotel, showing people walking in both directions, one or two carrying placards horizontally, the protest clearly tailing off. 'This was at about one o'clock,' she said.

'They started going home for lunch, I suppose.'

'That's Childers,' said Simmy, almost in a whisper. 'Look – he's walking up the hill. He definitely never went on the cruise. The boat doesn't get back until half past one.'

'I never heard him come in, then,' said Angie. 'I must have been busy with the lunch. He can only have been back about half an hour before she started shouting for help.'

'But . . . but . . .' Simmy was dumbfounded. 'This is amazing.' She stared at Tanya. 'Did you have any idea how important all this was going to be?' She flapped a hand at the laptop.

'Not at first. But people were assuming Mr Childers went on the cruise, and I just went through my phone for all the pictures I'd taken, to see if I'd got anything relevant. Then there was that photo of the murder victim in the news on Thursday, and we linked it up with this chap. It's all coincidence, basically.'

'The problem is, we all know different bits of the story,' said Simmy. 'We've all talked to different people and picked up odd details that the others don't know about. Just as an example, Chris and I met Moxon's new detective sergeant earlier today, and she told us a few things. Bonnie's been googling poisonous plants and probably hasn't told us everything she's found. Tanya's got these pictures. It's terribly chaotic.'

'I don't think it is, pet,' said Russell. 'There's a perfectly clear picture here. That's Tristan handing out drinks. There's Childers holding one of his paper cups. Candy looks as if she might well be pointing him out so Tristan would know which one he was. Childers most likely told her he was booked onto the cruise. He drinks the ginger cordial, immediately feels peculiar and decides to skip the boat ride and come back here. Where he dies half an hour later.'

'Longer than that,' said Angie, looking very pale.

'Not really,' said Simmy. 'If that's how it was, then it was pretty fast-acting.'

'You're saying that Tristan and Candy plotted together to kill Grant Childers?' said Bonnie. 'Because that's the conclusion Tanya and I reached, as well.'

'Not Candy,' said Russell. 'Remember how startled she was just now when we said Childers had been poisoned by a drink, rather than something solid. It seemed to be a whole new idea to her. And it was only then that she probably made the connection with Tristan's cordial. I dare say she's in a pretty bad state at this moment.'

'Slow down,' ordered Simmy. 'We need to go through it a step at a time. You're making it seem much too simple.'

There was a lull as they all gazed at the frozen picture on Tanya's screen, which she had brought up again. It showed Grant Childers' full face, his expression unreadable. 'Poor man,' whispered Angie. 'Why in the world would they want to poison him?'

'There's something connecting Dorothea Entwhistle to all this,' said Simmy, with sudden clarity.

'Pity none of you went to her funeral,' said Christopher, rather startlingly. They all looked at him, registering the *you*, which ought surely to have been *us*.

'He knew her,' Simmy explained to everyone, aware of their bewilderment. 'And I did too, just not by name. I saw the funeral flowers yesterday morning, and there was one that I think was made of datura. Devil's trumpet, by another name.'

'Closely related to something called *angel's* trumpet,' Bonnie interrupted. 'And both of them very poisonous.'

'And now that my mum and dad have just been to lunch with the very people we're accusing of murdering Mr Childers,' said Simmy. 'That strikes me as very sinister.'

'We only drank the wine – which both the Wilkinses drank as well,' said Russell facetiously. 'I think we've escaped with our lives.'

'We need Ben,' said Bonnie flatly. 'He'd know how to organise it all, and select the parts that are real evidence. Do you think Tanya's video is enough to take to the police? Is there anything else we need to work out first? Like motive. It's only half a story without that.'

'We need to be careful who we implicate,' said Angie. 'I'm still wondering where Stuart was today, that stopped him coming to lunch with the Wilkinses,' said Angie. 'They weren't happy about it. Daphne likes an even number, apparently.'

'You think he might be in cahoots with Tristan?' Russell asked.

'I don't know what to think,' she sighed. 'Don't forget that Daphne said she'd got property in Patterdale,' said Angie. 'Hartsop, I mean. She wants you, P'simmon, to buy a barn conversion off her.'

'That's not quite what she said,' her husband corrected her mildly. 'She said she might have a barn with planning permission for conversion. That's almost as bad as being sold a building plot. An awful lot of work to be done before you actually have a place to live in.'

'It keeps coming back to Patterdale, doesn't it?' said

Christopher crossly. 'And that's what's making it so personal for us. It's as if somebody knew we wanted to live there and connected that with the Childers man for some reason. Surely it can't be a complete coincidence that he was staying here when he died? It has to be connected, doesn't it?'

'Right,' said Simmy, with relief and approval both evident in her voice. 'Maybe we can start again from there.'

'We need Ben,' said Bonnie again. 'He'd do one of his flow charts.'

'I can do that. So can you,' said Tanya. 'Why are you being so wet about it?'

'Shut up,' snarled Bonnie.

Simmy tapped the table like a schoolteacher. 'Come on, you two. Bonnie, you're right that we're struggling without Ben, but Tanya's right as well. You've both done this before. Why don't I find you a piece of paper and we can start writing some of it down?'

Tanya leant down and pulled an A4 pad from a patchwork bag. 'I started, actually,' she said shyly. 'But I wasn't sure what you'd think of it.' She showed her preliminary workings, which comprised of little more than names placed around the page, and a few connecting lines.

Everybody craned their necks for a look and the next half-hour passed in a jumble of suggestions, hypotheses and sudden remembered details. Tanya did her best to keep her diagram clear, but by the end it was a hopeless mass of arrows and circles and question marks, with nothing in the way of clarity to show for their efforts. Dorothea Entwhistle had five underlinings and an asterisk, Candy Proctor was surrounded by question

292

marks. Stuart Carstairs and Tristan Wilkins were linked to most of the others, and Ninian Tripp made a shadowy appearance in one corner. The datura plant had a big thick circle around it, along with a query about glasshouses and funeral tributes.

'We're no closer to understanding the motive,' said Bonnie. 'Assuming it was Tristan who gave Grant the poisonous drink, why on earth would he do that?'

'It can only be to stop the new tourist park in Patterdale,' said Simmy. 'Surely?'

Tanya wrote it down.

'So how does he benefit from that?' It was Bonnie, quick to get to the central question.

Angie and Russell understood that they were being edged away from the central conversation by the young folk. The excited brainstorming had at some point left them behind. Angie found herself yearning for a mug of tea and Russell remembered that his dog had scarcely been out all day. He was also annoyed that his own perfectly constructed narrative had not been received with the enthusiasm it deserved. 'It all seems perfectly straightforward to me,' he muttered.

But the quest for a motive was gathering momentum. 'Obviously he wants to keep Patterdale as it is,' said Christopher, whose world-weary tone had only increased as time went by.

'But does he really believe those plans would ever have been given the go-ahead?' wondered Simmy. 'It felt like a pre-emptive strike, at that meeting we went to. Which makes it more sinister, somehow.'

'More devious, certainly,' said her father. 'Is this going

to go on much longer, because I should give the dog a walk before long? I can't see the point of all this chatter, when you've got something concrete to show the police. Just go down there now and hand over your phone, why don't you?'

'They'll be closed,' said Angie. 'You'll have to phone Moxon directly.'

Bonnie and Tanya shrank into their chairs, once again looking like children trying to keep up with people much older and wiser than themselves.

'Are you sure we should do that?' said Bonnie.

'Yes!' said Simmy, Angie and Russell in unison. Christopher merely rolled his eyes.

'Will you do it?' the girl asked. 'I don't know what to say.'

'Yes, yes,' said Simmy impatiently. 'And I'll come with you to see him. Whatever you want.'

Simmy called DI Moxon's mobile, and he answered fairly quickly in a relaxed tone. She visualised him drinking tea with his wife, taking a break from murder. 'We've got some evidence to show you,' she said. 'I think it's important.'

It was sweet, the way he reacted. Any other police officer would probably laugh. 'I'd better come and see it, then,' he said. 'Where are you?'

'At Beck View.' A hissing sound from Angie alerted her. Her mother was flapping a hand and shaking her head, mouthing 'NO-O-O'. 'But I think my mother would rather we saw you somewhere else,' she added.

Outside it was dry but grey. It was only an hour or so from sunset – not that there was any sign of the sun anyway. She looked again at her mother. 'Although I can't imagine where,' she said.

'I can open the police station. If it's real evidence, it would help if we had some formality in place when you reveal it. Can you be there in ten minutes?'

'Oh yes,' said Simmy.

Chapter Twenty-Four

Angie was more than half-asleep, nodding uncomfortably in her husband's fireside chair. Russell had insisted on taking the dog around the local streets, ignoring Angie's claim that the animal would be quite happy in the garden. 'I need to clear my head,' he said. Christopher had gone off on his own, saying he needed to get petrol for his car, and may as well do it now as later. 'Who knows what'll happen next?' he said. 'I'm learning that it's best to be prepared. For all I know, I'll be needed to drive somebody to Birmingham or Edinburgh at a moment's notice.'

Angie had just grunted and let him go.

When the doorbell rang, she was shaken awake, thinking it was Russell back again, and he must have forgotten his key.

But it was Stuart Carstairs, looking uncharacteristically abashed. 'Hey, Ange,' he said. 'Can I come in?'

She opened the door wider and waited for him to walk past her down the passageway to the kitchen. On balance, she was glad to see him, but weariness was the dominant sensation. She flopped back into the same chair, and sighed. 'I'm exhausted,' she said. 'We were awake most of the night.' Then she rallied. 'Where were you today? Daphne wasn't happy that you missed her lunch.'

'I couldn't face it, to tell you the honest truth. I'm ninety-nine per cent certain it was Tristan who poisoned your man. It can't be anybody else. I've gone through it a million times, and it keeps coming back to him.'

'It was him,' she nodded, feeling perfectly calm. 'The girls have gone to tell the police now. They've got evidence.'

He was struck dumb for half a minute. 'What?' he said then. 'What evidence?'

'I probably shouldn't say.'

'Must be about Dorothea, I suppose. She and Tristan were having a thing – did you know? They were growing those datura flowers in one of her greenhouses.'

'What on earth for?'

'Who knows? Some sort of game, I fancy. I think they were excited to be producing something that was so lethal. Lots of people are like that,' he added sententiously.

Angie's brain was working in slow motion. 'They plotted together to kill Grant Childers?'

'I doubt it. Dorothea got diagnosed with incurable cancer only six weeks before she died. It occurs to me she might have wanted to polish herself off before it got too unpleasant. That would make sense, and explain the toxic plants. Tristan would have been dragooned into helping her. He'd have wanted to make it easy for the poor old girl. We all liked her, after all.'

The sound of the front door opening and closing

announced Russell's return. The dog skittered down the passage, grinning from his overdue walk, followed by his owner. 'Russell,' nodded Stuart.

'He says Tristan poisoned Grant,' said Angie.

'We knew that already,' said Russell.

'He's just in the middle of explaining. Dorothea Entwhistle grew datura, and wanted to use it to kill herself if her cancer got too horrible. That's as far as we've got.'

'She was diagnosed six weeks ago,' Stuart repeated.

'Ah! Is it coincidence, then, that Childers booked in here at that same time?'

'No idea,' said Stuart. 'I don't pretend to know the whole story, not by a long way.'

'And Candy?' Russell asked. 'Where does she come in?'

Stuart looked blank. 'She doesn't, as far as I'm aware. Listen – all I'm doing is connecting the dots. Your man was poisoned with something botanical, and Tristan's the only one who fits the facts. And Dorothea – but she was dying.'

'She might have brewed up the lethal draught, though,' said Russell, who appeared to be deriving considerable enjoyment from the whole conversation. Angie was a lot less enthusiastic.

'Who knows?' said Stuart again.

'And we might never know,' said Angie. 'In any case, I've had enough of it all. I just want to crawl into bed and sleep for twelve hours.'

'If you go now, you'll be up at five,' said Russell. 'Try and last out another few hours. We can have a nice, quiet game of Scrabble, while everybody else is out there catching a murderer.'

Stuart took the hint and headed for the door. 'Sorry

if I've upset you,' he said, with a slightly puzzled air. 'I thought you'd want to know.'

'We're not upset,' said Angie. 'Just worn out. I know there's a whole lot more we should have asked you.'

Russell went to the door with Stuart. 'When did all this dawn on you?' he asked.

'Yesterday, at Dorothea's funeral. I hadn't given it much thought until then – been a bit busy with my own stuff, as it happens. Then I saw the wreath that Tristan sent – and thought "What a cheek!". It was a home-made effort, already going droopy. I recognised the flowers from when Dorothea showed them to me a few weeks back. He'd put something sentimental on the card, and called himself "Buzz". That was what we called him when he first started keeping bees. Then it hit me – he just couldn't help himself. Always was a big show-off. Thought he was beyond criticism, always knew what was best for everybody. It was a bloody cheek, you must admit – sending those exact same flowers to the funeral!'

They were on the doorstep, the road outside busy with Saturday evening traffic, streetlights giving it an almost wintry look. 'So you knew what they were, as well?' asked Russell. 'And you never said anything to the police?'

'They never asked me,' said Stuart, with a cheesy grin.

Simmy, Bonnie and Tanya met Detective Inspector Moxon on the pavement outside the police station, as agreed. He unlocked the door, pressed some buttons and switches and ushered them into a plain room down a short corridor. There were four chairs waiting for them, tidily arranged around a table.

'Thank you,' said Simmy, a number of times. 'It's very good of you to take us so seriously.'

'Remarkable as it might seem, I've learnt that it's the wisest approach,' he said.

Simmy recalled the Gibson woman calling Moxon 'soft'. It was probably true, she concluded. He showed a rare respect for the teenage detectives, which probably went some way to explaining the impression. It was almost as if he regarded them as friends, or even the family he and his wife evidently never had.

'I just have to leave you here for a minute,' he went on. 'I've got to make this official, which means filing a proper record. Talk among yourselves.' And he went out, closing the door behind him.

At first, none of them could think of anything to say. 'Why was Christopher in such a bad mood?' asked Bonnie, finally. 'Did you stop him from doing something? Or what?'

'We were going to see his sister in Penrith. When you phoned, we were just leaving. He doesn't like changes of plan, especially when it's because of something like this. He gets very conflicted about it. Although I thought he'd relaxed a bit earlier. We saw the new detective sergeant in a pub, and she came over to chat. She's nice. I told her about the datura flowers at the funeral.'

'What?' Bonnie stared at her blankly.

'Oh gosh – did I forget to tell you? There's been so much to think about, it got lost. Plus, I suppose once I'd told Detective Sergeant Gibson about it, I didn't think I needed to give it any more attention.'

'Explain.'

Simmy ran through what she had told the detective. 'It's probably not at all relevant. I can't even swear that they were datura flowers. But they were something unusual that I didn't recognise.'

'Have you remembered the name on the label yet?'

'I thought if I stopped trying, it would just come back of its own accord. The more I try, the more blank I get.'

Moxon came back, carrying a clipboard. He turned on a machine that could only be a voice recorder. 'Right, then,' he said at last. 'What's this evidence you're talking about?'

Tanya produced her laptop and showed him the footage from Sunday morning, explaining as it ran. 'What time was it?' he demanded. 'Why doesn't it show the time?'

'I never set it up for that. It was just before twelve o'clock. We can be sure of that, because that's when the boat sets off from Bowness.'

Moxon looked at Simmy. 'What time were you there? I'm right, aren't I, that you and your father walked down to the same spot on Sunday?'

'Right. It must have been a bit later. The boat was in the middle of the lake when we got there. And there wasn't any sign of people with a table giving out drinks. Candy and Tristan were parading up and down with their placards. We talked to them.'

'Well, this does help a lot,' he said, with a hint of reluctant admiration. 'It places Mr Childers at that spot at a specific time.' He looked slightly stunned. 'And he's obviously drinking something he'd got from that stall. The cup's identical to the others. And everything points to Mr Wilkins as the provider of the drink. But it's not a hundred per cent conclusive. Someone else could have

301

surreptitiously poured it out from a flask. That's what a defence lawyer would say. There's nothing to directly incriminate Wilkins. But we're almost there. This really is something of a breakthrough.'

'Hooray!' said Tanya.

'There must be something about you Harknesses. In your genes, maybe. It amazes me that you'd be there filming, at that very moment. What are the chances?'

'Well, I've been filming a lot of stuff lately. It's mostly for a school project. "Slice of Life" it's called. We're meant to capture ordinary events within a quarter of a mile of where we live. Things that represent what it's like to live where we do. The real surprise is that I found it again, among all the other stuff I've got on here. I had actually forgotten about it.'

'How did you know it was Mr Childers?'

'I didn't until Bonnie made the connection with the time and place. We found a picture of him on the news website, and worked out it was the same man. Then when we saw him with that drink, it started to seem important. But we ran it past Simmy and her parents first, just now. They confirmed that it was the right man.'

Simmy was gazing at the recording machine, half-listening and half-wondering how long this odd little meeting would take. Something suddenly clicked in her brain. 'Buzz!' she said. 'The funeral flowers were from somebody called Buzz.' The relief was out of all proportion. 'Thank goodness I remembered.'

'These are the flowers you told Gibson about?' Moxon said. 'We've been going through the list of people who sent funeral tributes. There were forty-one. Just about everybody from here to Ambleside is on the list.'

'But only one looked to be home-made,' said Simmy. 'And using datura flowers, which must have come from a greenhouse.'

The detective pursed his lips. 'Well, doesn't it seem very unlikely to you that the person who poisoned Mr Childers would advertise him- or herself by publicly contributing the source of that poison to a funeral?'

'That's what I said to DS Gibson,' Simmy admitted. 'But my dad thinks it would be typical of Tristan.'

'Who's Buzz, then?' asked Tanya.

'That shouldn't be too hard to discover, if we ask around,' said Moxon.

'Start with Candy Proctor,' said Simmy on a sudden whim. 'She knows everybody.'

Bonnie was jiggling in her chair. 'But you can just go and arrest Mr Wilkins, can't you? The other stuff can wait. You've got clear evidence in this video that he was giving out drinks in paper cups and Mr Childers had one of them.'

Moxon squared his shoulders. Even he wasn't going to take orders from such a scrap of a girl. And he couldn't even if he wanted to, as he went on to explain. 'I have to take this higher up. There has to be enough to convince the CPS that a prosecution is likely, based on this evidence.'

'So will you do it?' asked Bonnie, trying to be more conciliatory.

'Leave it with me. And thank you, ladies. You've given us some much-needed information, at last. I really shouldn't say this, but I have a feeling we couldn't have done it without you. Mind you, we're not there yet. You have to wonder whether it was actually possible to simply hand the man a paper cup full of a deadly drink in full view of a hundred people. Think of the planning needed. How could they be sure he would be there? And if he was there, who could say he'd be wanting a drink?'

'They'd have to have known every move he was going to make,' agreed Simmy.

'But it must have been Tristan Wilkins who gave it to him,' said Tanya, tapping her phone. 'He's right there in the video.'

'Christopher was right about that,' said Simmy. 'He was sure it was Tristan, days ago now.'

'And I'm fairly sure he keeps bees,' Tanya remembered. 'Maybe people call him "Buzz".'

'If it was him, he's got means and opportunity,' said Bonnie. 'But what on earth can the motive be?'

Simmy went back to Beck View, where Christopher was waiting for her. He appeared to be more relaxed than he'd been an hour earlier. Angie and Russell were in the kitchen with him, but there was no sign of preparations for an evening meal. 'We thought we'd go out for something to eat,' said Christopher. 'Your mother had a visitor, which meant she hasn't got around to fixing anything.'

Simmy looked at her parents in surprise. They never ate out. 'I thought you were dreadfully tired,' she said. 'Who was the visitor?'

'We are. Too tired to cook. But I've got my second wind now, and your father's up for it. It was Stuart – coming to tell me that Tristan Wilkins gave Grant Childers a fatal drink made out of datura from Dorothea Entwhistle's greenhouse. I told him we knew that already – that it appears to have been Tristan, I mean. He filled in one or two pieces of the picture, but I must admit I was almost past caring by that point. Anyway, let's go and eat. We were just waiting for you. How did it all go at the police station?'

'Fine, thanks. Moxon's going to apply for permission to arrest, or however they describe it.' She turned to Christopher. 'And I remembered the name on those flowers. The card was signed "Buzz".'

'That's old Tristan,' said Russell casually. 'Everyone called him that when he got so keen on beekeeping. Must be ten years ago now. I haven't heard anybody use it lately.'

'Dorothea Entwhistle would have done, I suppose?'

'Very much so. It might even have been her idea in the first place.'

'Dad – I've been meaning to ask, why didn't you go to her funeral? You didn't have anything else to do, and everybody else was there.'

Russell went pink and glanced at his wife. 'Notoriety,' he muttered. 'Everyone would be staring at us and wondering about the poisoned man. We didn't think we could face it.'

'He means me,' said Angie. 'I haven't been dealing with all this as well as I might. A funeral would have been the final straw.'

Christopher grinned. 'Straw!' he said, as if a very funny pun had been uttered. Nobody else smiled.

'So Tristan's well and truly in the frame,' said Russell. 'What a strange feeling that gives me. I never had him down as particularly clever or devious. If your theory's right, wouldn't he have had to plan every tiny detail, days in advance? For a start, he'd have to make the lethal drink, keep it safe, organise that protest as well as setting up a drink stall. I mean – that's not even legal, is it? Don't you need a licence or something? Then he'd have to hope Childers came by . . . I don't know. None of it sounds feasible to me.'

'He must have had help,' said Simmy. 'And it looks as if that could only have been from Candy.'

'Or Daphne,' Angie put in. 'She's the one with property in Patterdale – or expects to have. If she was in on it, the whole thing might make more sense.'

'One of them could have known that Childers was going on the lake cruise,' said Simmy. 'They might even have got the ticket for him.'

'No, he booked it on his computer,' said Angie. 'But they still might have known about it. He had plenty of time to meet them all and have a chat on Saturday. Tristan might have known everything Childers planned to do on Sunday.'

'So how are we going to catch him?' asked Christopher. 'Can the police just arrest him and force him to confess?'

'Obviously not,' said Russell impatiently. 'This is all pure speculation. Even if Tristan handed him the poisoned drink, he might not have done it deliberately. Somebody else could have planted it there.'

'Highly unlikely,' said Christopher. 'That really would require superhuman skills.'

'We need Ben,' said Simmy, as Bonnie had said several times through the week. 'And he's going to be here first thing tomorrow.'

The implications of this caused various reactions. Christopher groaned, Russell looked worried and Angie said, 'Really? That might be just the thing to straighten us out.'

'His mother doesn't want him distracted, though. I gather from Bonnie he's finding it all a bit overwhelming at uni. Apparently, there are people just as clever as him in the world, which came as a bit of a shock,' said Simmy.

Christopher smirked. 'Didn't I always say you overrated him?'

'Stop it,' Simmy snapped. 'You're deliberately trying to annoy me.'

'I suppose I am. It comes of having wasted most of the afternoon playing guessing games about a murder.'

'Honestly, Christopher, you never change, do you?' said Angie. 'What would your mother say if she could hear you talking like that?'

'She can't hear me, can she? And I hate to say it, but I think she'd make some sort of comment about me being more like you than her. You must have had a formative influence on me in the maternity ward.'

It was an old joke, that the babies had been swopped at birth, or at least been given too much exposure to each other's mother. In many ways their characters were closer to the other parent. Frances Henderson had been an unassuming woman, seeing the best in people and seldom taking much initiative. Angie Straw was much more scratchy and outspoken, wary of being under anyone else's control. 'Everyone marries their mother,' was a mantra Angie often quoted. Which only reinforced the notion that Simmy was more like quiet, restrained Frances and Christopher the outspoken one like Angie.

The talk continued as they walked the short distance to the Elleray pub. It was the default venue for Simmy, whenever a meal was suggested, and the walk was barely ten minutes. The food was satisfyingly straightforward.

Angie's second wind seemed to be holding up. 'I for one am still not altogether convinced that it was Tristan, you know. It all feels very tenuous to me, even after what Stuart told me. There must be all kinds of other explanations.'

'It was him,' said Christopher. 'I'm telling you.'

'You should have been with us at the lunch party, both of you,' said Russell. 'You could have watched out for clues. We didn't even realise there was any significance to the greenhouse – or the beehives. We had no idea about all that.'

'I still can't believe he'd have invited us if he'd poisoned Grant Childers. That's the thing that keeps coming back to me. I know he's a bit arrogant and self-important, but I don't think anybody would be that brazen.'

'It probably happens all the time,' argued Christopher. 'He probably wanted to check whether you suspected him. Or maybe it was his wife's idea and he had to go along with it.'

'I bet he wouldn't have invited us, though,' said Simmy. 'He must have heard about the other murder cases, with Ben and Bonnie being so clever at finding the killers.'

'A reputation that is not entirely justified,' Christopher pointed out. 'As I understand it, you mostly just stumbled into things and got the answer more by luck than anything else.'

'Nice to see you so busy,' Russell said, beaming his envious approval at the Elleray landlord who came over for a chat. 'Just how we like it, eh?'

There did not appear to be anything else to discuss

regarding Tristan and Childers and Dorothea Entwhistle. 'We've done all we can,' said Simmy.

At half past eight, when they were just finishing their coffee, a message pinged onto Simmy's phone. 'It's Moxon,' she said. 'Tristan Wilkins has been arrested and charged with premeditated murder.'

Angie sighed. 'And still we have no idea why. Even poor Grant Childers didn't know.'

Chapter Twenty-Five

Ben Harkness arrived at ten on Sunday morning, having got a train to Carlisle the previous evening with a fellow student, staying at his home overnight. From there he got an early bus.

'Just like a typical student in the olden days,' sighed Helen happily. 'Scrambling all over the country on public transport and expecting other people's parents to provide accommodation.'

'Just like we were,' said her husband.

'Well, not so much us as our parents,' Helen realised. 'Most of us had our own cars. Those were the glory days when students were a real elite.'

'I'm older than you. I had a harder time of it.'

Ben stayed for an hour before excusing himself and walking up to Corinne's to find his girlfriend.

The weather was dry, the cloud less oppressive than in recent days. 'Let's walk up to Troutbeck and see Simmy,' said Ben. 'I need some exercise.'

'Simmy's meant to be cooking a proper Sunday lunch for Angie and Russell. She won't have time to talk to us.'

'We'll take it slowly, and go to the Mortal Man first. By the time we get there, lunch'll have finished and they'll be glad to see us.'

'There's something to tell you,' said Bonnie nervously. 'Rather a big and complicated something.'

'Does it involve Simmy?'

'Oh yes. And Angie and Russell.'

'Then can we leave it till later? I want to tell you all about my course, and my new mates and the lecturer whose beard is eighteen inches long – and what we'll do in the Christmas vac, and stuff like that.'

'No problem,' said Bonnie, hugging his arm and grinning. 'I can hardly believe it's really you.'

They opted to walk along lanes and footpaths, through High Hay Wood, before joining the smaller of the two roads leading up to Troutbeck. It was an uphill hike of five miles or so, with views across Windermere to the woods on the western side. The youngsters paused at intervals to point out familiar landmarks and catch their breath. They talked much less than they'd expected to. The tree-lined tracks they used were shadowy and cool, the leaves turning yellow and brown. It was almost half past one when they reached the popular Troutbeck pub. 'I'm not really hungry,' Bonnie said. 'Isn't it weird the way exercise makes you want to eat less, not more?'

'There's a good biological explanation for it,' Ben told her. 'It's the main reason why people who walk a lot lose weight. Not the burning of calories, but the reduced appetite. But we'd better have something.'

They drank fruit juice and shared a sandwich, and were finished before two o'clock. 'Is it too soon to go to Simmy's?' wondered Bonnie impatiently. 'Christopher's going to be there as well. We don't want to miss them. They might be going to Patterdale again to look for a house.'

'They won't mind,' said Ben with confidence. 'They know I've only got one day here.'

'We needed you,' she said simply. The whole story of Grant Childers' death was threatening to burst out of her. 'Helen wouldn't let us tell you anything, but now they've arrested the man who did it, so it's safe. If you see what I mean.'

'Wait,' he told her. 'I want everybody to be there.'

'Poor Tanya,' Bonnie groaned. 'She's going to miss it. She isn't going to be happy about that.'

'I can fill her in later,' said Ben carelessly. 'If I'm home by five, there'll be plenty of time. You can come too, of course.'

'Do you think Simmy will drive us home? We'll have to walk all the way, otherwise.'

'Let's wait and see,' said Ben. 'No need to worry about it now.'

She looked up at him, trying to identify quite how he had changed. He was still her devoted boyfriend, with no signs of having outgrown her or found someone else. But he was less securely attached to her than before. He had other things to think about, other tasks and ambitions. She would never dare to take him for granted, or lapse into her old lethargic ways. She would have to read and study and think and listen if she was to be worthy of the great man he was destined to become. Despite knowing this, she was not afraid. Instead it gave her life a purpose it had always lacked. Ben Harkness was, after all, a geek. Most girls would be nervous of him, or simply bewildered. They would chafe at the lack of direct attention, and the even greater lack of interest in ordinary quotidian matters.

'What?' he said, when she gave a brief chuckle.

'I learnt a new word last week. "Quotidian". Isn't it great! I wanted to ask Mr Straw if he knew what it meant, but I haven't managed to yet.'

'One of my favourites,' laughed Ben. 'Atta girl.'

Simmy threw open her door in an unmistakable welcome. 'Hey, Ben! I wondered when I'd see you. How did you get here?'

'We walked,' said Bonnie. 'Have you finished lunch?'

'Ten minutes ago. We ate every scrap of the pork. The joint I got was too small. There might be some pudding left, though.'

'We're not hungry,' said Ben. 'I've come to hear the story. Bonnie hasn't told me a word.'

'She's a better man than I am, then. I'd never have managed to hold it back for a whole morning.'

'I'm literally bursting with it,' said the girl.

'No, you're not,' said Ben.

'Not literally, or you'd be splattered all over the wall by now,' said Russell, who had come out of the kitchen to greet them. 'Good to see you, boy,' he told Ben.

And then, after moving everybody into the little living room and finding them all a place to sit, the whole saga of Grant Childers and Tristan Wilkins and the poisoned drink was revealed. Bonnie did most of the talking, but Simmy and Angie regularly interrupted, especially to supply details the girl had been unaware of. After twenty minutes of this, Bonnie wailed, 'I've missed such a lot, haven't I? I've hardly been involved in it at all.'

'I'd gladly have swopped places with you,' said Angie drily.

'Well, that's it, more or less,' Simmy finished. 'Except the question of *Why?* What possible reason could Tristan have for wanting Childers dead? Every time we try to understand it, we end up thinking he must surely have needed him alive.'

Ben rubbed his nose, then tugged an earlobe. 'Seems fairly obvious to me,' he said. 'Surely the Wilkins man wanted the development to go ahead and was only pretending to be against it?'

They all stared at him. Christopher snorted and Simmy yelped 'No!' in disbelief.

'Explain,' ordered Bonnie.

'Well, everything points that way. It was common knowledge that Simmy and Chris want to live in Patterdale, right? Stuart Carstairs for one was keen to help if he could, because he's got a thing for you, Mrs Straw. He must have asked around, including Tristan Wilkins and Dorothea Entwhistle and loads of other people. Tristan and Dorothea were most likely having an affair, probably for the past twenty years or something. I dare say you'll find that she's left all her property to him, which would give him quite a nice fund for setting up a development company. Daphne Wilkins apparently owns a disused barn near Patterdale, as well. So, how about if Tristan and Dorothea hatch a plan to float the whole idea of a new tourist park up there, pretending to be dead against it? That way, they'd sow the seeds in people's minds, gauge opinion, and make everyone think they were on the side of the angels. They invited Candy's mate Childers to come and speak. But when they saw his speech, it was far *too good*. It risked turning the whole population against any sort of new building. So he had to go. The means were right there to hand, because Dorothea had her lethal cocktail all ready for when her cancer got too much. Candy Proctor was an innocent stooge, useful because she fancies Tristan and is fairly thick. Daphne's barn provides a handy cover story as well. Probably if the tourist park did get built, it would be a simple matter to hive off some of the materials and labour to do the conversion for peanuts. The whole thing would look like a win–win for all concerned. The only fly in the ointment was Childers, poor chap.'

'Yes, but—' Simmy's mouth opened and shut helplessly.

'The boy's a genius,' said Russell. 'An out-and-out gold-plated genius.'

'I said it was Tristan all along,' said Christopher quietly. Nobody took any notice.

'It's a very long way from sowing the seeds of an idea to actually getting the building done,' said Angie. 'Years and years.'

'Not necessarily,' said Ben. 'Wilkins knows all the right people. All he needed was a favourable climate, a few people murmuring that it wasn't actually such a bad plan, some sort of sop to the people of Patterdale, and bingo. Those lodges don't take much time to erect. I think the whole thing was brilliantly clever.'

'If it hadn't been for Tanya and her video, he'd have got away with it,' said Angie. 'Be sure you tell her we all realise that.'

'Her evidence will take pride of place at the trial,' said Ben. 'That should be more than enough for her.'

'It's the *only* evidence,' worried Bonnie. 'Are we sure they'll get a conviction?'

'That remains to be seen,' said Ben. 'All I've done is give you a reason why.'

'Which is what poor Grant Childers wanted to know, with his dying breath,' sighed Angie. 'He could never have guessed.'

'No,' said Simmy.

It was a week later that Simmy had a phone call from Daphne Wilkins. 'They've granted bail,' she said. 'But he's not allowed to communicate with you or your family. So I'm doing it instead, on my own account, not his. I wanted to tell you that the barn in Hartsop is yours if you want it. I'll give it to you. The conversion plans are all drawn up, so all you have to do is find builders and oversee the work. It could be finished by Easter, if the winter's not too foul.'

'But—' spluttered Simmy. 'Why? I mean – you can't be serious.'

'I'm leaving the area. I obviously can't stay here after what's happened. My husband can expect to spend much of his remaining life in prison. I intend to sell this house and move to France. And, to be honest, I feel I owe it to your parents to compensate them somehow. I could see your poor mother was suffering the after-effects of what happened. It's the least I can do.'

'Well . . . gosh. Thank you. I can hardly believe it.'

'You're welcome,' said Daphne.

* * *

Christopher was even less able to credit the news. 'She must be joking,' he said.

'She's not. I think she wants to rub Tristan's nose in it, and this is one way of doing that. She must be absolutely sick at it all.'

'I wonder what she thinks about Dorothea Entwhistle?'

'Probably wishes she could give all her stuff away as well. House, greenhouses – the lot.'

'You'd better be on the lookout for a mysterious fire, then. A woman scorned is a dangerous thing, remember.'

'And she's not the only one, is she? What about Candy Proctor? She came to see my parents yesterday, saying she'll never agree to give evidence against Tristan.'

'I don't imagine she's got much choice.'

'Nobody comes out of it very well, do they? All duped by the cunning Mr Wilkins.'

'Except Stuart. My dad's quite worried about the way my mother thinks he's the real hero of the hour.'

Christopher laughed. 'So we're going to live in Hartsop, are we? Is that close enough to Crookabeck for you?'

'I guess it'll have to be,' she said cheerfully.

REBECCA TOPE is the author of three bestselling crime series, set in the stunning Cotswolds, Lake District and West Country. She lives on a smallholding in rural Herefordshire, where she enjoys the silence and plants a lot of trees, but also manages to travel the world and enjoy civilisation from time to time. Most of her varied experiences and activities find their way into her books, sooner or later.

rebeccatope.com